THIEVES' WORLD™

is a unique experience: an outlaw world of the imagination, where mayhem and skulduggery rule and magic is still potent; brought to life by today's top fantasy writers, who are free to use one another's characters (but not to kill them off ... or at least not too freely!).

The idea for Thieves' World and the colorful city called Sanctuary™ came to Robert Lynn Asprin in 1978. After many twists and turns (documented in the volumes), the idea took off — and took on its own reality, as the best fantasy worlds have a way of doing. The result is one of F&SF's most unique success stories: a bestseller from the beginning, a series that is a challenge to writers, a delight to readers, and a favorite of fans.

Dramatis Personae

The Townspeople:

Hanse; Shadowspawn — Thief and bitter supporter of the lost glory of Ilsig. Also a friend to Prince Kadakithis and Tempus.

Illyra — Half-blood S'danzo seeress with True Sight.

    Dubro — Bazaar blacksmith and husband to Illyra.

Hakiem — Storyteller and confidant extraordinaire.

Jubal — Ex-gladiator and lynchpin of Sanctuary's organized crime. Wounded in the Stepson's assault which destroyed his mansion and his men.

    Saliman — His aide and only friend.

Lalo the Limner — Street portraitist gifted with magic he does not fully understand.

    Gilla — His indomitable wife.

Lastel; One-Thumb — Uptown merchant living a double life as the owner of the Vulgar Unicorn. Freed from a firey torture when Cime killed the mages who held him there.

Mor-am, Moria — Brother and sister sell-swords. Former hawkmasks cut adrift by Jubal's downfall.

Moonflower — S'danzo seeress. Teacher of Illyra and friend of Hanse.

    Mignuereal — Her eldest daughter.

Mradhon Vis — Foreign adventurer and sometime spy.

Omat, Hort, The Old Man (Panit) — Men of Sanctuary's fishing fleet.

The Magicians:

Ischade — Necromancer and thief. Her curse is passed to her lovers who die from it.

The Rankans living in Sanctuary:

Cime — Assassin, particularly of magicians. Her involvement with Tempus is both ancient and mysterious.

The Hell-Hounds — Zalbar, Quag, Armen: the Prince's bodyguard. Highly trained soldiers lately beset by internal discord.

Prince Kadakithis — Charismatic but naive governor of the town. Exiled to Sanctuary by his half-brother the Rankan Emperor.

Molin Torchholder; Torch — Archpriest of Vashanka. Next to the Prince the highest ranking imperial official in Sanctuary.

Stepsons; Sacred Banders — Members of a mercenary unit.

    Abarsis — Founder of the Stepsons. Slain by Jubal.

Tempus Thales; the Riddler — Hell-Hound. Nearly immortal mercenary through the power of Vashanka. Commander of the Stepsons.

Walegrin — Rankan army officer in charge of the Sanctuary garrison. Half-brother of Illyra the Seeress.

    Thrusher, Malm — His lieutenants.

The Gods:

Eshi — Ilsigi goddess of love, beauty and fertility.

Ils — Supreme diety of the vanquished Ilsigi pantheon.

Shalpa — Ilsigi patron god of thieves.

Vashanka — The Rankan Stormgod. Patron of their conquering armies.

STORM SEASON

Edited by
ROBERT LYNN ASPRIN & LYNN ABBEY

ACE BOOKS, NEW YORK

Exercise in Pain copyright © 1982 by Robert Lynn Asprin.
Downwind copyright © 1982 by C.J. Cherryh.
A Fugitive Art copyright © 1982 by Diana L. Paxson.
Steel copyright © 1982 by Lynn Abbey.
Wizard Weather copyright © 1982 by Janet Morris.
Godson copyright © 1982 by Andrew J. Offutt.

STORM SEASON

An Ace Book / published by arrangement with
the editors

PRINTING HISTORY
Ace edition / October 1982

ISBN: 0-441-78713-4

20   19   18   17   16   15   14

EDITOR'S NOTE

Those who have followed the first three volumes of THIEVES' WORLD are already aware that facts vary and contradict one another depending upon the character viewing or narrating an event. This fourth volume will be a bit more difficult to follow because of time-sequencing. While in the earlier volumes I have tried to keep the stories in the order in which they occur, this has proved to be impossible in STORM SEASON. The length of time covered by some of these tales is significant, causing the events to overlap or, in some cases, to occur within other stories. Rather than try to cut and splice the stories into a smooth chronology, I've left it to the reader to understand what is happening and construct his/her mental timeline as necessary. Just rest assured that all the stories herein occur between the end of SHADOWS OF SANCTUARY and the end of the STORM SEASON.

STORM SEASON

Table of Contents

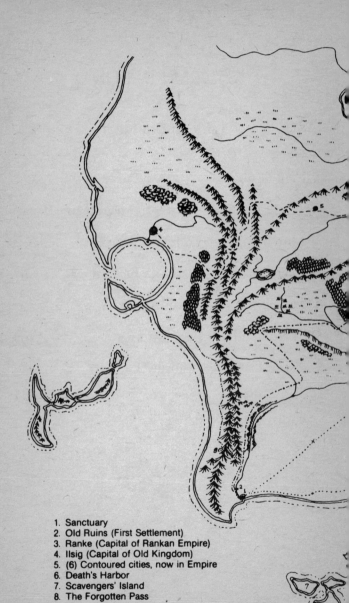

1. Sanctuary
2. Old Ruins (First Settlement)
3. Ranke (Capital of Rankan Empire)
4. Ilsig (Capital of Old Kingdom)
5. (6) Contoured cities, now in Empire
6. Death's Harbor
7. Scavengers' Island
8. The Forgotten Pass

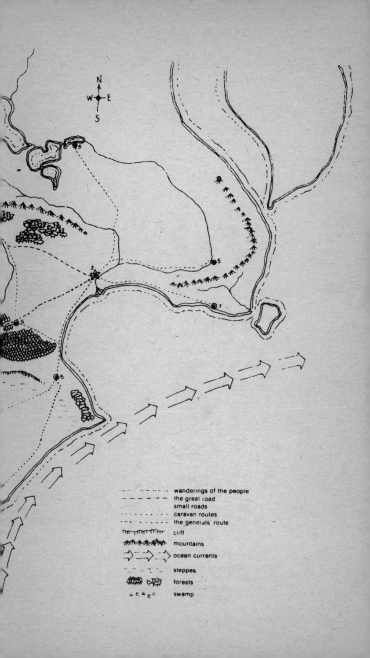

wanderings of the people
the great road
small roads
caravan routes
the generals' route
cliff
mountains
ocean currents
steppes
forests
swamp

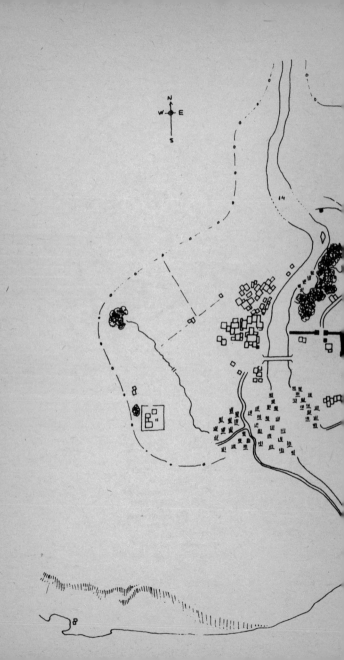

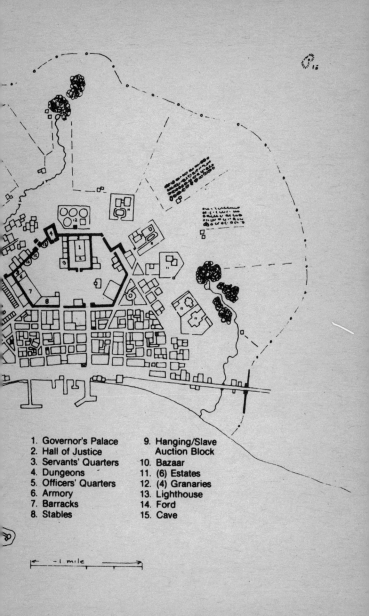

1. Governor's Palace
2. Hall of Justice
3. Servants' Quarters
4. Dungeons
5. Officers' Quarters
6. Armory
7. Barracks
8. Stables
9. Hanging/Slave Auction Block
10. Bazaar
11. (6) Estates
12. (4) Granaries
13. Lighthouse
14. Ford
15. Cave

⊢— ~1 mile —⊣

Storm Season

Introduction

Robert Lynn Asprin

It had been a long time since Hakiem, Sanctuary's oldest storyteller, had visited that section of town known only as the Fisherman's Quarters, but he still knew the way. Not much had changed: the stalls with their flimsy awnings to keep the sun off the day's catch; the boats bottom up along the pier and, on the beach, a few nets hung for drying and mending. All was the same—only more faded and worn—like the people . . . like the rest of the town.

Hakiem had watched Sanctuary's decline over the years; watched the economy dry up as the citizens became more desperate and vicious. He had watched and chronicled with the detached eye of a professional tale-spinner. Sometimes, though, like this—when a prolonged absence made the deterioration more apparent to the eye than the day-to-day erosion of his more favored haunts, he felt a pang of sorrow not unlike that he felt the day he visited his father and realized the man was dying. He had cut that visit short and never returned, preferring in his then-youth to preserve the memories of his sire in the joyful strength of his prime. Hakiem had always regretted that decision and, now that the town he had adopted and grown to love was in its death throes, he was determined not to repeat his earlier mistakes by abandoning it. He would stay with Sanctuary, sharing its pain and comforting it with his presence until either the town or he, or both, were dead.

Having renewed his resolve, the storyteller turned his back on the heartbreaking sight of the docks, once the pride of Sanctuary, now a ghastly parody of their own memory and entered the tavern which was his objective.

The Wine Barrel was a favorite haunt of those fishermen who wished to indulge in a bit of socializing before returning to their homes. Today was no exception and Hakiem easily located the person he sought. Omat was sitting alone at a corner table, a full tankard held loosely in his lone hand as he stared thoughtfully into the distance. For a moment Hakiem hesitated, reluctant to intrude on the one-armed fisherman's self-imposed isolation, but then curiosity won out over discretion and he approached the table.

"May I join you, Omat?"

The fisherman's eyes came into focus and he blinked with surprise. "Hakiem! What brings you to the docks? Has the Vulgar Unicorn finally run out of wine?"

The talespinner ignored the gibe and sank down onto one of the vacant stools. "I'm tracking a story," he explained earnestly. "A rumor which can only be fleshed out to audience-satisfying proportions with your assistance."

"A story?" Omat repeated, his gaze suddenly evasive. "Adventures only happen to your rich merchants or shadow-hugging cut-throats, not to us simple fisherfolk—and certainly not to me."

"So?" Hakiem asked, feigning surprise. "It

was some other one-armed fisherman who this very day told a garrison captain about the disappearance of the Old Man and his son?"

Omat favored him with a black glare. "I should know better than to expect secrecy in this town," he hissed. "Bad news draws curiosity-seekers like the Prince's gallows draw ravens. As they say, you can get anything in Sanctuary but help."

"Surely the authorities will investigate?" the storyteller asked, though he already knew the answer.

"Investigate!" the fisherman spat noisily on the floor. "You know what they told me—these precious authorities of yours? They say the Old Man must have drowned, he and his son both. They say the Old Man must've fallen overboard in a sudden squall. Do you believe that? The Old Man—fallen overboard? And him as much a part of his boat as the oarlocks. And Hort, who could swim like the fishes themselves before he could take a step. Drown? Both of them? With their boat still afloat?"

"Their boat was still afloat?" Hakiem pressed eagerly.

Omat eyed him for a moment, then leaned forward to share the tale at last. "For weeks now the Old Man has been taking Hort out, teaching him the tricks of deep-water boating. Oh, I know Hort'll never be a fisherman. I know it; Hort knew it, and so did the Old Man—but it was a handy excuse for the Old Man to show off a bit for his son. And, to Hort's credit, he played along—as patient with the Old Man as the Old Man had been with him. It warmed us all to see those two smile on each other again." The fisherman's own smile was brief as the memories crowded in on him, then he continued:

"Yesterday they went out—far out—beyond the sight of land or the other boats. I thought at the time that it was dangerous and said as much to Haron. She only laughed and told me not to worry—the Old Man was more than a match for the sea at this time of year." The fisherman took a long pull at his drink.

"But they didn't return. I thought perhaps they'd come ashore elsewhere and spent most of the night roaming the other piers asking for them. But no-one had seen them. This morning I took my boat out. It took 'til noon but I finally spotted the craft floating free, with its oars shipped. Of the Old Man and Hort I couldn't find a trace. I towed the boat in and sought out the City Garrison to report the disappearance. You already know what they told me. Drowned in a squall! And us still months away from the storm season. . . ."

Hakiem waited until the fisherman had lapsed into silence before he spoke. "Could it have been . . . some creature from the deep? I don't pretend to know the sea, but even a storyteller hears tales."

Omat regarded him steadily. "Perhaps," he admitted carefully. "I wouldn't risk the deep waters here in daylight, much less at night. Gods and monsters are both best left untempted."

"Yet you risked them today," the storyteller persisted, cocking his head to one side.

"The Old Man was my friend," the fisherman answered flatly. "But if it's monsters you want for your stories—then I suggest you seek after the two-legged kind that spend gold."

"What are you saying, Omat?"

Although they were already sitting close, Omat shot a furtive glance about the room to check for eavesdroppers. "Only this," he murmured. "I saw a ship out there—a ship that shouldn't have been there . . . shouldn't have been anywhere."

"Smugglers?"

"I've seen smuggler ships before, storyteller," the fisherman snarled. "We know them and they know us—and we give each other wide berth. If the Old Man were fool enough to close with a smuggler ship I'd have found him dead in his boat or floating in the water beside it. What use would a smuggler have for extra bodies?"

"Then, who?" the storyteller frowned.

"That's the mystery," Omat scowled. "The ship was far off, but from what I could make out it was unlike any ship I've ever seen, or heard of. What's more—it wasn't following the coast or making for the smuggler's island. It was putting out straight into the open sea."

"Did you tell this to the authorities?" Hakiem asked.

"The authorities," snorted the fisherman. "Tell them what? That my friends were stolen away by a ghost ship out of legend that sailed off over the horizon into uncharted waters? They would have thought I was drunk, or worse— added me to the collection of crazies that Kitty-cat's been gathering. I've told them too much as it is, though I've told you even more. Beware, storyteller, I'd not like losing another day's fishing because you put my name to one of your yarns and stirred the curiosity of those do-nothing guards."

Hakiem would have liked to inquire further about the "ghost ship out of legend," but it was apparent he was on the verge of overstaying his welcome. "I tell no story before I know its end," he assured his glaring host. "And what you've told me is barely the beginning of a tale. I'll hold my tongue until I've learned more, and even then I'll give you the first telling for free in payment for what you've given me now."

"Very well," Omat grumbled, "though I'd rather you skipped the tale and bought a round of drinks instead."

"A poor man must guard his coinage," Hakiem laughed, rising to go, then he hesitated. "The Old Man's wife . . . ?" he asked.

Omat's eyelids dropped to half-mast, and there was a wall, suddenly, between the two men. "She'll be taken care of. In the Fisherman's Quarter, we look after our own."

Feeling awkward, the storyteller fished a small pouch of coins from within his robes. "Here," he said, setting it on the table. "It isn't much, but I'd like to help with what little I can afford."

The pouch sat untouched.

"She'll not take charity from cityfolks."

For a moment the diminutive storyteller swelled to twice his normal appearance. "Then you give it to her," he hissed, "or give it to those who are supporting her . . . or rub it in a fish barrel until it reeks—" He caught himself, suddenly aware of the curious stares from the neighboring tables. In a flash the humble storyteller had returned. "Omat, my friend," he said quietly, "you know me. I am no more of the city than I am a fisherman or a soldier. Don't let an old woman's pride stand between her and a few honest coppers. They'll spend as well as any other when pushed across the board of a fishstall."

Slowly the fisherman picked up the pouch, then locked eyes with Hakiem. "Why?"

The storyteller shrugged. "The tale of the Old Man and the giant crab has paid me well. I would not like the taste of wine bought with that money while his woman was without."

Omat nodded and the purse disappeared from view.

It was dusk when Hakiem emerged from the Wine Barrel. Lengthening shadows hid the decay he had noticed earlier, though it was also true that his outlook had improved after his gift had been accepted. On an impulse, the storyteller decided to walk along the piers before returning to the Maze.

The rich smells of the ocean filled his nostrils and a slight breeze snatched at his robes as he digested Omat's story. The disappearance of the Old Man and his son was but the latest in a series of unusual occurrences: the war brewing to the north; the raid on Jubal's estate; and the disappearance and later reappearance of both Tempus and One-Thumb—all were like the rumble of distant thunder heralding a tempest of monumental proportions.

Omat had said the storm season was months off, but not all storms were forged by nature. Something was coming, the storyteller could feel it in the air and see it in the faces of the people on the streets—though he could no more have put a name to it than they could have.

For a few moments he debated making one of

his rare visits to a temple, but as always the sheer number of deities to be worshipped, or appeased, daunted him. With petty jealousies rampant among gods and priests it was better to abstain completely than risk choosing wrong.

The same coins he could have given as an offering might also buy a glimpse of the future from a bazaar-seer. Of course, their ramblings were often so obscure that one didn't recognize the truth until after it had happened. With a smug grin, Hakiem made up his mind. Instead of investing in gods or seers he would quest for insight and omen in his own way—staring into a cup of wine.

Quickening his step, the storyteller set his course for the Vulgar Unicorn.

EXERCISE IN PAIN

by

Robert Lynn Asprin

There must be trouble. Saliman had been gone far too long for his mission to be going smoothly. Some might have had difficulty judging the passage of time during the period of time between sundown and sunrise, but not Jubal. His early years as a gladiator in the Rankan capital had included many sleepless nights before arena days, or Blood Days as those in the trade called them; he knew the darkness intimately. Each phase of the night had its own shade, its own texture—and he knew them all . . . even with his eyes blurred with sweat and tears of pain as they were now.

Too long. Trouble.

The twin thoughts danced in his mind as he tried to focus his concentration, to formulate a contingency plan. If he was right; if he was now alone and wounded—what could he do? He couldn't travel far pulling himself painfully along the ground with his hands. If he encountered one of those who hunted him, or even a random townsperson with an old grudge, he couldn't defend himself. To fight, a man needed legs, working legs. He knew that from the arena, too.

The oft-repeated words of his arena instructor

sprang into his mind, crowding out all other
thoughts.

"Move! Move, damn you! Retreat. Attack. Retreat. Circle. Move! If you don't move, you're
dead. If I don't kill you myself, your next opponent will! Move! A still fighter's a dead fighter.
Now move! *move!*"

A half-heard sound wrenched Jubal's fevered
thoughts back to the present. His hand dropped
to his dagger hilt as he strained to penetrate the
darkness with his erratic vision.

Saliman?

Perhaps. But in his current state he couldn't
take any chances. As his ally knew his exact
location, the information could have been forced
out of him by Jubal's enemies. Sitting propped
against a tree with his legs stretched out before
him, Jubal cast about looking for new cover. Not
two paces away was a patch of knee-high weeds.
Not much, but enough.

The ex-gladiator allowed himself to fall side-
ways, catching himself on one hand and easing
his body the rest of the way to the ground. Then it
was reach, pull; reach, pull, slowly making his
way towards and finally into the weed patch.
Though he used his free hand to maintain his
balance, once one of the broken arrowshafts
protruding from his knees scraped along the
ground, sending a sheet of red agony through his
mind. Still, he kept his silence, though he could
feel sweat running off his body.

Reach, pull. Reach.

Safely in the weeds now, he allowed himself to
rest. His head sank completely to the ground.
The dagger slid from its scabbard and he held it
point down, hiding the shine of its blade with his

forearm. Trembling from the efforts of his movement, he breathed through his nose to slow and silence his recovery. Inhale. Exhale. Wait.

Two figures appeared, patches of black against deeper black, bracketing the tree against which he had recently lain.

"Well?" came a voice, loud in the darkness. "Where is my patient? I can't treat a ghost."

"He was here, I swear it!"

Jubal smiled, relaxing his grip on the dagger. The second voice was easy to recognize. He had heard it daily for years now.

"You're still no warrior, Saliman," he called, propping himself up on one elbow. "I've said before, you wouldn't recognize an ambush unless you stumbled into it."

His voice was weak and strained to a point where he scarcely recognized it himself. Still, the two figures started violently at the sound rising from a point near their ankles. Jubal relished their frightened reaction for a moment, then his features hardened. "You're late," he accused.

"We would have been quicker," his aide explained hastily, "but the healer here insisted we pause while he dug up some plants."

"Some cures are strongest when they are fresh," Alten Stulwig announced loftily as he strode toward Jubal, "and from what I've been told—" He stopped suddenly, peering at the weeds around his patient. "Speaking of plants," he stammered, "are you aware that the particular foliage you're laying in exudes an irritating oil that will cause the skin to itch and burn?"

For some inexplicable reason the irony contained in this recitation of dangers struck Jubal as hilarious, and he laughed for the first time since the Stepsons had invaded his estate. "I think, healer," he said at last, "that at the moment I have greater problems to worry about than a skin-rash." Then exhaustion and shock overtook him and he fainted.

*   *   *

It wasn't the darkness of night, but a deeper blackness—the blackness of the void, or of a punishment cell.

They came for him out of the black, unseen enemies with daggers like white-hot pokers, attacking his knees while he struggled vainly to defend himself. Once, no twice, he had screamed aloud and tried to pull his legs close against his chest, but a great weight held them down while the torturer did his work. Unable to move his hands or arms, Jubal wrenched his head about, drooling and gibbering incoherent, impotent threats. Finally his mind slipped onto another plane, a darker plane where there was no pain—no feeling at all.

*   *   *

Slowly the world came back into focus, so slowly that Jubal had to fight to distinguish dream from reality. He was in a room . . . no, in a hovel. There was a guttered candle struggling to give off light, crowded in turn by the sun streaming in through a doorway without a door.

He lay on the dirt floor, his clothes damp and clammy from his own sweat. His legs were wound from thigh to calf with bandages . . .

lumpy bandages, as if his legs had no form save for what the rags gave them.

Alten Stulwig, Sanctuary's favored healer, squatted over him, keeping the sun's rays from his face. "You're awake. Good," the man grunted. "Maybe now I can finish my treatment and go home. You're only the second black I've worked on, you know. The other died. It's hard to judge skin tone in these cases."

"Saliman?" Jubal croaked.

"Outside relieving himself. You underestimate him, you know. Warrior or not, he kept me from following my better judgment. Threatened to carve out my stomach if I didn't wait until you regained consciousness."

"Saliman?" Jubal laughed weakly. "You've been bluffed, healer. He's never drawn blood. Not all those who work for me are cut-throats."

"I believed him," the healer retorted stiffly. "And I still do."

"As well you should," Saliman added from the doorway. In one hand he carried a corroded pan, its handle missing; he carried it carefully, as if it, or its contents, were fragile. In his other hand he held Jubal's dagger.

When he attempted to shift his body and greet his aide, Jubal realized for the first time that his arms were bound over his head—tied to something out of his line-of-vision. Kneeling beside him, Saliman used the dagger to free Jubal's hands, then offered him the pan, which proved to be half-full of water. It was murky, with twigs and grass floating in it—but it did much for removing the fever-taste from the slaver's mouth.

"I shouldn't expect you'd remember," Saliman continued, "but I've drawn blood at least four times—with two sure kills—all while getting you out of the estate."

"To save my life?"

"My life was involved too," Saliman shrugged. "The raiders were rather unselective about targets by then—"

"If I might finish my work?" Stulwig interupted testily. "It has been a long night—and you two will have much time to talk."

"Of course," Jubal agreed, waving Saliman away. "How soon before I can use my legs again?"

The question hung too long in the air, and Jubal knew the answer before the healer found his voice.

"I've removed the arrows from your knees," Stulwig mumbled. "But the damage was great . . . and the infection—"

"How long?" This time the slaver was not asking; he demanded.

"Never."

Jubal's hand moved smoothly, swiftly past his hip, then hesitated as he realized it was not holding the dagger. Only then did his conscious mind understand that Saliman had his weapons. He sought to catch his aide's eye, to signal him, before he realized that his ally was deliberately avoiding his gaze.

"I have applied a poultice to slow the spread of the infection," Alten went on, unaware that he might have been dead, "as well as applied the juice of certain plants to deaden your pain. But we must proceed with treatment without delay."

"Treatment?" the slaver glared, the edge momentarily gone from his temper. "But you said I wouldn't be able to use my legs—"

"You speak of your legs," the healer sighed. "I'm trying to save your life—though I've heard there are those who would pay well to see it ended."

Jubal heard the words and accepted them without the rush of fear other men might feel. Death was an old acquaintance of all gladiators. "Well, what is this treatment you speak of?" he asked levelly.

"Fire," Stulwig stated without hesitation. "We must burn the infection out before it spreads further."

"No."

"But the wounds must be treated!" the healer insisted.

"You call that a treatment?" Jubal challenged. "I've seen burned legs before. The muscle's replaced by scar tissue; they aren't legs—they're things to be hidden."

"Your legs are finished," Stulwig shouted. "Stop speaking of them as if they were worth something. The only question worth asking is: do you wish to live or die?"

Jubal let his head sink back until his was staring at the hovel's ceiling. "Yes, healer," he murmured softly, "that is the question. I'll need time to consider the answer."

"But—"

"If I were to answer right now," the slaver continued harshly, "I'd say I'd prefer death to the life your treatment condemns me to. But that's the answer a healthy Jubal would give—now, when death is real, the true answer requires more thought. I'll contact you with my decision."

"Very well," Alten snarled, rising to his feet. "But don't take too long making up your mind.

Your black skin makes it difficult to judge the infection—but I'd guess you don't have much time left to make your choice."

"How much?" Saliman asked.

"A day or two. After that we'd have to take the legs off completely to save his life—but by then it might only be a choice of deaths."

"Very well," Jubal agreed.

"But in case I'm wrong," Stulwig said suddenly, "I'd like my payment now."

The slaver's head came up with a jerk, but his aide had fore-reached him. "Here," Saliman said, tossing the healer a small pouch of coins, "for your services and your silence."

Alten hefted the purse with raised eyebrows, nodded and started for the doorway.

"Healer!" Jubal called from the floor, halting the man in mid-stride. "Currently only the three of us know my whereabouts. If any come hunting us and fail to finish the job, one, or both, of us will see you suffer hard before you die."

Alten hesitated then moistened his lips. "And if someone finds you accidentally?"

"Then we'll kill you—accidentally," Saliman concluded.

The healer looked from one set of cold eyes to the other, jerked his head in a half-nod of agreement and finally left. For a long time after his departure silence reigned in the hovel.

"Where did you get the money?" Jubal asked when such thoughts were far from his aide's mind.

"What?"

"The money you gave Stulwig," Jubal clarified. "Don't tell me you had the presence of mind to gather our house-funds from their hiding places in the middle of the raid?"

"Better than that," Saliman said proudly, "I took the records of our holdings."

From the early beginnings of Jubal's rise to power in Sanctuary, he had followed Saliman's advice—particularly when it concerned the safety of his wealth. Relatively little of his worth was kept at the estate but was instead spread secretly through the town as both investments and caches. In a town like Sanctuary there were many who would gladly supplement their income by holding a package of unknown content for an equally unknown patron.

Jubal forced himself up into a sitting position. "That raises a question I've been meaning to ask since the raid: why did you save me? You placed yourself in physical danger, even killed to get me out alive. Now, it seems, you've got the records of my holdings, most of which you've managed. You could be a wealthy man—if I were dead. Why risk it all in an attempt to pluck a wounded man from the midst of his enemies?"

Saliman got up and wandered to the doorway. He leaned against the rough wood frame and stared at the sky before he answered. "When we met—when you hired me—you saved me from the slave block by letting me buy my freedom with my promises. You wouldn't have me as a slave, you said, because slaves were untrustworthy. You wanted me as a freeman, earning a decent living for services rendered—and with the choice to leave if I felt my fortunes might be better somewhere else."

He turned to face Jubal directly. "I pledged

that I would serve you with all my talents and
that if I ever should leave I would face you first
with my reasons for leaving. I said that until then
you need never doubt my intentions or loyal-
ties. . .

"You laughed at the time, but I was serious. I
promised my mind and life to the person who
allowed me to regain my freedom on his trust
alone. At the time of the raid I had not spoken to
you about resigning, and while I usually content
myself with protecting your interests and leave
the protecting of your life to yourself and others,
I would have been remiss to my oath if I had not
at least tried to rescue you. And, as it turned out, I
was able to rescue you."

The slaver studied his aide's face. The limbs
were softer and the belly fuller than the angry
slave's who had once struggled wildly with the
guards while shouting his promises—but the
face was as gaunt as it ever had been and the eyes
were still bright with intelligence.

"And why was that resignation never offered,
Saliman?" Jubal asked softly. "I know you had
other offers. I often waited for you to ask me for
more money—but you never did. Why?"

"I was happy where I was. Working for you
gave me an unusual blend of security and excitement with little personal risk—at least until
quite recently. Once, I used to daydream about
being an adventurer or a fearless leader of men.
Then, I met you and learned what it took to lead
that sort of life; I lack the balance of caution and
recklessness, the sheer personal charisma necessary for leadership. I know that now and am

content to do what I do best: risking someone else's money or giving advice to the person who actually has to make the life-and-death decisions."

A cloud passed over Saliman's expression. "That doesn't mean, however, that I don't share many of your emotions. I helped you build your web of power in Sanctuary; helped you select and hire the hawkmasks who were so casually butchered in the raid. I, too, want revenge—though I know I'm not the one to engineer it. You are, and I'm willing to risk everything to keep you alive until that vengeance is complete."

"Alive like this?" Jubal challenged. "How much charisma does a cripple have? Enough to rally a vengeful army?"

Saliman averted his eyes. "If you cannot regain your power," he admitted, "I'll find another to follow. But first I'll stay with you until you've reached your decision. If there's anyone who can inspire a force it's you—even crippled."

"Then your advice is to let Stulwig do his work?"

"There seems to be no option—unless you'd rather death."

"There is one," Jubal grinned humorlessly, "though it's one I am loathe to take. I want you to seek out Balustrus, the metal-master. Tell him of our situation and ask . . . no, beg him to give us shelter."

"Balustrus?" Saliman repeated the name as if it tasted bad. "I don't trust him. There're those who say he's mad."

"He's served us well in the past—whatever

else he's done," the slaver pointed out. "And, more important—he's familiar with the sorcerous element in town."

"Sorcery?" Saliman was genuinely astounded.

"Aye," Jubal nodded grimly. "As I said, I have little taste for the option, but it's still an option nonetheless . . . and perhaps better than death or maiming."

"Perhaps," the aide said with a grimace. "Very well, I'm off to follow your instructions."

"Saliman," the slaver called him back. "Another instruction: when you speak to Balustrus don't reveal our hiding place. Tell him I'm somewhere else—in the charnel houses. I trust him no more than you do."

*   *   *

Jubal bolted awake out of his half-slumber, his dagger once again at the ready. That sound—nearby and drawing closer. Pulling himself along the floor toward the doorway the slaver wondered, for the first time, just whose hovel Saliman had hid him in. He had assumed it was abandoned—but perhaps the rightful owner was returning. With great care he poked his head out the bottom corner of the doorway and beheld—

Goats.

A sizable herd meandered toward the hut, but though they caught the ex-gladiator's attention, they did not hold it. Two men walked side-by-side behind the animals. One was easily recognized as Saliman. The other's head came barely to Saliman's shoulder and he walked with a rolling, bouncy gait.

Jubal's eyes narrowed with suspicion and puzzlement. Whatever Saliman's reason for revealing their hideaway to a goat-herd it had better be a good one. The slaver's mood had not been improved by the time the men reached the doorway. If anything it had darkened as two goats strayed ahead of the rest of the herd and made his unwilling acquaintance.

"Jubal," Saliman declared, hardly noticing the goats that had already entered the hovel. "I want you to meet—"

"A goat-herd?" the slave spat out. "Have you lost your mind?"

"Not a goat-herd," the aide stammered, surprised by Jubal's erupting anger. "He's a Lizerene."

"I don't care where he was born—get him and his goats out of here!"

Another goat entered as they argued and stood at Jubal's feet, staring down on him with blandly curious eyes while the rest of the herd explored the corners.

"Allow me to explain, my lord," the little man said quickly and nervously. "It's not where I'm from but what I am: the Order of Lizerene . . . a humble order devoted to the study of healing through sorcery."

"He can mend your legs," Saliman blurted out. "Completely. You'll be able to walk—or run—if you wish."

Now it was Jubal's turn to blink in astonishment, as he absently shoved one of the goats aside. "You? You're a wizard? You don't look like any of the magicians I've seen in town."

"It's a humble order," the man replied, fussing with his threadbare robe, "and, then again, liv-

ing with the goats does not encourage the finery
my town-dwelling colleagues are so proud of."

"Then, these *are* your goats?" Jubal shot a dark
look at Saliman.

"I use them in my magics," the Lizerene
explained, "and they provide me with suste-
nance. As I said: it—"

"I know," Jubal repeated, "it's a humble order.
Just answer one question: is Saliman right? Can
you heal my legs?"

"Well—I can't say for sure until I've examined
the wounds, but I've been successful in many
cases."

"Enough. Begin your examination. And,
Saliman—get these damn goats out of the hut!"

By the time Saliman had gotten the animals
into the yard the Lizerene had the bandages off
and was probing Jubal's legs. It was the first time
the slaver had seen the wounds and his stomach
rebelled at the sight of the damage.

"Not good . . . not good at all," the magician
mumbled. "Far worse than I was told. See
here—the infection's almost halfway up the
thigh."

"Can you heal them?" Jubal demanded, still
not looking at the wounds.

"It will be costly," the Lizerene told him, "and
with no guarantee of complete success."

"I knew that before I sent for you," the slaver
snarled. "Your profession always charges high
and never guarantees their work. No sellsword
would stay alive if he demanded a sorceror's
terms."

The wizard looked up from his examination.
His expression had gone hard. "I wasn't speaking of my fee," he corrected his patient, "but of

the strain to your body and mind. What is more it
is your strength, and not mine which will determine the extent of your recovery. Strength of
muscle and of spirit. If I and others have fallen
short in our healings it is because most arrogant
warriors have greater egos than skills and are
also lacking—'' he caught himself and turned
again to the wounds. "Forgive me, my lord,
sometimes being of a 'humble order' is wearing
on the nerves."

"Don't apologize, man," Jubal laughed. "For
the first time I begin to have some faith in your
ability to do what you promise. What is your
name?"

"Vertan, my lord."

"And I am Jubal—not 'my lord,' " the slave
told him. "Very well, Vertan. If strength is what's
needed then between the two of us we should be
able to renew my legs."

"How much strain to the mind and body?"
Saliman asked from the doorway.

Jubal glared at his aide, annoyed by the inter-
ruption, but Vertan had already turned to face
Saliman and did not see.

"A fine question," the Lizerene agreed. "To
grasp the answer you must first understand the
process." He was in his own element now, and
his nervousness melted away. "There will be
two parts to the healing. The first is relatively
simple, but it will take some time. It involves
drawing out the infection, the poisons, from the
wounds. The true test lies in the second phase of
the healing. There is damage here, extensive
damage—and to the bones themselves. To mend
bone takes time, more time that I'd venture
m'lord Jubal wishes to invest. I would therefore

accelerate the body processes, thereby shortening the time required. While in this state you will consume and pass food at an incredible rate—for the body needs fuel for the healing. What would normally require days will transpire in hours; the processes of months compacted into weeks."

"Have you ever used this technique before?" Saliman asked.

"Oh, yes," Vertan assured him. "In fact, you know one of my patients. It was I who healed Balustrus. Of course, that was back in the capital before he changed his name."

"Balustrus," Jubal scowled, an image of the crippled metal-master flashing in his mind.

"I know what you're thinking," the Lizerene injected hastily, "but I have done much to perfect my skills since then. I was surprised, though, that he recommended me. At the time he was not at all pleased with the results of my work."

"I see," the slaver murmured. He shot a look at Saliman who nodded slightly, acknowledging that the metal-master would have to be investigated more closely. "But, if I follow your program I *will* be able to use my legs—normally?"

"Oh yes," Vertan assured him confidently. "The key factor is exercise. Balustrus remained abed throughout the process, so his joints fused together. If you have the strength and will to work your legs constantly you should regain full mobility."

"Do that for me and I'll pay you double your fee, however large, without question or complaint. When can you begin?"

"As soon as your man there takes his leave of our company," the sorceror said.

"What?" Saliman exclaimed, rising to his feet. "You said nothing about—"

"I'm saying it now," Vertan cut him short. "Our methods are generally known, but our techniques are guarded. If one undisciplined in our order were to learn them and then attempt to duplicate our efforts without complete understanding of the signs and dangers, the results would be not only disastrous but demeaning to our humble order. No-one but the patient may witness what I propose to do. The laws of our order are most strict about this."

"Let it pass, Saliman," Jubal ordered. "I had other plans for you. I get no pleasure or support from having others see me in this weakened condition—even you. If I am to rebuild my force I will need two things: my normal physical health, intact; and current information of happenings in Sanctuary. The healing is my task; one you cannot help me with. But, for the information I must rely on you, as I have so many times in the past." He turned to the Lizerene. "How long will your healing take?"

The healer shrugged. "The time is not exact. Perhaps two months."

Jubal spoke again to Saliman. "Return to town and don't come back for three months. You have access to most of our hidden funds; use them and live well. Anyone hunting hawkmasks will not think to look among the wealthy.

"That hunting should serve as a weeding to test the fitness of our remaining swords. Learn their whereabouts and watch them—but let none know I'm still alive. After three months we'll meet and decide who is to be included in the new organization."

"If you are as wealthy as your words," Vertan interjected cautiously, "might I make an additional suggestion?" Jubal cocked an eyebrow, but indicated the wizard should continue. "There are several wizards in Sanctuary who have the power to ferret out your location. If I were to provide a list of their names and estimates of their bribe-price, you could insure your safety during the healing process by paying them not to find you."

Saliman snorted. "That way they'll take our money and still sell their services to the first hunter that asks. How trustworthy do you really think your colleagues are, healer?"

"No more or less trustworthy than a sell-sword," the Lizerene countered. "Every person has weaknesses, though some are weaker than others. While a few might be unscrupulous enough to accept double-service at least you can eliminate the danger from the honest practitioners."

"See that it's done," Jubal instructed Saliman. "There're two other things I'll want when you return. Find Hakiem and let him accompany you to witness my recovery—"

"The storyteller? Why?"

"He has amused us with his tales in the past," Jubal smiled, "as well as providing occasional bits of timely information. Sharing this story with him will guarantee that all will hear of my return to power."

Saliman frowned but did not protest further. "What else?"

"A sword," Jubal stated, his eyes suddenly fierce. "The finest sword you can find. Not the prettiest, mind you: the best steel with the

keenest edge. There will some who will be less
than happy at the news of my recovery and I
want to be prepared to deal with them."

*   *   *

"That's enough for today," Vertan announced
shakily, removing his hands from Jubal's knees.

Like a drowning man encountering a log, the
healer grabbed the goat tethered nearby and
clung to it while the animal bleated and struggled to free itself. The slaver averted his eyes,
nauseated by the now-familiar ritual.

The first day he had watched intently and
what he had seen was now branded into his
memory. Though he had always loathed magic
and its practitioners he now admitted a grudging
admiration of the little wizard who labored over
him. He would rather face a hundred swords
than subject himself to what the Lizerene endured voluntarily.

Vertan drew the poison from Jubal's legs as
promised, but what the ex-gladiator had not
realized was that the wizard drew it into his own
body. He had seen Vertan's hands after the first
session: swollen and misshapen; dripping pus
from deep-cracked skin—caricatures of hands
in the flickering candlelight. The poison was
then transferred to one of the goats whose body
would then undertake to heal the invading infection. Over a dozen of the herd now had swellings
or sores from taking part in the treatments. Jubal
was astounded, frightened by the volume of
poison in his ravaged legs. While several animals now coped with his infection, thereby lessening its power, it had all passed through Vertan. Rather than being annoyed with the little

wizard's frequent recuperative rests, Jubal was amazed at the Lizerene's tenacity.

"A few . . . more days . . . will complete this phase of the treatment," Vertan said weakly, releasing the goat. "Then the real trial begins."

* * *

Jubal gagged at the smell wafting from Vertan's kettle. He had known odors before which others found revolting: the rotting smell of blood and entrails which the wind carried from the charnel house to his estate; the stink of unwashed bodies, alive or dead; the clinging aroma of the excretions of penned animals; the acrid bite of the stench of the swamp at low tide. All these he had suffered without comment or complaint, but this . . . Whatever bubbled in Vertan's pot was an abomination. No such odor had ever been generated by nature or civilization—of that Jubal was certain.

"Drink," Vertan ordered, thrusting a ladle into the slaver's hands. "Two swallows, no more."

The contents of the ladle were still bubbling; they had the appearance and texture of vomit— but Jubal drank. The first swallow was surprisingly cool on his tongue but the second had the warmth and pulse of something alive. Jubal took it down with the same detached resolve he had used to kill his first helpless, crippled opponent and handed the ladle back to the wizard.

With a satisfied nod, the Lizerene tossed the utensil back into the kettle, then extended his hands, palms down, until they were each a few inches above Jubal's knees. "Brace yourself, swordsman," he ordered. "You're about to begin learning about pain."

Something moved under the skin of the slaver's right knee, sending a quick stab of agony along his leg. Another piece moved, grating against the first. Then the movement began in his left knee. Despite his resolve an animal howl of pain escaped Jubal's lips, a wordless note that rose and sank as the pieces of his shattered kneecaps shifted and realigned themselves. The world had faded from knowledge when Vertan's voice came to him through the red mists.

"Now move your legs. *Move them!* You must flex your knees."

With a giant effort Jubal bent his right knee, sliding his foot along the dirt floor. The pain was beyond sound now, though his mouth strained with silent screams.

"More. You must bend it completely. More, swordsman! Do you want to be a cripple? *More!* The other knee—more! Move it!"

Spittle ran down from the corner of the slaver's mouth; he soiled himself from the agony but he kept moving, bending first one knee then the other. Right knee—straighten. Left knee—straighten. Right knee . . .

He was disoriented in time and space. His entire world had been reduced to the effort of repeating the simple exercise.

"Where's that will you bragged about," the torturer taunted. "More! Bend those knees completely. Move!"

*   *   *

He was growing used to the taste of Vertan's vile potion. It still disgusted him, but the repeated doses had made the nausea familiar and therefore acceptable.

"Today you stand," the wizard announced
without fanfare.

Jubal hesitated, a piece of roast goat-meat
halfway to his lips. As promised he was now
eating five meals for every one the Lizerene ate.
"Am I ready?"

"No," Vertan admitted. "But there's more involved here than your knees. Your muscles,
especially your leg muscles, must be worked if
you are to keep any strength in them. Waving
your feet in the air isn't enough for your legs;
they must bear weight again—and the sooner the
better."

"Very well," the slaver agreed, finishing the
last of the meat and wiping his hands on his
sleeves. "Let's do it now—before I've got to re-
lieve myself again." That function, too, had in-
creased five-fold.

Seizing the wall with one hand, Jubal drew his
feet under him then pushed with his legs. Standing up had once seemed so simple; nothing he
ever thought about. Now sweat popped out on
his brow and his vision blurred. He kept pushing; by now agony was as familiar as the
Lizerene's face. Slowly, his hands scrabbling
against the walls, he rose until his weight was on
his feet.

"There," he stated through clenched teeth,
wishing he could stop the waving motion of the
floor and walls around him. "As you said, nothing is impossible if the will is strong enough."

"Good," Vertan said with a malicious laugh,
"then you won't mind walking back and forth a
bit."

"Walking?" Jubal clutched at the wall, a wave

of dizziness washed over him. "You said nothing about walking!"

"Of course," the wizard shrugged. "If I had, would you have attempted to stand? Now, walk—or don't you remember how?"

*   *   *

The thunderstorm raged, giving added texture to the night. Jubal practiced alone without Vertan's supervision. This was not unusual now that his mobility was returning. He slept and woke according to the demands of his healing body and was often left to exercise by himself.

The rain had driven the goats away from the hut; they sought and usually found better shelter, so even his normal audience was absent. Still, the slaver practiced, heedless of the sucking mud at his feet. He held a stout branch in one hand—a branch the length of a sword.

Block, cut, block behind. Turn and duck. Cut at the legs. Move. Move. Move! Over and over he practiced a death-dance he had learned as a gladiator. The pain was a distant ache now, an ache he could ignore. He had something else on his mind now.

Turn, cut. Move. Block, turn, block, cut! Finally he stopped, the raindrops collecting in the wrinkles of his forehead.

Slow—all of it. Slow.

To the untrained eye his swordwork might seem smooth and expert, but he knew he had a mere fraction of his old speed. He made to test his suspicions; he stooped and picked up two clods of dirt with his left hand and tossed them

into the air. He swung at them with his impro-
vised weapon. One clod splattered as the limb
connected with it but the other splashed into the
mud with a sound Jubal heard as a death knell.

One! There had been a time when he could hit
three. The healing was going far too slowly, taking too much of his strength. At times he felt his
reflexes were getting worse instead of improv-
ing. There was only one solution.

Moving quietly he crept back into the hut,
listening carefully to the unchanging rhythm of
the wizard's soft snores. The kettle of vile potion
was bubbling vigorously, as always. The slaver
carefully dipped the ladle in and lifted it to his
lips. For a week now he had been sneaking extra
swallows, relying on the Lizerene's growing
fatigue to blind that normally watchful eye. Still,
a few swallows had not made a difference.

Ignoring the smell and taste, Jubal drained the
ladle, hesitated, then refilled it. He drained it a
second time then he crept back into the rain to
continue his practice.

*　　　*　　　*

"Jubal, are you there?"

The slaver rose from his pallet at the sound of
his aide's voice. His counting had been correct. It
was three months since Vertan's arrival.

"Don't come in," he cautioned, "I'll be out in a
moment."

"Is something wrong?" his aide asked in a
worried voice. "Where's Vertan?"

"I sent him away," the slaver responded,
leaning heavily against the wall of the hut. He
had been anticipating this moment, but now that

it was here he found himself filled with dread. "Is the storyteller with you?"

"I'm here," Hakiem said for himself. "Though just the news that you are indeed alive is story enough for a dozen tellings."

"There's more," Jubal laughed bitterly, "believe me—there's more. You won't regret your trip."

"What is it?" Saliman insisted, alerted by the odd tone of the slaver's voice. "Wasn't the cure successful?"

"Oh, I can walk well enough," Jubal grimaced. "See for yourselves." With that he stepped through the doorway and into the sunlight.

Saliman and Hakiem each gasped at the sight of him; open astonishment was written large on their faces. If the slaver had any doubts of his recent decision, the confirmation was now before him. He forced himself to smile.

"Here's the finale for your tale, Hakiem," he said. "Jubal will be leaving these parts now. Where so many others have failed, I myself have succeeded in out-witting Jubal."

"What happened?" Saliman stammered.

"What the Lizerene said would happen—if we'd had the wit to listen to him closely. He healed my legs by speeding my body's processes. Unfortunately he had to speed them all—not just those in my legs."

Jubal was old. His hair was white and his skin had the brittle, fragile texture of parchment once wet then left to dry in the sun. Though his muscle tone was good there was none of a young man's confidence in his stride or stance—only the careful, studied movements of one who knows his natural days are nearing an end.

"It's as much my fault as his," the ex-gladiator admitted. "I was sneaking extra doses of his potion, thinking it would speed the healing. By the time he realized what was happening the damage had been done. Besides, he filled his part of the bargain. I can walk, even run—just as he claimed. But as a leader of men, I'm finished. A common merchant with a cane could beat me in a fight—much less the swordsmen we had planned to challenge." A silence fell over the group, one which Jubal felt with ever-increasing discomfort. "Well, Hakiem," he said with forced cheerfulness, "you have your story. Tell it well and you'll have wine money for a year."

The old talespinner sank slowly into his favored squat and scratched absently. "Forgive me—I had been expecting a better ending."

"So had I," Jubal snarled, his carefully rehearsed poise slipping before Hakiem's insolence. "But I was given little choice in the final outcome. Am I not right, Saliman? Look me in the eye and tell me that at this moment you are not pondering where you may go now in search of someone who can give you your revenge? Or are you going to lie and say you think I still have a fighting chance against Tempus?"

"Actually, that was one of the things I meant to speak to you about," Saliman admitted, looking away. "I've done much thinking in the time since we parted and my current feeling is that under no circumstances should we pursue Tempus at all."

"What—but he . . ."

"He did nothing anyone else wouldn't have done had he the strength," Saliman said over

Jubal's objections. "The fault was ours. We were far too open at the end, flaunting our wealth and power, strutting through the streets in our hawkmasks—an easy target for anyone with the courage and skill to oppose us. Well, someone did. If you issue enough challenges someone, sooner or later, is going to call you. Gladiators know the penalty of pride—of displaying strength when it isn't necessary. A wise opponent will listen quietly and use knowledge against his enemy. Tempus has done what we should have done."

Jubal listened with growing astonishment. "Then you're saying we just let him go unmolested?"

"Our goal has always been power, not vengeance," Saliman insisted. "If we could ever seize power without confrontation, that's the route we'd take. Is confronting Tempus the only way to regain control over Sanctuary? If not— then we should avoid it."

"You keep saying 'we.' Look at me. What good is a leader who can't fight his own battles?"

"Like Prince Kitty-cat? Like Molin Torchholder?" Saliman asked with a dry chuckle. "Or the Emperor himself?"

"How often have you used your sword in the last two years?" Hakiem interrupted. "I may have missed some accounts, but as near as I can figure it's only once—and you could have avoided that fight."

"I used it the day of the raid—" Jubal replied, unimpressed.

"—And it didn't help you then—when you were at the peak of health and skill," his aide picked up the thread of the argument. "There're

ways to fight other than with a sword. You've
been doing it for years but your gladiator's brain
won't let you admit it."

"But I can't fight alone," the slave insisted, his
greatest fear finding voice at last. "Who would
join with an old man?"

"I would," Saliman assured him, "if that old
man were you. You have your wealth, you know
the town and you have a mind that can use power
like your hands used a sword. You could run the
town. I'm sure enough of it to stake my future on
it."

Jubal pondered a moment. Perhaps he was
being hasty. Perhaps there were others like
Saliman. "Exactly how would we build a secret
organization? How could we be unseen, unknown and still be effective?" he asked carefully.

"In many ways it would be easier than working openly as we have in the past," Saliman
laughed. "As I see it—"

"Excuse me," Hakiem got to his feet, "but I fear
you are getting into matter not safe for a tale-
spinner to hear. Some other time I will listen to
your story—if you're willing to tell it to me,
still."

Jubal waved farewell to the storyteller, but his
mind was already elsewhere carefully weighing
and analyzing the possibilities Saliman had set
forth. He just might be able to do it. Sanctuary
was a town that thrived on greed and fear, and he
was well-versed in the usage of both.

Yes. Barring any major changes in the town, he
could do it. Pacing thoughtfully, he called for
Saliman to brief him on everything that had
happened in Sanctuary since the raid.

DOWNWIND

by

C. J. Cherryh

i

There was enterprise among the sprawl of huts
and shanties that was the Downwind of
Sanctuary. Occasionally someone even found
the means of exacting a livelihood out of the
place. The aim of most such was to get out of
Downwind as quickly as possible, on the first
small hoard of coin, which usually saw the en-
trepreneurs back again in a fortnight, broke and
slinking about the backways, sleeping as the des-
titute immemorially slept, under rags and
scraps and up against the garbage they used for
forage (thin pickings in the Downwind) for the
warmth of the decaying stuff. So they began
again or sank in the lack of further ideas and died
that way, stark and stiff in the mud of the alleys
of Downwind.

Mama Becho was one who prospered. There
was an air to Mama Becho, but so there was to
everyone in Downwind. The stink clung to skin
and hair and walls and mud and the inside of the
nostrils, and wafted on the winds, from the offal
of Sanctuary's slaughterhouses and tanneries
and fullers and (on days of more favorable wind)
from the swamp to the south; but on the rare days

the wind blew out of the north and came clean, the reek of Downwind itself overcame it so that no one noticed, least of all Mama Becho, who ran the only tavern in the Downwind. What she sold was mostly her own brew, and what went into it (or fell into it) in the backside of her shanty-tavern, not even Downwinders had courage to ask, but paid for it, bartered for it and (sometimes in the dark maze of Downwind streets) knifed for it or died of it. What she sold was oblivion and that was a power in Downwind like the real sorcery that won itself a place and palaces across the river that divided Sanctuary's purgatory from this neighboring hell.

So her shanty's front room and the alley beside was packed with bodies and areek with fumes of brew and the unwashed patrons who sprawled on the remnants of makeshift furniture, itself spread with rags that had layered deep over un-laundered years, the latest thrown to cover holes in the earlier. By day the light came from the window and the door; by night a solitary lamp provided as much smoke as light over the indistinct shapes of lounging bodies and furnishings and refuse. The back room emitted smoke of a different flavor and added a nose-stinging reek to the miasma of the front room. And that space and that eventually fatal vice was another of Mama Becho's businesses.

She moved like a broad old trader through the reefs of couches and drinkers, the flotsam of debris on the floor. She carried clusters of battered cups of her infamous brew in stout red fists, a mountainous woman in a tattered smock which had stopped having any color, with a crazy twist of grizzled hair that escaped its wooden skewers and flew in wisps and clung to her cheeks in sweaty strings. Those arms could heave a full ale keg or evict a drunk. That scowl, of deepset eyes like stones, of jaws clamped tight and mouth lost in jowls, was perpetual and legendary in the Downwind. Two boys assisted her, shadow-eyed and harried and the subject of rumors only whispered *outside* Mama Becho's. Mama Becho had always taken in strays, and no few of them were grown, like Tygoth, who might be her own or one of the foundlings, and lounged now with half-crazed eyes following the boys. Tygoth was Mama Becho's size, reputed half her wit, and loyal as a well-fed hound. There was besides, Haggit, who was one of Mama's eldest, a lean and twisted man with lank greasy hair, a beggar, generally: but some mornings he came home, limping not so badly as he did in Sanctuary's streets, to spend his take at Mama Becho's.

So enterprise brought some coin to the Downwind in these days of unrest, with Jubal fallen and the Stepsons riding in pairs down the street, striking terror where they could; and coin inevitably brought the bearer to Mama Becho's, and bought a corner of a board that served as a bench, or a pile of rags to sit on, or for the fastidious, the table, the sole real table with benches, and a draft of one of Mama Becho's special kegs or even (ceremoniously wiped with a grimy rag) a cup and a flask of wine.

Mradhon Vis occupied the table this night as he had many nights, alone. Mad Elid had tried him again with her best simper and he had scowled her off, so she had slunk out the door to try her luck and her thieving fingers on some drunker prey. Thoughts seethed in him tonight that would have chilled Elid's blood, vague and half-formed needs. He wanted a woman, but not Elid. He wanted to kill, someone, several some-ones in particular, and he was no small part drunk, imagining Elid's screams—even Elid might scream, which he would like to hear, which might ease his rage at least so long as he was mildly drunk and seething. He had no real grudge against Elid but her persistence and her smell, which was nothing which deserved such hate. It was perhaps because, looking at her, with her foolish grin that tried to seduce and dis-gusted him instead, he saw something else, and darker, and more terrible; and smelled behind her reek a delicate musk, and saw hell behind her eyes.

Or he saw himself, who also had traded too much of himself and sold what he would have kept if he had had the luxury.

But generally the whores and the bullies let Mradhon Vis alone. That was tribute of a kind in Mama Becho's, to an outsider, and not a large man. He was foreign. It was in his dark face and in his accent. And if he was watched, still no one had seriously tried him, excepting Elid.

He paid for the special wine. He maintained his solitude through a slice of gritty stoneground bread and some of Mama Becho's passable bean soup, and kept his surreptitious watch over the door.

Night after night he spent here, and many of his days. He lodged across the alley, in space Mama Becho rented for more than it was worth—excepting her assurance that it would stay inviolate, that the meager furnishings would always be there, that there would never be

some sly opening of the door when he was out or
while he was asleep. Tygoth made his rounds of
Mama's properties all night with stick in hand,
and if anything was not what it ought to be, then
corpses floated down the White Foal in the
morning.

That was good so long as his small hoard of
coin lasted, and it was running low. Then the
reckoning came.

The woman-mountain rolled his way and
loomed beside him, setting down a second cup
of wine and repossessing the empty. "Fine
stuff," she said, "this."

He laid down the coin she wanted. Fingers the
match of Tygoth's picked it off the scarred table
with incongruously long curved nails, ridged
like horn. "Thank 'ee," she said sweetly. Her face
in its halo of grizzled hair, its mound of
cheeks—grinned to match the voice, but the eyes
in their suety pits were black and almond and
glittered like eyes he had seen the other side of
swords-point. She fed him on the best, gave him
sleeping space like a farmwife some fatted hog;
he knew. She would be sure she had all the
money first and then go on to other things—
Mama Becho dealt in souls, both men and
women, and she named the services, when the
coin was gone. She had him in her eye—a man
who could be useful, but having weaknesses—a
man who had tastes that cost too much. She
scented helplessness, he reckoned; she smelled
blood and made sure that he bled all he had—
and oh, she would be there when he had run out
of money, grinning that snake's grin at him and
offering him his choices, knowing he would die
without, because a man like him did die in the

Downwind when the money ran out along with any hope of getting more. He would not beg, or sell what sold in the Downwind; he would kill to get out; or kill himself with binges of Downwind brew, and Mama knew what a delicate bird she had in her nets—delicate though he had survived half a dozen battlefields: he could not survive in the Downwind, not as Downwinders did. So it was possession that gleamed in Mama's deepset eyes, the way she regarded one of her treasured pewter cups or looked at one of her boys, assessing its best use and on whom it was best bestowed.

She kept a private den backstairs, that ragpiled, perfume-stinking boudoir with the separate back door, out of which her Boys and Girls came and went on her errands, out of which wafted the fumes of wine and expensive krrf—he lived opposite that door like the maw of hell, had been inside once, when he let his room. She had insisted on giving him a cup of wine and taking him to Her Room when explaining the rules and the advantages her Boys' protection afforded. She had offered him krrf—a small sample, and given him to know what else she could supply. And that den continued its furtive visitors, and Tygoth to walk his patrol, rapping on the walls with his stick, even in the rain, tap-tap, tap-tap, tap-tap in the night, keeping that alley safe and everything Mama owned in its place.

"Come backstairs," Mama would say when the money ran out. "Let's talk about it." Grinning all the while.

He knew the look. Like Elid's. Like—

He drank to take a taste from his mouth, made the drink small, because his life was measured in such sips of his resources. He hated, gods, he hated. Hated women, hated the bloodsucking lot of them, in whose eyes there was darkness that drank and drank forever.

There had been a woman, his last employer. Her name was Ischade. She had a house on the river. And there was more than that to it. There were dreams. There was that well of dark in every woman's eyes, and that dark laughter in every woman's face, so that in any woman's arms that moment came that turned him cold and useless, that left him with nothing but his hate and the paralysis in which he never yet had killed one—whether because there was a remnant of selfwill in him or that it was terror of her that kept him from killing. He was never sure. He slept alone now. He stayed to the Downwind, knowing she was fastidious, and hoping she was too fastidious to come here; but he had seen her first walking the alleys of the Maze, a bit of night in black robes, a bit of darkness no moon could cure, a dusky face within black hair, and eyes no sane man should ever see. She hunted the alleys of Sanctuary. She still was there . . . or on the river, or closer still. She took her lovers of a night, the unmissable, the negligible, and left them cold by dawn.

She had sent him from her service unscathed—excepting the dreams, and his manhood. She called him in his nightmares, promising him an end—as he had seen her whisper to her victims and hold them with her eyes. And at times he wanted that end. That was what frightened him most, that the darkness beckoned like the only harbor in the world, for a man without hire and patronage, for a Nisibisi wanted by law at home and stranded on the wrong side of a war.

He dared not become too drunk. The night Mama Becho ever thought he had all his money on him, which he had—Then they would go for him. Now it was a game. They tested him, learned him and his resources, whether he was a thief or no, what skills he had. So he still baffled them.

And watched the door. Desperately casual, pretending not to watch.

All of a sudden his heart lurched an extra beat and began to hammer in his chest, for the man he had been waiting for had just come through the door; and Mradhon Vis sipped his wine and gave the most blunt disinterested stare that he gave to all comers, not letting his eyes linger in the least on this young ruffian, darkhaired, darkskinned, who came here to spend his money. The man came closer, edged past his back, and sat down at the end of the same table, which made staring inconvenient. Mradhon feigned disinterest, finished his wine, got up and walked away through the debris and out the open door, where drinkers and drunks took the fresher air, leaned on walls or sprawled against them or sat on the two benches.

So Mradhon took his place, his shoulders to the wall in the shadows, and stood and stood until his knees were numb, while the traffic came and went in and out Mama Becho's door, until soon Tygoth would take up his vigil in the alleyway.

Then the man came out again, reeling a little in satiation—but not that much, and not lingering among the loiterers by the door.

ii

The quarry passed to the right and Mradhon
Vis leaned away from his wall, stepped over the
sprawled legs of a fellow hanger-on and went
after the young man, along the muddy streets
and alleyways. The wine had lost its effect on
him in his waiting, but he pretended its influence in his step—he had learned such strategems
in his residency in the Downwind. He knew the
ways thereabouts, every door, every turning that
could take a body out of sight in a moment. He
had studied them with all the care with which in
other days he had studied broader terrain, and
now he stalked this shanty maze, knowing just
when his step might sound on harder ground,
when his quarry, turning a corner, might chance
to see him, and where he might safely lag back or
take a shorter way. He had not known which way
this man might go; but he had him now, and
knew every way that he might take, no matter
which way he might turn. It had been a long wait
already—for this man, this current hope of his,
who visited Becho's with money, who also liked
his wine, and bought krrf in the back room.

He knew this man—who did not know him.
Knew him from a place across the river, in the
Maze, in a place where he had courted Jubal's
employ, once in better days. And if there was a
chance left to him, it was this. He had tracked
this man on another night and lost him; but this
night he knew the ground, had set the odds in his
own favor in this hunt.

And the man—youth—was at least some part
drunk.

The way crossed the main road, past a worse and worse tangle of hovels, past the flimsy shelters of the hopeless, the old, the desolate, and now and again a doorway where someone had taken shelter against the wind, eyes that saw everything and nothing in the dark, witnesses whose own misery enveloped them and left only apathy behind.

Down a side track and into an alley this time, and it was a dead end: the quarry entered it and Mradhon knew—knew the door there, as he knew every turn and twist of this street. He thrust himself around the corner, having heard the steps go on.

"You," Mradhon said. "Man."

The youth whirled, hand to belt, with the quick flash of steel in the blackness.

"Friend," Mradhon said. He had his own knife, in case.

If the young man's mind had been fumed, it was shocked clear now. He had set himself in a knifeman's crouch and Mradhon measured it as too far for any simple move.

"Jubal," Mradhon said ever so softly. "That name make a difference to you?"

Still silence.

"I've got business to talk with you," Mradhon said. "Suppose we do that."

"Maybe." The voice came tightly. The crouch never varied. "Come a little closer."

"Why don't you open that door and let's talk about it."

Another silence.

"Man, are we going to stand here for the world to watch? I know you, I'm telling you. I'm by myself. The risk is on my side."

"You stand there. I'll open the door. You go in first."

"Maybe you've got friends in there."

"You're asking the favors, aren't you? Where did I get you on my heel? Or were you waiting on the street?"

Mradhon shrugged. "Ask me inside."

"Maybe I'll talk to you." The voice grew reasoned and calm. "Maybe you just put away that knife and keep your hands where I can see them." The youth inserted his knife in the seam of the door and flipped up the latch inside, pushed it open. The inside was dark. "Go first, about six steps across the room."

"Let's have a light first, shall we?"

"Can't do that, man. No one in there to light it. Just go on."

"Sorry. Think I'll stand here after all. Maybe you'll change your living after tonight; maybe you'll slip me after this. So I'll have my say here—"

"Have it inside." A second figure stepped into the alley out of the dark doorway, and the voice was female. "Come on in. But go first."

He thought about it. The pair of them stood in front of him. "One of you get a light going in there."

The second figure vanished, and in a moment a dim light flared, casting a faint glow on the youth outside. Mradhon calculated his chances, slipped his own knife into its sheath and went, with a prickling sensation at his nape—a short step up to the floor with the man at his back, a flash of the eye about the single room, the tattered faded curtain at the end that could conceal anything; the woman; a single cot this side,

clothing hung on pegs, water jugs, pots and pan-
nikins set on a misshapen brick firepit at the
right on the rim of which the lamp sat. The
woman was the finer image of the man, dark hair
cropped close as his, like twins—brother and
sister at least. He turned. The brother shut the
door behind him with a push of his foot.

"Mama Becho's," the brother said. "That was
where you were."

"You're Jubal's man," Mradhon said and ignored the knife to walk over to the wall nearest
the clothes, where a halfwall jutted out to shield
his back from the curtain. "Still Jubal's man, I'm
guessing, and I'm looking for hire."

"You're crazy. Out. There's nothing for you
here."

"Not so easy." He saw one cloak on the pegs.
The man wore one. There was some clothing, not
abundant. He fingered the cloak, letting them
follow his train of thought, and looked at them
again, folded his arms and leaned back against
the wall. "So Jubal's got troubles, and maybe he's
in the market. I work cheap—to start. Room and
board. Maybe your man can't support anything
more right now. But times change. And I'm willing to ride through this—difficulty. Better days
might come. Mightn't they? For all of us."

The woman made a quiet move that took her to
the side. She sat down on the cot, and that put
their hands on different levels, at different angles
to his vision. He recognized the stalking and
the angle the man occupied between him and the
door, the curtain at his shoulder, so he moved
again a couple of paces along the wall, slipped
his hands both into his belt (but the one not far

from his knife) and shrugged with a wry twist of his mouth.

"I tell you I work cheap," he said, "to start."

"There's no hire," the man said.

"Oh, there has to be," Mradhon said softly, "otherwise you wouldn't like my leaving here at all, and I've walked in here in good faith. It's your pick, you understand, how it goes from here. An introduction to your man, a little earnest coin—"

"He's dead," the woman said, and shook his faith in his own bluff. "The hawkmasks are all like us—looking for employ."

"Then you'll find it. I'll throw in with you— partners, you, me, the rest of you."

"Sure," the man said, and scowled. "You've got the stink of hire about you already. What coin? The prince's?"

Mradhon forced a laugh and leaned back again. "Not likely. Not likely the Hell-Hounds or any of that ilk. My last hire turned sour, and a post in the guard—no. Not with your complexion—or mine. Your man, now—So he and you are lying low a while, and maybe I've got reasons for doing the same. There are people I don't want to meet. No better service I can think of—than a man who might be building back from a little difficulty. Don't give me that. Jubal's gone to cover. Word's around. But one of those hawkmasks might suit me . . . keeping my face out of the sight of two or three."

"I'm afraid you're out of luck."

"No," the woman said, "I think we ought to talk about it."

Mradhon frowned, trusting her less, liking it

not at all that it was the woman that took that twist, that looked at him from the cot and tried to demand his attention away from her brother? cousin? with a quiet, incisive voice.

Then the curtain moved, and a darkskinned man in a hawkmask stood there with a sword aimed floorward in his hand. "We talk," the man said, and Mradhon's heart, which had leapt several beats while his fingers, obeying previous decision, stayed still . . . began to beat again.

"So," Mradhon said cockily enough, "I was wondering when the rest of us would get into it. Look—I'm short of funds . . . a little bit for earnest, so I can reckon I'm hired. I'm particular about that."

"Mercenary," the young man said.

"Once," Mradhon said. "The guard and I came to a parting of the ways. It's this skin of mine."

"You're not Ilsigi," said the mask.

"Half." It was a lie. It served, when it was convenient.

"You mean," the youth said, "your mother really knew."

Heat flamed up in Mradhon's face. He gripped the knife and let it go again. "When you know me better," Mradhon said softly, "I'll explain it all . . . how women know."

"Cut it," the woman said. She tucked her feet up within her arms.

"What would it take," the hawkmask said, "for you to consider yourself hired?"

Mradhon looked at the man, his heart pounding again. He sat down on the edge of the firepit, making himself easy when his instincts were all otherwise. He thought of something exorbitant, remembered the hawkmasks' fallen fortunes.

"Maybe a silver bit—Maybe some names, too."

"Maybe you don't need them," the hawkmask said.

"I want to know who I'm dealing with. What the deal is for."

"No. Mor-am; Moria; they'll deal with you. You'll have to take your orders there—Does that gall you?"

"Not particularly," Mradhon said, and that too was a lie. "As long as the money's regular."

"So you knew Mor-am's face."

"From across the river. From days before the trouble. I dealt with a man named Stecho."

"Stecho's dead."

The tone put a wind down his nape. He shrugged. "So, well, I suspect a lot were lost."

"Stabbed. On the street. Tempus' games. Or someone's. These are hard times, Vis. Yes, we've lost a few of us. Possibly someone talked. Or someone knew a face. We don't wear the masks outside, Vis. Not now. You don't talk in your sleep, do you, Vis?"

"No."

"Where lodging?"

"Becho's."

"If," the voice grew softer still, difficult, for its timbre, "if there were a slip, we would know. You see, it's your first job to keep Mor-am and Moria safe. If anything should happen to the two names you knew—well, we'd suspect, I'm afraid, that you'd made some kind of mistake. And the end of that would be very bad. I can't describe enough—how bad. But that won't happen; I know you'll take good care. Go back to your lodgings. For now, go there. We'll see about later."

"How long?" Mradhon asked tautly, not favoring this threatening and believing every word of it. "Maybe I should move in here—to keep an eye on them."

"Out," said Mor-am.

"Money," Mradhon said.

"Moria," the hawkmask said.

The woman uncurled from the cot, fished a bit from the purse she wore and offered it to him.

He took it, snatched it from her fingers without a look, and strode for the door. Mor-am got out of his way and he opened it, stepped out into the foul wind and the dark and the reek of the alley, and walked, out onto the main way again.

Doubtless one of them would follow him. His mind seethed with possibilities, and murder was one. For less than the silver, any one of them would kill. He sensed that. But there was the chance too that the hire was real: their casualties were real, and they could not get too many offers now.

He padded as quickly as he could toward his own territory down the main road, down which the last few stragglers moved, homeless and searching, muddle-minded, some, which kleetel left of one when its use had been too long; or moving with purpose it was unwise to stare at. He strode along in a world of faceless shapes and lightless buildings, everything anonymous as himself. Hooves sounded in the dark, moving in haste, and in a moment the streets were clear, himself among the lurkers that hid along the alleys: a quartet of riders passed toward the bridge, Stepsons, Tempus' men. They were gone in a moment and life poured back onto the street.

So the business out by Jubal's estate con-

tinued, and Tempus settled in. A shiver ran
down Mradhon's spine, for the inconvenience of
the neighborhood. He wanted out—desperately
he thought of Caronne—if he had had the funds.
But they hunted spies. War with Nisibis was on
them. Any foreigner was suspect, and one who
really happened to be Nisibisi—

Most especially he avoided the main ways
after that, grateful for the anonymity of Mama
Becho's, which lay off the main track the carts
and the riders took. Something in him shivered,
remembering the hire he had just accepted, pay
which had set him against the new occupants of
the estate. Tempus' men hunted hawkmasks as
they hunted spies and foreigners; and gods knew
it was no prettier way to go.

The alleyways unwound, almost home territory now. A beggar or two always huddled near
Mama Becho's, one wakeful enough tonight to
put out a claw and want a coin—a true cripple,
perhaps, or too sick to make the bridge to richer
streets. A dry spitting attended his lack of charity.

Then for one heart-stopped moment he heard a
sound behind, and turned, but there was nothing
but the moon on a muddy alley and the tilt-
walled buildings leaning together like some
fever dream of hell in the dark.

Followed, he thought. He quickened his pace,
on the verge of home, and came to the alleyway
by Mama's, where the drinking continued, and
the hangers-about-the-door still loitered, but
fewer of them. He walked into that alley and
Tygoth was there, to his relief, a hulking stick-
carrying shadow making his rounds.

"It's Vis," Mradhon said.

"Huh," was Tygoth's comment. Tygoth rapped against the wall with his stick. "Walk with you?"

Tygoth did, taking his duty seriously, rapping the wall as he went, rapping at the door of his lodgings, opening the door for him like the servant of some palatial home, across from the lighted parchment window that was Mama Becho's own.

"Coin," Tygoth said, and held out his hand. Mradhon laid the nightly fee in the huge palm, and the sturdy fingers closed. Tygoth went into the room and fetched the little light from its niche by the door, stumped away with it to Mama Becho's back door and opened that to light it from that inside, then came back again, shielding the flame with his monstrous hand. With greatest care he went inside and set it in its place.

"Safe," Tygoth declared then, a murmurous rumble, and walked off tapping his stick against the walls.

Mradhon looked after that shambling shadow, then went in and barred the door.

Safe.

So he had a bit of silver to bolster his dwindling coppers, and a bar on the door for the night, but it was in his mind that this Mor-am and Moria would change their lodgings tonight and not show up again.

He hoped. It was more surety than he had had the day before.

In the safety of his room he pinched out all but the nightwick and lay down to his sleep, hoping for sleep, but knowing that there would be dreams.

There always were.

*   *   *

Ischade, the wind whispered coming from the river and riffling through the debris outside. He dreamed her walking the streets of Downwind this time, her black robes unsullied, and the stench became the musk that surrounded her, like the smell of blood, like the smell of dead flowers or old, dusty halls.

He waked in sweat, more than once. He lay awake and stared into the dark: the draft had put the wick out. It always did. He reminded himself that there was the silver; he felt it in the dark, like a talisman, proving that that meeting had been real.

He needed anonymity and gold. He needed power that could put locks on doors. He put fanatic hope in this Jubal, who had once had both.

Whenever he shut his eyes he dreamed.

iii

There was silence in the small company, a prolonged silence inside the cramped quarters that had been one of their safe shelters, with Mor-am sulking in a crouch against the wall and Moria folded in the other corner, her arms about her knees. Eichan occupied the cot, crosslegged, arms wrapped about his huge chest, his dark head lowered, uncommunicative. What could be done had been done. They waited.

And finally the scurrying came in the alley outside, which brought heads up and got

Mor-am and Moria to their feet: no attack, not likely. Two of their own were on the street now, watching.

"Get it," Eichan said, and Moria unlatched the door.

It was Dzis, who stepped owlishly into the faint light they afforded inside—no mask, not on the streets these days: all Dzis managed was dirt, and the stink that armored all Downwind's unwashed. "He went where he said," Dzis said. "He's snugged in at Becho's alley."

"Good," Eichan said, and got up from the cot, taking his cloak across his arm. "You stay here," he said to Mor-am and Moria. "Use the drop up the way. Keep on it."

"You didn't have to give our names," Moria said. She trembled with rage, whether at Eichan or at her brother. "Any objection if we settle that bastard outright?"

"And leave questions unanswered?" Eichan flung on the cloak. He towered, difficult to conceal if one suspected it was Eichan. "No. We can't afford that now. You've cost us a safe hole. You live in it. And watch yourselves."

"There'll be watchers," Moria said, hoping that there would.

"Maybe," said Eichan. "And maybe not." He followed Dzis back out the door and pulled it after him. The latch dropped. The lampflame waved shadows round the walls.

Moria turned round and looked at her brother, a burning stare.

Mor-am shrugged.

"Hang you," Moria said.

"Oh, that's not what they do to hawkmasks lately. Not the ones on our trail."

"You had to go to Becho's, had to have it, didn't you? You let someone follow you, stinking stewed—*get off it*, hear me? Get off that stuff. It'll kill you. It almost did. When the Man gets back—"

"There's no guarantee he's coming back."

"Shut up." She darted a frantic glance at the door, where one of the others could still be listening. "You know better than that."

"So—they got him good this time, and Tempus wins. And Eichan goes on pushing and shoving as if the Man was still—"

"Shut up!"

"Jubal's not in shape to do anything, is he? They go on hunting hawkmasks in the street and none of us know when we'll be next. We live in holes and hope the Man gets back. . . ."

"He'll settle with them when he does. If we keep it all together. If—"

"If. If and if. Have you *seen* that lot that's moved in on the estate? Jubal'll never go back there. He won't face them down. Can't. Did you hear the riders in the street? That's permanent."

"Shut up. You're stiffed."

Mor-am walked over to the wall and pulled his cloak off the peg.

"Where do you think you're going?"

"Out. Where there's less noise."

"Don't you dare."

He slung it on and headed for the door.

"Come back here." She grabbed at his arm, futile: he had long ago outweighed her. "Eichan will have your head."

"Eichan doesn't care. He feeds us pennies and gives silver out with our names for the asking."

"You won't go after him. Eichan said—"

"Eichan said. Stay out of my business. No, I won't cut the bastard's throat. Not tonight. I've got a headache. Just let me alone."

"All right, all right, I won't talk to you, just stay inside."

He pulled the door open and went out it.

"*Mor-am!*" she hissed.

He turned and held up a coin. "Enough to get me really drunk. But only enough for one. Sorry."

He whirled and left, a flurry of a ragged cloak. Moria closed the door, crossed the room, flung herself down to sit on the cot with her head in her hands and the blood pounding in her temples. She was scared. She wanted to hit something. Anything. Since the raid had scattered them with half their number dead, it was all downhill. Eichan tried to hold it together. They had no idea whether he had what he claimed to have, whether Jubal was even still alive. She doubted it sometimes, but not out loud. Mor-am's doubts were wider. She did not fully blame him: tonight she hated Eichan—and remembered it was Mor-am himself who had led the outsider to them. Drunk. Stoned on krrf, using far too much.

And Becho's—any place was dangerous if they frequented it, if they set up a pattern, and her brother had a pattern. His habits led him here and led him there. There was the smell of death about him, that terrified her. All the enemies the slaver Jubal had ever accumulated (and they were many) had come to pick bones now that his power was broken; from the days that hawk-masks used to swagger in gaudy dress through the streets, now they wore ragged cloaks and slunk into any hole that would keep them. And that was, for all of them, a bitter change.

Mor-am^ could not bear it. She gave him money, doled it out, hers and his; but he had lied to her—she knew he had; and gotten that little more that it needed for Becho's. Or he had cut a purse or a throat, defying Eichan's plain orders. He was committing slow suicide. She knew. They had come up together out of this reek, this filth, to Jubal's service, and learned to live like lords; and now that it was back to the gutter again, Mor-am refused to live on those terms. She held onto him with all her wit and talents, covered for him, lied for him. Eichan might kill him himself if he had seen him go; or beat him senseless: she wished she had the strength to pound the idiocy out of him, flatten him against a wall and talk sense to him. But there was no one to do that for him. Not for years.

*   *   *

Mor-am flung off down the street, striding along with purpose none of the sleepers in doorways challenged, getting off the main road as quickly as he might.

But something stirred another way. A beggar dislodged himself from his doorway near an alley and shuffled along until he reached shadows, then moved quite differently, hunkering down when he thought it might serve and running spryly enough when there was need.

Then other beggars began to move, some truly lame, but not all.

And one of them had already gone, scuttling

along alleys as far as a shack near Mama Becho's, at the back of which the White Foal river flowed its sluggish, black-glistening way beneath the bridge.

Guards dozed there, about the walls, unlikely as guards as he was unlikely as a messenger, in rags, one a little urchin-girl sleeping in the alley, who looked up and went back to her interrupted nap, a huddle of bony limbs; and one a one-legged man who did the same; but that hulk nearest the door got up and faced the messenger.

"Got something," the messenger said, "himself'd want to hear."

The guard rapped at the door. In a little time it opened on the dark inside, and a shutter opened, affording light enough to someone who had been inside all along.

The messenger went in and squatted down in a crouch natural to his bones and delivered what he had heard.

So Moruth listened, sitting on his bed, and when the messenger was done, said: "Put Squith on it, and Ister."

Luth-im left, bowing in haste.

Mama's latest boarder. Moruth pondered the idea, hands clasped on his knees, smiling and frowning at once because any link between his home territory and the hawkmasks he hunted made him uneasy. There was, in the dark, on the back side of the door, a mask pinned with an iron nail, and there was blood on it that had dried like rust in the daylight; but only those that came to this shack and had the door closed on them could see it. It was a joke of sorts. Moruth had a sense of humor, like his half-brother Tygoth shambling along the alleys by Mama's, rapping

his stick and mumbling slackwitted nonsense.
He had one now, and ordered Luth-im himself
followed: the urchin was summoned to the door
and given a message to take.

So Tygoth would know.

"Good night," Moruth told his lieutenant, and
the man closed the shutters and the door, leaving
him his darkness and his sleep.

But he kept rocking and thinking, pondering
this and that, shifting pieces on his mental map
of Downwind alleys, remembering this and that
favor owed, and how to collect.

Hawkmasks died, and either they were loyal
(which seemed unlikely) or ignorant where Jubal
lay, even in extremity. He had had three so far.
The one nailed to the door had told him most,
where these two lodged; but so far he had not
pounced. He knew the homes and haunts of
others.

And suddenly the trail doubled back again, to
Mama's, to his own territory. He was not
amused.

*   *   *

And just the other side of the bridge, in a
curious gardened house with well-lighted windows casting a glow on the same black water. . . .

Ischade received quite another messenger, a
slave and young, and handsome after a foreign
fashion, who appeared at her gate disturbing
certain wards, who came up the path only after
hesitating some long time, and stood inside her
dwelling as if he were dazed.

He was a gift, constantly held out to her. He

had come and gone frequently, sent by those who had offered her employ, and stood there now staring at the floor, at anything but herself. Perhaps he had known in the beginning that he was not meant to come back to his masters; or that his handsomeness was to have attracted her and offered a reward; he was not stupid, this slave. He was scared, perpetually, sensing something, if only that his mind was not what it ought to be when he was here, and he would not, this time, look at her, not at all. She was, on one level, amused, and on another, vexed with those who had sent him—as if she were some beast, to take what was thrown to her, even so delicate an offering as this.

But they dared not come themselves. They were that cautious, these adherents of Vashanka, not putting themselves within this room.

She was untidy, was Ischade; her small nest of a house was strewn not with rags but with silks and cloaks and such things as amused her. Her taste was garish, with unsubtle fire-colored curtains, a velvet throw like a puddle of emerald, and it all undusted, unkept, a ruby necklace like a scatter of blood lying atop the litter on a gilded table—a bed never made, but tossed with moire silks and hung with dusty drapes. She loved color, did Ischade, and avoided it for her dress. Her hair was a fall of ink about her face; her habiliments were blacker than night; her eyes—

But the slave would not look at them.

"Look up," she said, when she had read the message, and after a moment he must. He stared at her. The fear grew quiet, because she had that skill. She held him with her eyes. "I did a service for one your masters knew—lately. They seem to think this obligates me. Nothing does. Do they realize this?"

He said nothing, shaped a no with his lips. He had no wish to be party to any confidences, that was clear. Yes, or no, or whatever she wanted to hear; the mind, she thought, was unfocussed like the eyes.

"So. Do you know what this says?"

No, the lips shaped again.

"They want the slaver. Jubal. Does that amuse you?"

No answer at all. There was fear. It bubbled against her nerves like strong wine, harder and harder to resist, but she played with it, stronger than they judged she was, despising them—and perhaps a little mad. At times she thought she was, or might become so, and at others most coldly sane. Humor occurred to her, a private laughter, with this gift so obviously proffered, this—bribe. Animal she was not. She knew always what she did. She moved closer and her fingers touched his arm while she wove a circle round him like some magic rite. She came full circle and looked up at him, for he was tall. "Who were you?" she asked.

"Haught is my name," he said, all but a whisper, she was that close, and he managed then to look past her.

"And were you born a slave?"

"I was a dancer in Caronne."

"Debt?"

"Yes," he said, and never looked at her the while. She had, she thought, guessed wrong.

"But not," she said, "Caronnese."

There was silence.

"Northern," she said.

He said nothing. The sweat ran on his face. He never moved: could not, while she willed; but never tried: she would have felt a trial of her hold.

"They question you, don't they, about me?—each time. And what do you tell them?"

"There's nothing to tell them, is there?"

"I doubt that they are kind. Are they? Do you love them, these masters of yours? Do you know what you're really for?"

A flush stained his face. "No," she said sombrely, answering her own question. "Or you'd run, even knowing what you'd pay." She touched him as she might some fine marble, and there was such hunger, such desire for something so fine—it hurt.

"This time," she said after measuring that thought, "I take the gift . . . but I do with it what I like. My back door, Haught, is on the river, a great convenience to me; and bodies often don't surface, do they? Not before the sea. So they won't expect to find you . . . So just keep going, do you hear? Serves them right. Go somewhere. I set you free."

"You can't—"

"Go back to them if you like. But I wouldn't, if I were you. This message doesn't need an answer. Don't you reckon what that means? I'd keep running, Haught—no, here." She went to the closet and picked clothing, a fine blue cloak—many visitors left such remembrances behind. There were cloaks, and boots, and shirts—all manner of such things. She threw it at him; went to the table and wrote a message. "Take this back to them if you dare. Can you read?"

"No," he said.

She chuckled. "It says you're free." She took a purse from the table (another relic) and gave that into his hand. "Stay in Sanctuary if you choose. Or go. Take my word. They might kill you—but they might not. Not if they read that note. Do as you please and get out of here."

"They'll find me," he protested.

"Trust the note," she said, "or use the back door and the bridge."

She waved her hand. He hesitated one way and the other, went toward the front and then fled for the back, for the riverside. She laughed aloud, watching his flight from her doorway, watched him run, run down the riverside until the dark swallowed him.

But after the laughter was dead she read the message they had sent her a second time and burned it in the lamp, letting the ashes fall and scorch an amber silk, carelessly.

So Vashanka's faction went on wanting her services, and offered three times the gold. She cared nothing for that at present, having all she cared to have. She cared not to be more conspicuous, no, not if they offered her a palace for her services. And they could.

How would that be, she wondered, and how long till neighbors rebelled at the steady disappearances? She could buy slaves . . . but enter the Prince's court, but live openly—?

The thought amused, the way irony might. She could herself become Jubal, in a trade that would well suit her needs. A pity she had already taken hire—

But the irony of it palled and the bitterness stayed. Perhaps the Vashanka-lovers suspected what they did. Perhaps they had some inkling of her motives or the need—and so they sent the likes of Haught, a messenger they expected to have had thus silenced on the first visit, then to supply her with more and more; or a lure they dragged past her with cynical cruelty, to ascertain how much they believed was truth—what she was, and how long her restraint might go on.

She thought on Haught and thought, as she had each time he came to her; and that too they had surely intended. The hunger grew. Soon it would be too strong.

"Vis," she said aloud. The images merged in her mind, Vis and Haught, two dark foreigners, both of whom she had let go—because she was not pitiless. There was hell in the slave's eyes, like hers. Time after time he had passed that door in either direction, and the hell grew, and the terror that was itself a lure—one could develop such a taste, for the beauty and the fear, for gentility. Like a drug. She had more pride.

She had had no intention of going out at all tonight. But the restlessness grew, and she hated them for that, for what they had done, that now she would kill, the way she always killed—but not in the way they thought. It was the luck that followed her, the curse an enemy had laid on her.

She slung on her black cloak and pulled up the hood as she went out by that back way as well, through the small vine-tangled garden and past the gate to the river walk, pace, pace, pace along the unpaved way.

And pace, pace, pace along the bridge, a striding of small slippered feet, soft against the wooden planks; and onto the wet pavings and then the paveless alleys of the Downwind. She hunted, herself the lure, as the slave had been—

Perhaps she would find him, lingering too long in his flight. Then she would have no compunction. A part of her hoped for this, and savored the trust there might be at first, and then the terror; and part of her said no.

She was fastidious. The first accoster she met disgusted her, and she left him dazed by the close encounter of her eyes, as if he had forgotten why he was in this place at all; but the second took her fancy, being young and with that arrogance of the street tough, the selfish self-doubt that amused her in its undoing, for most of that ilk recognized her in their heart of hearts, and knew that they had met what they had hated all their twisted lives—

That kind was worth the hunt. That kind had no gentler core, to wound her with regret. This one had no regret in him, and no one in all the world would miss him.

There was an abundance of his kind in Sanctuary and its adjuncts; it was why she stayed in this place, who had known so many cities: this city deserved her . . . like the young man who faced her now.

She thought of Haught still running, and laughed a twisted laugh, but soon the assailant/ victim was too far gone to hear, and in the next moment she was.

iv

"Money," Mor-am said, sweating. His hands shook and he folded his arms about his ribs under his cloak, casting a furtive look this way and that down the alley of Shambles Cross, on the Sanctuary-ward side of the bridge. "Look,

I've got a man in sight; it just takes a little to get him here. Meanwhile even Downwind takes money—leading a man anywhere takes money."

"Maybe more than you're worth," the man said, a man who frightened him, even in the open alley, alone. "You know there's a string on you. You know how easy it is to draw it in. Maybe I should just say—produce the man. Bring him here. Or maybe we ought to invite you in for a talk. Would you like that,—hawkmask?"

"You've got it wrong." Mor-am's teeth chattered. The night wind felt cold even for the season; or it was Becho's stuff working at his stomach. He locked his arms the tighter. "I take chances for what I get. I've got connections. It doesn't mean I'm—"

"If we hauled you in," the man said, ever so softly with the animals grunting softly in the distance, doomed to the axe in the morning, "if we did that they'd just change all the drops and meeting places, wouldn't they? So we dribble coin into your hand and you supply us names and places and times, and they do work—don't they? But if they should be wrong—maybe I've got someone supplying me yours. Ever wonder that, Wriggly? Maybe you're not the only hawkmask who wants to turn coat. So let's not make up tales. Where? Who? When?"

"Name's Vis. At Mama Becho's."

"That's a tight place. Not easy to get at."

"That's my point. I get him to you."

There was a silence. The man brought out silver pieces and dropped them into Mor-am's hand, then clenched fingers on his as they closed. "You know," the Rankan said, "the last one named your name."

"Of course." Mor-am tried not to shake. "Wouldn't you want revenge?"

"Others have. You knew they would."

"But you want them brought out of the Downwind. And I do that for you." He clenched his jaw, a grimace against the chattering of his teeth. "So maybe we get to the big names. I give you those—I deliver them to you just like the little ones. But that's another kind of price."

"Like your life, scum?"

"You know I'm useful. You'll find I can be more useful than you think. Not cash. A way out." His teeth did chatter, spoiling his pose. "For me and one other."

"Oh, I don't doubt you'll be cooperating. You know if the word gets out on the streets how we got our hands on your friends—you know how long you'd last."

"So I'm loyal," Mor-am said.

"As a dog." The man thrust his hand back at him. "Here. Tomorrow moonrise."

"I'll get him." Mor-am subdued the shivering and sucked in a breath. "We negotiate the others."

"Get out of here."

He went, slow steps at first, and quicker, still with a tendency to shiver, still with a looseness in his knees.

*   *   *

But the man climbed the stairs of a building near that alley and made his own report.

"The slave is gone," one said, who in his silk and linen hardly belonged in the Shambles, but neither did the quarters, that were comfortable

and well-lit behind careful shutters and sealing
of the cracks. Two of the men were Stepsons,
who smelled of oil and light sweat and horses,
whose eyes were alike and cold; three had the
look of something else, a functionary kind of
coldness. "Into the Downwind. I think we can
conclude the answer is no. We have to extend
our measures. Someone knows. We take the
hawkmasks alive and eventually we find the
slaver."

"We should pull the slave in," another said.

"No," said the first. "Too disruptive. If convenient . . . we take him."

"This woman is inconvenient."

"We hardly need more inconvenience than
we've had. No. We keep it quiet. We destroy no
leads. We want this matter taken out—down to
the roots. And that means Jubal himself."

"I don't think," said the man from the street,
"that our informer can be relied on that far.
That's the one who ought to be pulled in, kept a
little closer . . . encouraged to talk."

"And if he won't? No. We still need him."

"A post. Security. Get him into our steady
employ and we'll learn where all his soft spots
are. He'll soften up fast. Just twist the screws now
and then and he'll do everything he has to."

"If you make a mistake with him—"

"No mistake. I know this little snake."

A chair grated. One of the Stepsons had put his
foot on the rung, folded his arms with elaborate
disdain for the proceedings.

"There are quicker ways," the Stepson said.

No one said anything to that. No one debated,
but slid the discussion aside from it, arguing

only the particulars and a slave who had finally run.

*   *   *

The bridge was always the worst part, coming or going. It narrowed possibilities. There was one way and only one way, afoot, to come into the Downwind, and Mor-am took it, sweating, feeling his heart pounding, with a little edge of black around his vision that might be terror or something in the krrf that he had bought, that tunnelled his vision and made his heart feel like it was starting and stopping by turns, lending an unreality to the whole night, so that he paused in the middle of the bridge and leaned on the rail, wishing that he could heave up his insides.

Then he saw the man following—he was sure that he was following, a walker who had also paused on the bridge a little ways down from him and delayed about some pretended business.

Sweat broke out afresh on him. He must not seem to see. He pushed himself away from the rail and started walking again, trying to keep his steps even. The shanties of Downwind lurched in his view under the moon, closer and closer, like the crazy pilings of the fishing-dock beside it and the sway and flare of someone's lantern near the water below. He found himself walking faster than he had intended, terror taking over.

Others used the bridge. People came and went, a straggle of them passing him in the dark, passing his pursuer and still he kept his steady pace. But one of them had veered into his path and sent his hand twitching after his knife, coming rapidly toward him.

Moria. His heart turned over as he recognized his sister face to face with him. "Walk past me," he hissed at her in desperation. "There's someone on my track."

"I'll get him."

"No. Just see who it is and keep walking."

They parted, expert mimery: importunate whore and disgusted stroller. He found his breath too short, his heartbeat pounding in his ears, trying to keep his wits about him and to concoct lies Moria would believe, all the while terrified for what might be happening behind him. There might be others. Moria might be walking into ambush set for him. He dared not turn to see. He reached the end of the bridge, kept walking, walking, walking, toward the shelter of the alleys. It was all right then, he kept telling himself; Moria could take care of herself, would recross the river and find her own way home. He was in the alleys, in his element again, of beggars crouched by the walls and mud squelching underfoot.

Then one of the beggars before him unfolded upward out of the habitual wall-braced crouch, and from behind an arm encircled him, bringing a sharp point against his throat.

"Well," a dry voice cackled, "hawkmask, we got you, doesn't we?"

*   *   *

Moria did not run. Gut feeling cried out for it, but she kept her pace, in the waning hours of the night, with thunder rumbling in the south and

flashing lightning in a threatening wall of cloud.
It was well after moonset. Mor-am had not gotten
home.

And there was a vast silence in the Downwind.
It was not nature, which boomed and rumbled
and advised that the streets and alleys of
Downwind would be aswim. The street-dwellers
were up seeking whatever scrap of precious
board or canvas that could be pilfered, carrying
their clutter of shelter-pieces with them like the
crabs down by seamouth, making traffic of their
own—It was none of these things; but it was
subtle change, like the old man who always had
the door across from their alley-door not being
there, like no hawkmask watcher where he ought
to be, in the alley across the way; or again, in the
alley second from their own. They were gone.
Eichan might have pulled them when their lair
became unsafe.

But Mor-am had been followed on the bridge,
and that follower had not led her back to Mor-
am, when she had turned round again after passing him. Panic ran hot and cold through her
veins, and guilt and self-blame and outright terror. She had become alone, like that, in the space
of time it took to walk the bridge and turn round
again; and find that the follower did not lead her
to Mor-am, or to anything; he himself had hesitated this way and that and finally recrossed the
bridge.

Mor-am would be at home, she had thought;
and he was not.

She kept walking now, casual in the mutter of
thunder, the before-storm movements of the
street people, moving because if something had
gone wrong, nowhere was really safe.

They hunted hawkmasks nowadays; and
Eichan had cast them adrift.

There was one last place to go and she went to
it, toward Mama Becho's.

The door still spilled light into the dark, where
a few patrons sprawled, drunk and unheeding of
the storm. Moria strode into it in a gust of wind,
but the bodies sprawled inside in sleep were
amorphous, heaped, drunken. There was no sign
of Mor-am. A further, darker panic welled up in
her, her last hope gone.

He still might be hiding, she tried to tell herself; might have gone to earth and determined to
stay there; or it was bad and he was still running.
Or even sleeping off a drunk.

Or dead. Like the murdered hawkmasks. Like
one who had been nailed to a pole by the bridge.

She turned and strode for the door, almost
colliding with the human mountain that suddenly filled it.

"Drink," Tygoth suggested.

"No."

He lifted his stick. "You come here to steal—"

"Looking for someone." Her mind leapt this
way and that. "Vis. Boarder of yours."

"Asleep."

She dodged past and ran, down the alley, the
only lighted alley in the Downwind, that got the
light of the ever-lit lantern at Mama Becho's
door.

"Vis," she called softly, rapping at the door.
Her hands clenched against the wood. "Vis,
wake up, get out here. Now." She heard Tygoth
coming, shambling along after her, rapping the
wall with his stick. "Vis, for the gods' sake, wake
up."

There was movement from inside.

"It's Moria," she said. The rapping was closer. "Let me in."

The door opened, a rattling of the latch. She faced a daggerpoint, a half-dressed man wild-eyed and suspecting murder. She showed her empty hands.

"Trouble?" Tygoth said behind her.

"No trouble," Vis said, and reached out and caught her by the wrist in a crushing grip, pulling her inside, into the dark. He closed the door.

*   *   *

They brought Mor-am through the dark muffled in a foul-smelling, greasy cloak; gagged and with a bandage over his eyes and his hands so long tied behind his back that they had gone beyond acute pain to a general numb hurt that involved his chest and arms as well. He would have run but they had had his knees and ankles tied too, and now he was doing well to walk at all, with his knees and ankles beyond any sensation of balance, just stabbing pain. They jerked him along in the open air, and he remembered the hawkmask they had nailed to the pole near the bridge; but they had not yet hurt him, not really, and he was paralysed with hope, that this was all some irritation of the men he worked for; or fear, that they were his own brothers and sisters, who had found out about his treason; or, or, or—His mind was in tatters. They were near the bridge now. He heard the moving of the water far away at his left, heard the mutter of thunder, that confounded itself with the sounds about him. The image flashed to him of a sodden body crucified against a pole, in the early morning rain.

*   *   *

"Just put more men on it," the Stepson said, never stirring from where he sat, in the too great warmth of the room. The naivete of the operation appalled him. But there were necessities and places too little apt for his kind. "If you can do it without sounding the alarm through every alley in the Downwind." Something had gone wrong. The abruptness of the vanishing, uncharacteristic of the informer, smelled of interventions. "This had better not go amiss," his companion said meaningfully to the man who sat and sweated across the table. "It was far too productive. And you've botched the other avenue tonight, haven't you? That contact more than failed. It went totally sour. We don't like incompetence."

*   *   *

"I haven't seen him," Mradhon Vis said, in the dark, in the narrow room. The woman—Moria—had a knife; he was sure of that, sure where she was too, by her breathing. He kept where he was, having all the territory measured, thinking, in one discrete side of his mind, that he dealt with a fool or they thought he was one, a solitary woman coming at him like this.

But a vision of dark robes flashed through the dark of his vision, with cold, with the scent of musk; she was solitary, female, and he held in his hand the knife he slept with, safer than women.

"Why didn't you go to your own?" he sneered at her. "Or is this the testing? I don't like games, bitch."

"They've cut us off." The voice quavered and steadied. He heard her move at him and brought the knife up. It met her body and she stopped, dead still, hard-breathing. "You took our pay." It was a hiss through clenched teeth. "*Do* something to earn it. Help me find him."

"Smells, woman. It smells all the way."

"He's into something. He's dealing in something. Krrf. Gods know what." The voice cracked. "Vis. Come with me. Now. After this— I'll swear to you you'll get money. You'll be in. I've got contacts I'll swear for you. Get my brother. He's dropped through a crack somewhere. Just come with me. Riverside. We've got to find him."

"How much ."

"Name it. I'll get it."

A woman who was faithful. To something. He stared at the dark, doubting all of it, standing in the den Mama Becho owned and listening to the promise of gold to get him out of it.

"Back off," he said, shoving her away, not wanting her knife in him, and he reckoned it was drawn. "I'll get my shirt. Don't make any moves. Just tell me where you reckon to look for this lost lamb."

"Riverside." She caught her breath, a moving of cloth in the dark. "That's where they turn up—the hawkmasks they murder."

He stopped, his shirt half on. He cursed him-

self, thought of the gold and made his mind up to
it.

"You'll pay for this one."

*   *   *

Mor-am kicked. They jerked him off his feet
and carried him, battering him against some narrow passage as he struggled, with the reek of wet
stone and human filth and suddenly warm and
windless air. They set him on his feet again and
jerked the blindfold off. The room came clear in a
haze of lamplight, a cot, a ragged small man
sitting on it crosslegged amid a horde of others,
the human refuse of the Downwind standing and
squatting about the room. Beggars. He felt hard
fingers working at the knot at the back of his
skull, freeing him of the gag: he choked and tried
to spit out the dirty wad and the same hard fingers pried it from his mouth, but his hands they
had no intention to release. They only let him
stand on his own, and his knees wanted to give
under him.

"Hawkmask," the man said from the bed, "my
name is Moruth. Have you heard it?"

No, he said, but his tongue stuck to his mouth
and muffled it. He shook his head.

"Right now," Moruth said quietly, an un-
pleasant voice with the accent of Sanctuary's
Maze and not the Downwind, "right now you'd
be thinking that you shouldn't know that name,
that taking that blindfold off means you're already a dead man and we don't care what you
see. Might be. That might be. Turn around."

He stood still. His mind refused to work.

"Turn 'round."

Hands jerked him about, facing the closed door. A mask was pinned there with a heavy iron nail. Terror came over him, blank terror, image of Brannas nailed to the pole. They spun him about again facing Moruth.

"You want to live," Moruth said. "You're thinking now you'd really like to live, and that this is an awful place to die." Moruth chuckled, a dry and ugly sound. "It is. Sit down—sit *down*, hawkmask."

He looked, reflexively. There was nowhere. A crutch hooked his ankle and jerked. He hit the dirt floor on his side and rolled, fighting to get his knees under him.

"Let me tell you a story," Moruth said softly, "hawkmask. Let me tell you what this Jubal did. Remember? Kill a few beggars, he said, and put the informer-sign on them, so's the riffraff knows what it is to cross Jubal the slaver, ain't it so?" The accent drifted to Downwind's nasal twang. "Ain't that what he did? And he killed us, killed boys and girls that never done no hurt to him—to impress them as might want to squeal on his business. It weren't enough he offs his own, no, no, he cut the throats of mine, hawkmask. You know something about that."

He knew. He shivered. "I don't. I don't know anything about it.—Listen, listen,—you want names—I can give you names; I can find out for you, only you let me out of here—"

Moruth leaned forward, arms on ragged knees, grinned and looked appallingly lean and hungry.

"I think we've got one what'll talk, doesn't we?"

*   *   *

Haught flinched in his concealment beneath the bridge. Screams reached him, not fright, but a crescendo of them, that was pain; and they kept on for a time. Then silence. He hugged himself and shivered. They began again, different this time, lacking distinction.

He bolted, having had enough, finding no more assurance even in the dark; and the thunder cracked and the wind skirled, blowing debris along the shore.

Of a sudden something rose up in his way, a human form in the ubiquitous rags of Downwind, but with an incongruous long blade shining pure as silver in the murk. Haught shied and dodged, ex-dancer, leapt an unexpected bit of debris and darted into the alley that offered itself, alley after alley, desperate, hearing someone whistle behind him, a signal of some kind; and then someone blocked the alley ahead.

He zigged and dodged, feinted and lost: the cloak caught, and the fastening held; he hit the wall and the ground, and a hand closed at his throat.

* * *

"Escaped slave," Moria said, crouching by the man they had knocked down. She had her knife out, aimed for the ribs; but the throat was easier and quieter, and Mradhon was in the way. "Kill him. We can't afford the noise."

"Something started him," Mradhon said.

The slave babbled a language not Rankan, not Ilsigi, nothing she knew, sobbing for air. "Shut up," Mradhon said, shaking him and letting his hand from the man's throat. Mradhon said something then, the same way, and the slave stopped struggling and edged up against the wall. He talked, an urgent hiss in the gloom, and Mradhon kept the knife at his throat.

"What's that?" Moria asked, clenching her own hilt in a sweating fist. "What's that babble?"

"Keep still," Mradhon said, reached with his fist and the hilt of his knife and touched the slave gently on the side of the cheek. "Come show us, seh? Come show us the place. Fast."

"What place?" Moria demanded, shoving Mradhon's arm.

Mradhon ignored her, hauling the slave to his feet. She got up too, knife aimed, but not meaning to use it. The slave had straightened up like a human being, if a frightened one, and moved free of Mradhon's grip, travelling with lithe speed. Mradhon followed and she did, as far as the opening of the alley.

"River," the slave said, delaying there. "By the bridge."

"Move," Mradhon said.

The slave rolled his head aside, staring back at them, muttered something.

"Seh," Mradhon repeated. "Move it, man." Mradhon set an empty hand on his shoulder. The slave gave a gasp for air like a diver going under and headed down the next alley, stopping again when they reached a turning.

"Lost," the slave said, seeming to panic. "I can't remember; and there were men—men with swords—and the screams—It was the house by the bridge, that one—"

"Get moving," Moria hissed frantically and

jabbed him with the blade. The slave flinched, but Mradhon stayed her hand with a grip that almost broke her wrist.

"He's likely still alive," Mradhon said. "You want my help, woman, you keep that knife out of my way; and his."

She nodded, wild with rage and the delay. "Then quit stopping."

"Haught," Mradhon said. "Stay with us."

They went, running now, with no pauses, down the twisting ways even she did not know; but it was Mradhon's territory: they passed through a shanty alleyway so close they had to turn their shoulders and came out upon sight of the bridge.

It was quiet, excepting the wind, the dry, muttering thunder. A lightning flash threw the pilings of the bridge and the house by the pier into an unnatural blink of day, exposed a bridge vacant of traffic.

"There," said the slave, "there, that was the place—"

"Better stay back here," Mradhon said.

"It's quiet," Moria said. Her voice shook despite herself. "Man, hurry up." She pushed at him and got shoved in turn. He caught a fistful of her shirt and jerked at her.

"Don't shove. Get your mind working, woman, cool down, or I'm off this."

"I'll get round by the windows," she said, shivering. "I'll find out. But if you run out on me—"

"I'll be working up the other side. Haught and I. If it's even odds we take them. If it isn't we pull off, hear, and refigure."

She nodded and caught her breath, trotted off with a looseness of her knees she had not felt since her first job; felt as vulnerable as then, everything gone wrong. She sorted her mind into order, pretending it was not Mor-am in there, in that long quiet, where screams had been before.

She took a back alley, disturbing only an urchin-girl from her rest, going round the long way, where boards might gape and afford sight or sound, but none did. She kept going, focussed now, lost in the moment-by-moment calculations, and found the windows she hoped for, shuttered, but there was a crack.

She listened, and something went twisted inside. It was a quiet voice, that described streets with deadly accuracy, a strained voice that told no lies.

. . . Mor-am's. Giving away all they had.

And more than three of them in there.

"There's another house," her brother volunteered all too eagerly, "by the west side. There's a way from there out into a burned house. . . . We used that in the old days. . . ."

Shut up, she wished him, having difficulty holding her breath.

Something moved behind her. She whirled, knife thrusting, and got the man in the belly, leapt, and saw others.

"Ai!" she yelled, slashing wild, a howl that was the last shred of honor: *It's all up, it's done*— She tried to run.

There were still more, arrived from out of nowhere, a sweep of men and knives in the dark, rushing the house and alley from the riverside.

She stabbed and killed; the urchin-girl shrieked and ran into shadows as beggars scattered and guardsmen shouted orders.

Fire streaked Moria's side. She slashed and stumbled back; and back as wood cracked and the house erupted with shouting and with knives, and the back way opened, pouring out bodies.

She fell. Someone stepped on her back as she lay there, and she braced and rolled against the shanty wall as the battle tended the other way. She crawled for the alley, scrambling to her feet as she reached the corner of the shanty.

Someone grabbed her from the back and dragged her aside; the slave Haught pinned her knifehand under his arm and a hand muffled her as they hit the dark leanto together, a knot of three.

"Keep low," Mradhon hissed in her ear as tumult passed their hiding-hole. A man died not far from them in the first pattering of rain. She lay still, feeling the pain in her side when she breathed, feeling for the rest as if she had been clubbed.

Mor-am!

Fire glared, a quick flaring up of orange light in the direction of the shanty.

She struggled then. The two of them held her.

"You can't help him," Mradhon said, his arms locked round her.

"She's hurt," said Haught. "She's bleeding."

They tended her, the two of them. She hardly cared.

*   *   *

"It's him," the Stepson said, looking disdainfully at the human wreck they deposited on the road across the bridge. Rain washed the wounds, dark threads of blood trailing in a wash of water over the skin. The guard toed the informer in the side, elicited a little independent movement of the arm, lit in lightning-flashes. "Oh, treat him tenderly," the Stepson said. "Very tenderly. He's valuable. Get a blanket round him."

"We lost the rest," his companion said tautly. There was rage beneath his tone.

The Stepson looked up. A shadow stood there in the lightnings, in the rain, an unlikely cloaked shape, a darkness by the bridge.

When the lightning next flashed it was gone. Fire danced on the water, full of tricks and shadows on this side of the bank. The blaze might have taken all of Downwind, but for the rain. It was dying even now.

Six horsemen thundered across the bridge from Sanctuary to Downwind, securing the road.

"You'd better send more," the garrison officer said. "They're like rats over there, small but a lot of them. You saw that."

The Stepson fixed the man with a chill, calm eye. "I saw catastrophe. *Two* of us could have turned the town upside down if that were the object. Perhaps you misunderstood. But I rather doubt it. Six could raze the town. But that wasn't what we wanted, was it?" He looked down at the moaning informer, then collected his companion and walked away.

*   *   *

"Drink," Mradhon said. Moria drank, holding the cup herself this time, and stared blearily at the two men, Mradhon leaning over her, Haught over against the wall. It was decent food they gave her. She wondered where they got the money, dimly, in that vague way she wondered about anything. She was curious why these two kept treating her as they did, when it cost them, or why two men she had never met had proved dependable when those she had known best had not. It confounded her. They never used that language they both spoke, not since that night. Haught had put on freeman's clothing, if only that of Downwind. He had scars. She had seen them, when he dressed. So did Mradhon Vis, but different ones, made with knives.

So did she, inside and out. Maybe that was what they had in common, the three of them. Or that they wanted what she knew, names and places. Or that they were just different, thinking differently, the way people did who had not grown up in the Downwind, and that kind of maze of foreignness she never tried to figure.

She just took it that they wanted something; and so did she, which was to fill a nebulous and empty spot and to keep fed and warm and breathing.

Mor-am was dead. She hoped so. Or things were worse than she had figured.

A FUGITIVE ART

by

Diana L. Paxson

The fleeing King ran towards the Gate, the
strained lines of his back and arms, and the
bunched muscles of his thighs, eloquent of desperation. His face was shadowed and his crown
rolled in the dust; behind him lay a confusion of
arms and weapons, and the bloodied sword of
his conqueror raised against a sunset sky.

"And here we have the last King of Ilsig, pursued by Ataraxis the Great. . . ." Crimson
damask rustled stiffly as Coricidius the Vizier
motioned towards the mural that glowed on the
ancient wall. He bowed to the Prince and his
companions. The other guests at the reception
stood in a respectful half-circle on the chequered
marble of the floor.

Lalo the Limner, trailing self-consciously a
few steps behind, squinted at the painting and
wondered if he had made the sky too lurid after
all. What would they think, these great lords of
Ranke who had been sent by the Emperor to
evaluate Sanctuary's preparations for the war?

Prince Kadakithis flushed with pleasure and
peered more closely at the figure of his ancestor.
Coricidius fixed Lalo with an eye like a moulting
eagle's, summoning him. His aged skin was pallid above the vehemence of his gown.

He should not wear that color, thought Lalo,

suppressing an impulse to duck behind one of
the gilded pillars. Coricidius always affected
him that way, and he had almost refused the task
of refurbishing the Presence Hall for this visit
because of it. But however discredited the Vizier
might be in Ranke, in Sanctuary his power was
second only to that of the Prince-Governor (indeed, some said that his influence counted for
more).

"Remarkable—such freshness of line, such
originality!" One of the Imperial Commissioners
bent to examine the brushwork, chins quivering
with enthusiasm.

"My Lord Raximander, thank you. May I present the artist! Master Lalo is a native of
Sanctuary . . ."

Lalo hid his paint-stained hands behind his
back as they all looked at him, curious as if he
had been in Meyne's Menagerie. It must be only
too obvious that he lived in the city—the battered buildings through which the painted King
was fleeing belonged to the Maze.

Exuding attar of roses and geniality, Lord Raximander turned to Lalo.

"You have great talent, but why do you stay
here? You are like a pearl on the neck of a
whore!"

Lalo stared at him, then realized that the man
was not mocking him—neither the Prince nor
the Vizier had ever ventured west of the Processional, and the Maze had not been included on
the Commissioners' sight-seeing tour. He stifled
a grin, thinking of these popinjays at the mercy
of some of his old friends from the Vulgar Unicorn—like alley-cats with some Lady's pet
love-bird, they would be.

The other Commissioners were looking at the painting now—the General, the Archpriest Arbalest, Zanderei the Provisioner and an undistinguished relative of the Emperor. Lalo listened to them commenting on its naive charm and primitive vigor and sighed.

"Indeed—" came a soft voice close to his ear. "What recognition can you expect in this city of thieves? In Ranke they would know how to appreciate you. . . ."

Lalo jumped, hearing his own thoughts vocalized, and saw a slight man with clipped greying hair and a skin weathered brown, draped in dove-grey silk. Zanderei . . . after a moment his memory supplied the name, and for a moment he imagined he recognized amused understanding in the Commissioner's eyes. Then blandness masked them, and as Lalo opened his mouth to reply, Zanderei turned away.

A meek nonenity, Lalo had thought him when the Prince introduced the Commissioners to them all, and now Zanderei was a mouse once more. Lalo frowned, trying to understand.

A youthful eunuch, somewhat overaware of the splendor of his new purple satin and fringe, approached with a tray of pewter goblets. It was wine of Caronne, the whisper ran, cooled by snow that had been packed in sawdust all the way from the northern mountains whose possession was now being disputed so bitterly. The Commissioners took new goblets, and Coricidius motioned the slave away.

Lalo, whose cup was almost empty, looked after him longingly, but did not quite have the confidence to call him back again. *I should have used myself as a model for the cowardly Ilsig*

King, he thought bitterly. *Too many people here remember when I was drinking myself to death and Gilla took in laundry from the merchants' wives, and I am afraid they will laugh at me. . . .*

And yet he had painted the walls of the Temple of the Rankan gods, he had decorated this hall, and the Prince himself had complimented him. Why could he not be satisfied? *Once my dream was to paint the truth beneath the skin,* he thought then. *What do I want now?*

The air pulsed with polite conversation as rich merchants of Sanctuary pretended they were accustomed to such affairs, the Rankans tried to look as if they were enjoying this one, and the Prince and his officers uneasily enjoyed the Empire's belated recognition while wondering whether it was to their advantage.

Except for Coricidius—Lalo reminded himself. Rumor had it that the Vizier would stop at nothing to spend what remained of his old age back in the capital.

A wave of scent set Lalo to coughing, and he turned to confront Lord Raximander's beaming face.

"Why not return to the Capital with me?" the Commissioner said expansively. "A new talent! My wife would be so pleased."

Lalo smiled back, his vision expanding in images of marble columns and pavements of porphyry that far outshone the face-lifted splendors of Prince Kittycat's hall. Would Gilla like to live in a palace?

"But we need not waste the few weeks I have to spend here—"

Lalo's skin chilled as Lord Raximander went on.

"A picture of me, for instance—you could do that here in the palace as a small demonstration of your skill."

Before Raximander had finished, Lalo was shaking his head. "Someone must have misinformed you—I never do portraits!"

Some of the others, attention attracted by the raised voices, had drifted toward the mural again. Zanderei was watching with a faint smile.

Coricidius motioned towards the wall with a bony finger. "Who poses for all your pictures, then?"

Lalo twitched like a nervous horse, trying to find an answer that would not alienate them . . . Anything but the truth, which was that a sorcerer's spell had enabled—nay, compelled him, to portray the true nature of his sitters' souls. After a few disastrous attempts to paint Sanctuary's wealthy, Lalo had learned to choose his models from those among the poor who were still uncorrupted.

"My lord, that one was done from imagination," he said truthfully, for the Ilsig King had been inspired by his memories of fleeing through the Maze just ahead of local bullies when he was a boy. He did not tell them that he had got the Hell-Hound Quag to boast of his feats on campaign while he posed for the figure of the Rankan Emperor.

One of the eunuch pages scurried towards them and Coricidius bent to hear his message. Released from his gaze, Lalo stepped backward with a sigh.

"You are too sensitive, Master Limner," Zanderei said softly. "You must learn to accept what each day brings. In these times, ideals are an expensive luxury."

"Do *you* want a portrait too?" Lalo asked bitterly.

"Oh, I would not be worth the trouble—" Zanderei smiled. "Besides, I know how I appear to the world."

Cymbals crashed, and as Lalo's startled pulse began to slow he realized that the other end of the room was flaring with the colored silks of the dancing girls. He should have expected it, having watched them rehearse almost every afternoon while he worked on the paintings here.

Such a commotion, he thought, *for a few strangers who will make notes on Sanctuary as most artists make portraits—recording only the surface of reality—and then will be gone.*

Happily abandoning their conversations, the Commissioners let the purple-clad pages usher them to couches below the dais on which the Prince was already enthroned. The dancers, chosen from among the more talented of Kadakithis' lesser concubines, moved sinuously through the ornate topography of their dance, pausing only from time to time to detach a veil.

Trembling with reaction, Lalo drifted towards the row of pillars that supported the vaulted and domed ceiling. Someone had left a goblet on the marble bench, nearly full. Lalo took a long swallow, then made himself put it down again. His heart was pounding as loudly as the drums.

Why am I so afraid? he wondered, and then wondered how he could be anything else, in a town where footpads dogged your steps by day,

and if you heard a scream after dark you ran not
to help but to bar your door. *It must be better in
the Capital . . . there must be somewhere Gilla
and I could live in safety.*

He lifted the goblet once more, but the wine
tasted sour and he set it back half-full. Coricidius
would not care if he left the celebration now that
he had exhibited both the pictures and their
creator. Lalo wanted to go home.

He got to his feet and stepped around the pillar, then halted, startled as something in front of
him seemed to move. After a moment he
laughed, realizing that it was only his reflection
in the polished marble that faced the wall. Dimly
he could see the glitter of embroidery on his
festival jerkin, and the sheen on his full
breeches, but they could not disguise the stoop
of his narrow shoulders or the way his belly had
begun to round. Even the thinning of his ginger
hair was somehow mirrored there. But through
some quality of the dark marble or some trick of
the light, Lalo's face was as shadowed as that of
the Ilsig King.

*   *   *

Lalo worked his way around the outside of the
Presence Hall to the side door. The corridor
seemed quiet after the clamor of music and the
wine-fueled babble of conversation, and the
government offices that occupied the spaces between the Hall and the outside of the Palace were
empty and dark. As he had expected, the side-
door leading to the courtyard was bolted tight.
With a sigh he went the other way, passed
through the Hall of Justice that fronted the Palace

as quickly as he could, and out through one of the great double doors that led onto the porch and broad stair.

Torches had been fixed in the pillars at the top and bottom of the stair, and their fitful light gleamed on the armour of the guards who stood at attention on each of the four wide steps, and glowed on the purple pennon tied to each spear, then rayed out across the inner courtyard in uneven ribbons of brightness and shadow, as if the soldiers had become part of the Palace architecture.

Lalo paused for a moment, noting the effect. Then he saw that the first guard was Quag, nodded, and received in answer the flicker of an eyelid in the wooden patience of the Hell-Hound's face.

Lalo's sandals crunched on grit as he crossed the flagstones of the inner courtyard, punctuating the patter of applause that drifted from the Palace, at this distance as faint as the sound of wavelets on a shore. He supposed that the concubines had stripped off their final veils. He must remember not to show Gilla the sketches he had made of them practicing.

One of Honald's many nephews was on duty in the guardbox set into the massive archway of the Palace Gate. Tonight the double doors were opened wide, and Lalo passed through unquestioned, though he remembered a time when all he owned would not have been enough to bribe the Gatekeeper to let him enter here. He felt dizzy, although he had hardly had any wine.

Why can't I be satisfied with what I have? he wondered. *What is wrong with me?*

He crossed the expanse of Vashanka's Square

more quickly, heading diagonally towards the West Gate and the Governor's Walk. For a moment the east wind brought him the rank, fuggy smell of the Zoo Gardens, then it shifted and he felt on his face the cool breath of the sea.

He halted just outside the Gate and with a sigh reversed his cloak so that its dull inner lining concealed his festival clothes. It was well known in the appropriate places that Lalo never carried money—in the old days he had never had any, and now Gilla controlled the family treasury—but he would not want anyone to make a mistake in the dark.

A waxing moon was already brightening the heavens, and the rooftops of the city made a jagged silhouette against the stars. Not since he was a boy, slipping from his pallet behind his father's workbench to join his friends' adventuring, had Lalo seen Sanctuary at this hour with sober eyes. Just now, with all its sordidness obscured by shadow, it seemed to him to be possessed of a kind of haphazard but enduring integrity.

His feet had carried him almost to Shadow Lane without his attention when they encountered something soft. He leaped awkwardly aside to avoid stepping into the contents of a honeypot which someone had emptied into the street to stink and steam, until the rain washed it into the city's underground maze of sewers and it was carried off by the tide. He had been into those tunnels once, on a dare, through an entry shaft near the Vulgar Unicorn. He wondered if it were still there. . . .

What am I doing, getting sentimental about Sanctuary! thought Lalo as he inspected the sole of his sandal to see if any ordure remained. *I must have had more wine than I thought!* He had heard that in Ranke, armies of street cleaners scoured the streets every night to rid the city of the refuse of the day. . . .

He remembered the flatteries of Lord Raximander and that strange man, Zanderei, and he remembered the days when his one desire had been to get out of Sanctuary. It seemed to him that his life had consisted of cycles in which he dreamed of escape, found new hope for life in Sanctuary, discovered that his hope was unjustified, and began to plan flight once more.

This last time, when he had found that if he stuck to mythological subjects and chose his models carefully he could turn Enas Yorl's gift to a blessing, he had been sure that his troubles were over. But now here he was, bewailing his fate again.

I should have learned better by now . . . he thought morosely, *but what is there to learn? Will anything but death stop this wheel or make it take a different path?*

Houses leaned close together above him now, cutting off the sky. In some of the windows lamplight glowed, though most of them were tightly shuttered, edged and chinked with light that dappled the worn cobbles below. Lalo winced as a murmur of voices exploded into abuse. A mangy dog that had been nosing at something in the gutters looked up at the noise, then went back to its meal.

Lalo shuddered, visualizing death as a starving jackal-hound waiting to spring. There must be some other way—he told himself, for however much he hated his life, he feared death more.

Human shadows slid from the shadows behind him, and he forced himself to walk steadily, knowing that at this hour, in this part of Sanctuary, it was indeed death to be visibly afraid. By daylight the area shared in the quasi-respectability of the Bazaar, but by night it belonged to the Maze.

From ahead came the sound of drunken song and a burst of laughter. Torchlight danced around the corner followed by the singers, a group of mercenaries emboldened by numbers to make the pilgrimage to the ale casks of the Vulgar Unicorn.

As the light reached them, the shapes that had followed Lalo slipped back into alleys and doorways, and Lalo himself edged beneath the overhang of a tenement until the soldiers had gone by. He had almost reached Slippery Street now, and the cul-de-sac which for twenty years had been his home.

Now, at last, Lalo allowed himself to hasten, for in all the ups and downs of his fortunes there had been one constant, and that was the knowledge that he had a home, and that Gilla waited for him there.

The third step of the staircase squeaked, as did the seventh and the eighth. When Lalo had become fashionable and had, for the first time in his life, had money, he and Gilla had bought the building in which they lived and repaired, among other things, the staircase. But the stairs still squeaked, and Lalo, hearing the lullaby Gilla was singing to their youngest child halt a moment, knew that she had heard him coming home.

Breathing a little faster than he would have

liked after the climb, he opened the door.

"You're home early!" The floor quivered beneath her steps as Gilla came through the door of what had once been the adjoining apartment. Lalo saw beyond her the curly head of their youngest, whom they still called the baby even though he was now nearly two years old, and the outstretched arm of an older child.

"Is everything all right?" Lalo unfastened his cloak and hung it on the peg.

"It was only a nightmare—" softly she closed the door. "And what about you? I was sure you would be at the Palace all night, imbibing the wine of paradise with all the great ones and their gilded ladies." The carved chair groaned faintly as she sat down and lifted her massive arms to pat the elaborate curls and coils of her hair.

"There weren't any ladies—" tactfully he passed over the dancing girls, "just an unlikely mixture of military and priests and government men, like a stew from the Bazaar!"

She set her elbow on the table and rested her head on her hand. "If it was such a bore why did you stay so long? Don't tell me they wouldn't let you go?" Her eyes narrowed and he flushed a little beneath the acuity of her gaze. Deliberately he began to unhook his vest, waiting for her to speak again.

"Something happened—" she said then. "Something's troubling you."

He draped his vest across another chair and sat down in it with a sigh.

"Gilla, what would you say to the idea of leaving Sanctuary?" Beyond her he could see his first study for the picture of Sabellia which graced the great Temple now. Gilla had been his model, and for a moment he saw a double image of woman and Goddess, and her bulk took on a monumental dignity.

She put down her arm and sat up straight. "Now, when we are secure at last?"

"How secure can anyone be, here?" He hunched forward, running stubby craftsman's fingers through his thinning hair. Then he told her how they had praised his picture, and what the future Lord Raximander had offered him.

"Ranke!" she exclaimed when he had finished. "Clean streets and quiet nights! But what would I do there? All the fine ladies would laugh at me. . . ." For a moment she looked curiously vulnerable, despite her size. Then her eyes met his. "But you said he wanted a portrait—Lalo, you can't do that—you'll end up in the Imperial dungeons, not the court!"

"Even there? Surely there must be some honest men and virtuous women at the heart of the Empire!" Lalo said wistfully.

"Will you never grow up? We are doing very well as we are—you have a position, people like what you do, and the children will be well-apprenticed and married when the time comes. And now you want to go chase some other dream? Why can't you make up your mind?"

He put his hands over his aching eyes and shook his head. If only he knew—there was something missing in him, something that he sought in each new thing he tried to do . . . *What use has it been to have my heart's desire?* he thought, *if I myself am still the same?*

After a little he heard the chair scrape and felt her coming to him, and sighed again, more deeply, as the strength and softness of her arms enclosed him. She had scented her skin with oil of sandalwood, and he could feel the opulence of her body through the thin silk of the night-robe she wore.

It changed nothing, but in her arms he could forget his perplexities for at least a little while. Gilla kissed him on his bald spot and drew away, and with a sense of having made a truce with fate he followed her into the other room.

*   *   *

"Thieves!"

Lalo jerked upright, shocked from sleep by Gilla's scream and the crash that had shaken the room. Was it morning? But everything was still dark! He rubbed his eyes, still half-drugged by dreams of marble terraces and applause.

Shadows moved and feet that no longer troubled to be stealthy thudded on the floor . . . hard hands grasped Lalo's shoulders and he cried out. Then something hit the side of his head and he sagged against the hard hands that prisoned him.

"Murderers! Assassins!"

His head still ringing, Lalo recognized Gilla in the voice, and in the dark bulk that heaved upward from the bed to fling another assailant against the wall. Water spattered his cheek and he smelt roses as the vase that had stood on the bedside table flew past him and shattered against someone's skull. Men caromed into each other swearing as Gilla groped forward. There was no sound from their neighbors—he had not really expected it—they would ask their questions when morning came.

"In Vashanka's name, somebody silence the sow!" In the half-light a drawn sword gleamed dimly.

"No!" he croaked, gasped in air and cried out, "Gilla, stop fighting—there are too many—Gilla, please!"

There was a final convulsion, then silence. Flint rasped steel and a little light sparked into life. Gilla lay sprawled like a fallen monument. For a moment Lalo felt as if a great hand had closed on his chest. Then there was movement in the tangle of limbs. Gilla rolled over and levered herself to her feet without spending a glance on the man who had cushioned her fall.

"Savankala save me, she's squashed me flat . . . Sir, help me—don't leave me here. . . ."

Sir? But the man on the floor was a Hell-Hound—Lalo recognized him now.

"I don't understand . . ." he said aloud, and as he turned the light was quenched and he blinked at darkness again.

"Carry him," said a deep voice. "And you, woman, be still if you want to see him whole again."

Sick from the blow and aching from rough handling, Lalo did not resist as they shoved his sandals onto his feet and thrust an old smock over his head and marched him along the empty streets back to the Palace. But instead of rounding the outer wall to the dungeons, as Lalo had dismally expected, they hustled him through the Palace Gate and along the side of the building and down a little staircase to the basement.

Then, still without a word of explanation, he was thrust into a dank hole smelling of dry rot and full of things to stumble over to shiver, and

wonder why they had brought him here, and
gnaw his paint-stained fingers while he waited
for dawn . . .

*   *   *

"Wake up, you Wrigglie scum! The Lord
wants to talk to you—"

Lalo surfaced, groaning, from a dream in
which he had been taken prisoner and dragged
through the night until . . . Something hit him
hard in the ribs and he opened his eyes.

It was morning, and it had not been a dream.
He saw flaking white-washed walls, and splintered crates and furniture heaped on the bare
earth of the floor. It was not a prison then. A little
pallid light filtered down to him through one
barred window set high in the wall.

He forced himself to sit up and face his tor-
mentors.

"Quag!"

At Lalo's exclamation, the Hell-Hound's
pitted-leather face became, if possible, a richer
shade of terra cotta, and his eyes slid away from
the painter's gaze. Lalo followed the look to the
doorway, and suddenly began to understand
what power had brought him here, though he
was as far as ever from comprehending why.

Coricidius hunched in the doorway like a sick
eagle, with his cloak clutched around him
against the early morning chill, and a face like
curdled milk. He eyed Lalo sourly, hawked and
spat, and then stepped stiffly into the room.

"My Lord, am I under arrest? I've done nothing—why have you brought me here?" babbled
Lalo.

"I want to commission some portraits . . ." The lined face twitched with the faintest of malicious smiles.

"What?"

Coricidius snorted in disgust and motioned to one of the guards to set a folding camp-stool in the middle of the room. Joint by joint, the old man lowered himself until he settled fully upon it with a sigh.

"I have no time to argue with you, dauber. You say you don't do portraits, but you will do them for me."

Lalo shook his head. "My lord, I *can't* do pictures of real people . . . they hate them . . . I'm no good at it."

"You're too good at it." Coricidius corrected him. "I know your secret, you see. I've had your models followed, and talked to them. I could kill you, but if you refuse me, I have only to tell a few of your former patrons and they will save me the toil."

Lalo clutched at the folds of his smock to hide the trembling of his hands. "Then I am doomed—if I do portraits for you, my secret will be known as soon as they are seen."

"Ah, but these pictures are not for public display." Coricidius hunched forward. "I want you to make a likeness of each of the Commissioners who have come fron Ranke. I shall tell them that it is a surprise for the Emperor—that no one must see it until it is done . . . and before that happens, some accident to the painting is certain to occur. . . ." The Vizier was shaking with subtle tremors that ran along each limb to end in a grimace which Lalo took minutes to recognize as laughter.

"But not before I have seen it," the old man went on, "and learned the weaknesses these peacocks hide from men . . . They have come to power in the Court since my time, but once I know their souls I can constrain them to help me return to favor again!"

Lalo shivered. The proposal had a certain superficial logic, but there were so many things that could go wrong.

"But perhaps I have simply not yet found the right stick to make the donkey go . . ." Coricidius went on. "They say you love your wife—" he peered at Lalo disbelievingly. "Shall we blind her and send her to the Street of the Red Lanterns while we keep you prisoner?"

I should have gone away . . . thought Lalo. *I should have taken Gilla and the children out of here as soon as I had the money to go . . .* Once he had seen a rabbit transfixed by the shadow of a stooping hawk. *I am that rabbit, and I am lost . . .* he thought.

And after all, the internal dialogue went on, *what are all these plots and counterplots to me? If I can help this Rankan buzzard return to his own foul nest then at least Sanctuary will be free of him!*

"All right . . . I will do what you say . . ." Lalo said aloud.

*   *   *

Lalo, brow furrowed and an extra brush held between his teeth, leaned closer to the canvas, concentrating on the line the soft brush made. When he was painting, his hand and eye became a single organ in which visual impressions were transmitted to the fingers and to the brush which was their extension without mediation by the consciousness. Line, mass, shape and color, all were factors in a pattern which must be replicated on the canvas. The eye checked the work of the hand and automatically corrected it without either interpretation or reaction from the brain.

". . . and then I was promoted to be under-warden of the great Temple of Savankala in Ranke." The Archpriest Arbalest settled a little more comfortably in his chair, and Lalo's sensitive fingers, responding, adjusted a line.

"An excellent position, really, right at the heart of things. Everybody who is anybody pays homage there eventually, and whoever transmits their petitions to the god can gather quite a lot of useful information in time." Smiling complacently, the Archpriest smoothed the brocaded saffron folds of his gown.

"Mmnn—very true—" murmured Lalo with the fraction of his mind that was not mesmerized by his work.

"I wish you would let me look at what you are doing!" the priest said petulantly. "It is my face you are immortalizing, after all!"

Shocked into awareness, Lalo stepped back from the easel and looked at him.

"Oh no, my Lord, you must not! It has been strictly ordered that this picture shall be a surprise. None of the sitters is to see it until the entire painting is revealed to the Emperor. If you try to look I will have to call the guard. Indeed, it is as much as my life is worth to let anyone see the picture before its time!"

And that, at least, was perfectly true, thought Lalo, daring to look at the canvas with conscious

eyes at last. Against the crude backdrop of a
pillared hall had been sketched the rough out-
lines of five figures. The one on the far left had
been filled in yesterday with the picture of Lord
Raximander, the first of the Commissioners to
serve as model here. He looked like a pig—
complacently self-indulgent, with just a hint of
stubborn ferocity in the little eyes.

Lalo wondered that the Commissioners had
consented to it. Since they came they had been
busy with inspections and meetings, and listening to interminable reports. Perhaps they were
glad of a chance to sit still. Or perhaps they
feared the consequences of refusing to contrib-
ute to a gift for their Emperor, or possibly they
really were eager to have their visit to this out-
post of Empire immortalized. Raximander, at
least, had appeared to take the sitting as tacit
agreement from Lalo to paint another portrait
which the Commissioner *would* be allowed to
see.

Now the picture of the Archpriest was almost
complete beside Lord Raximander's. If the thing
had been meant seriously, Lalo would have
wanted several hours more to work on the finishing of the gown and hair, but it was already
sufficient for the Vizier's purposes. Lalo looked
at it with normal vision for the first time and
repressed a sigh.

Why had he dared to hope that just because the
man was a priest he would be virtuous? But
Arbalest was not a pig—more of a weasel, Lalo
thought, noting the covert cunning of his gaze.

"If you are tired we can end the sitting now."
He bowed to the priest. "I will not need your
presence for what remains."

When the priest had gone Lalo refilled his mug from the pitcher of beer provided by Coricidius. Aside from the infamous manner of the commission, the Vizier had not treated him badly. Having blackmailed him into painting, the old man was at least allowing him to do so in comfort. They had set aside a pleasant room on the second floor of the Palace for his use—at the front next to the roof garden so that windows on three sides gave him light—working conditions, at least, were ideal.

But the painting was an abomination. Lalo forced himself to look at it again. He had sketched in columns and a carven ceiling just in case someone should catch a glimpse of the canvas from far away. But the faces with which he was filling the foreground made the rich surroundings seem a travesty.

Everyone at the Palace appeared to believe the tale that the painting was a bribe to the Emperor, and some, believing that this must give Lalo some influence, were already toadying to him. Even to Gilla, Lalo had had to pretend that the midnight arrest was a mistake and the commission real. But if she did not believe him, for once she had the sense to let the subject alone.

Would others do the same? What if the project became so famous that people insisted on seeing the picture? What if one of his sitters proved nimble enough to get a good look before Lalo could call the guard?

Lalo sighed again, drained his mug, and told the Hell-Hound currently on duty to bring the third subject in.

*   *   *

Lalo sat on a low stool next to the table where he had laid out his painting things, waiting, like them, for the fourth of the Commissioners to arrive for his sitting. He supposed that he had been lucky to get in Arbalest and the royal relative yesterday—he glanced at the third picture with distaste. "Something-*axis*," the man's name was, but already he had trouble remembering. Not surprising—his portrait revealed a bovine complacence that avoided evil mainly through lack of energy.

And these are the pride of Ranke! thought Lalo. He found himself almost grateful to Coricidius. *I would never have known*—he grimaced at the painting again—*I would have uprooted my family to seek my fortune in the capital, innocently certain it must be superior to Sanctuary. But there, the evil is only better disguised. . . .*

From the courtyard below he could hear the even tramp of bullhide sandals—the Prince's Guard was drilling again. These days, even the City garrison marched and polished their armor, but whether it was in hopes of being sent to the war or the opposite, he did not know. Nor, at this moment, did he care. He found it hard to believe that any new invader could make things any better, or worse, in Sanctuary.

Still, the incessant marching made him nervous, as if his former certainties were illusions, and just around the corner lay some new threat that he could not see. Restlessly he paced to the window, and was just turning back when the guard brought the fourth sitter in.

"My Lord Zanderei!" Lalo bowed to the man to whom he had spoken at the reception. "Please be seated—" he indicated the sitter's chair.

"I am sorry to have kept you waiting, Master Limner," the man said plaintively, settling himself. "I was detained at the warehouses. There seems to be some confusion regarding the grain supplies set aside for the war . . ."

Lalo busied himself with his paints to hide a grin. He could well imagine that the web of bribes, kickbacks, substitutions and out-and-out shortchanging characteristic of business in Sanctuary would make "confusion" an understatement. Why had they sent such a clerkly little mouse to deal with the situation here? Glancing at him again, Lalo realized that Zanderei had one of the least remarkable faces he had ever seen.

I suppose it comes of a life-time of deference, he thought. The man displayed no individuality at all. But for the first time in this project Lalo found himself eager to set brush to canvas, knowing that once he did, no dissimulation could hide the truth of the man from him.

"Am I posed correctly? I can turn my head the other way if you like, or fold my hands . . ."

"Yes, clasp your hands—your head is very well as it is. You must relax, sir, and think how near your business is to its conclusion . . ." Lalo poured thinner into the cup and dipped his brush.

"Yes," Zanderei echoed softly. "I am almost done. A week or less will show me if I have accomplished all I was sent to do. The conflict draws very close to us now." His thin lips curved in the faintest of smiles.

Lalo's eyes narrowed. He drew his brush through the light ochre and began.

A half hour went by, and an hour. Lalo worked

steadily without really being conscious either of
the passage of time or of what he was doing.
Zanderei was light and shadow, color and texture and line—a problem in interpretation. The
artist adjusted to the changing light and even
gave his model permission to move from time to
time without emerging from the trance which
was his art and his spell.

Then, from the Hall of Justice below, the gong
for the fourth watch began to toll. Zanderei got to
his feet, grey robes shifting like shadow around
him. Lalo, fighting his way back to awareness
like a man awakening from sleep, saw that dusk
was beginning to gather in the corners of the
room.

"I am sorry. I must go now." Zanderei took a
few steps forward, more smoothly than Lalo
would have expected, considering how long the
man had been sitting still.

"Oh, of course—forgive me for keeping you so
long."

"Are you finished? Will you want me to come
to you again?"

Lalo looked at the picture, wondering if he had
captured the reality of this man. For a moment he
did not understand what he saw. He glanced
quickly at the other portraits, but they had not
changed, and paint still glistened wetly where
he had given a last touch to Zanderei's hair. But
he had never been unable to recognize the model
in one of his portraits before . . .

He saw a face like stone, like steel, a face with
no life but in the eyes, and there only an ancient
pain. And in the hands of this image, a bloodied
knife was gripped fast.

Coricidius wanted to see these men's

grief for his work, for himself, for his family left fatherless.

The canvas had caught fire and was beginning to crackle merrily now. Bright flame fattened on the paint-soaked cloth and cast demon-flickers on the face of Zanderei.

"No!" The cry burst from Lalo's lips, and as Zanderei straightened, Lalo's hand closed on the paint pot and he flung it at the other man.

It struck Zanderei's shoulder, and red paint splashed like blood across the grey robe.

The assassin exploded towards him and Lalo scrambled frantically around the table, snatching up more paint pots, brushes, anything he could throw. One of them hit Zanderei's forehead, and as paint sprayed across his face he hesitated for just a moment to mop his eyes.

And in that moment Lalo kicked over the table and ran.

*   *   *

Lalo hugged his chest as if he could muffle the drumming of his heart and stared around him.

He had confused memories of having fled down the corridor that edged the upper half of the Presence Hall, towards the back of the Palace, down the stairs by the dais, and then still farther, into a part of the Palace he did not know. Though the floor was still marble, the slabs were cracked and discolored, and plaster was chipping from the wall. Then he heard crockery clattering nearby and realized he must be hard by the kitchens.

At least, he thought gratefully, Zanderei the Commissioner would be even more out of place here than he. Cautiously he turned into another passageway and moved forward. But as he eased open the door at the end of it, he heard once more a faint pattering behind him—the steps of one who from long training ran so lightly his footfalls were only a whisper of fine leather on polished stone.

Stifling a moan, Lalo burst through the door, dashed across the wooden floor and the platform that opened out onto the kitchen courtyard, and flung himself into the first concealment he found.

It had looked like a cart, and as Lalo sank into its contents he realized what it was. Not the honey-wagon, thank the gods, but the cart into which they had collected the garbage from several days' worth of princely meals. Gagging, Lalo wriggled deeper into the mass of turnip peelings and sour curds, soggy rice and pastry crusts and meat trimmings and bones.

He thought grimly, *As long as I can retch, I'm still alive . . .*

The cart moved beneath him and he heard the stamp of a hoof on stone. He realized then that not only was he alive, he might even escape, for if the horse was hitched, it must be time for the garbage to be taken away. He waited, breathing shallowly, for the endless minutes until he heard voices and the wagon lurched with the weight of somebody climbing onto the driver's bench. Then they began to move.

Faster . . . Faster! Lalo prayed as he was jounced deeper into the reeking mass. The clatter of wooden wheels on stone was deafening, then there was a pause, a moment's conversation with Honald at the Gate, and the duller vibration as the wagon trundled across the pounded earth of Vashanka's Square.

Then the cart shuddered to a halt. Lalo strained his ears for the night-noises of Sanctuary, but heard instead shouting and the clamor of an alarm.

"Is that smoke? Theba's paps, it's the Palace! Leave the wagon, Tam, we can give the beasts their slops in the morning!" The wagon heaved again and Lalo heard two sets of footsteps pounding back the way they had come.

He settled back down, realizing with wonder that for the moment at least, he was saved.

And what will I do now? Zanderei would tell everyone that Lalo had killed the guard and started the fire. If caught, he would be cast into the dungeons, if they did not kill him out of hand. And if he offered to demonstrate his skill in his defense, he might wish that they had . . .

He could not return to the Palace to accuse the 'Commissioner', but if he could reach the Maze he could hide indefinitely—there were still a few who owed him favors there.

And then . . . Zanderei would either assassinate Prince Kadakithis, or go peacefully home. The former seemed more likely, for one does not return a honed blade to the sheath without blooding it, and in that case Coricidius would fall as well.

And what would become of Sanctuary? The thought troubled his satisfaction. What kind of tyrant would the Empire send to avenge its son? For all his clumsiness, at least Prince Kittycat meant well, and if they must be ruled by foreigners, surely the ones they were accustomed to would be best.

And it's all in my hands . . . Trying to control

laughter, Lalo unwisely took too deep a breath, and began to cough again. *Here I wallow in the Prince's garbage, deciding what his fate shall be!* Power bubbled in his veins like wine of Caronne. *I could send word to Coricidius—he started this, he might believe me . . . or—*he remembered rumors he had heard about Shadowspawn—*I might be able to get word to the Prince himself . . .*

But first I have to get out of here!

Cautiously Lalo poked his head over the rim of the cart. There was a whiff of smoke in the air, and above the wall he could see torches winking like glowworms in the upper windows of the Palace, but he saw no glare of fire—perhaps they had put it out in time. The cart in which he was sitting was parked just outside the Zoo Gardens, a few feet from the Processional Gate.

Sighing with relief, Lalo clambered over the side and began to strip off his smock and brush away the worst of the filth that coated him—

—And stopped, feeling a gaze that was not the dispassionate stare of the mangy lions beyond the barrier. He turned then, and looked across the square to the Palace Gate from which a familiar grey-robed figure had just emerged. For a moment fear froze him again, but he was still glowing with the inebriation of power. He let his smock fall to the ground.

Zanderei's robe was of rich silk, while his own worn shirt and stained breeches would attract no attention. If he could entice the Rankan into the town, Lalo would be on his own ground, and the City itself might rid him and the Prince of their enemy.

Grinning nervously, Lalo walked into plain

view, and then urged his stiff limbs into an awkward dash through the Gate as Zanderei and half a dozen Hell-Hounds leaped into motion across the Square after him.

Looking back over his shoulder at every other step, Lalo pressed his cramped limbs to greater speed along the Processional Way. Hearing the guards close behind him, he dodged among the merchants' houses to Westgate Street and down Tanner's Row, heading for the Serpentine. And as he ran, the blood began to course freely through his limbs once more, and he shed middle-age and awkwardness as he had shed his ruined smock, and his fear.

Lalo leaped over a handcart that had been abandoned in the road and paused to send it spinning broadsides. That would not long delay them, but he could hear mercenaries laying bets on a dogfight in the next street. Laughing like the boy who had raced through these streets so long ago, he let his pursuers follow him around the corner, slid eel-like through the crowd, and laughed again as the tinny clash of weapons told him that the Hell-Hounds and the mercenaries had met.

But what about Zanderei? Lalo waited in the shadow of a quiet doorway and watched the gap at the entrance to the street. Night had fallen, and the moon, now almost at the full, was drawing free of the distorting smoke of the City and transforming the shape and shadows of the street with its own deceptive dappling. How could he tell which one—

Ah, there, a shadow moved of itself, and Lalo knew that his enemy was here.

So soon! Shock tingled through his veins and

set every hair on end. *I must run . . . the man moves too subtly—before those who would attack him for the silk he wears can note him, he is away. I am a dead man if I cannot trap him somehow.* The glory he had tasted seemed now as inconstant as the moon. In a moment Zanderei would reach his hiding place.

And yet it was almost as if he had done all this before—he remembered a time in his boyhood, when he had come with his mates into the Maze in search of excitement and been set upon there. He had escaped by—he looked up and saw that this house too had an external stair. Without allowing himself time to think of failure, Lalo launched himself upward.

The wooden structure swayed alarmingly. Lalo clutched at a railing and nearly fell when it gave way beneath his hand. He could hear loud voices inside—a window opened and then slammed shut as he was seen, and for a moment the quarreling was stilled. Then he was on the roof, leaping over trays of drying fruit and ducking under clotheslines. He saw the dark shape behind him and jerked one end of the line free so that the hanging clothes clung damply to the man who was following him.

Something flashed by his cheek in the moonlight like a line of white fire. Lalo threw himself across the gap between two buildings, clutched at the ledge of a parapet and lay across it, gasping, staring at the quivering blade that matched the one he had seen in the throat of the slain guard. He hauled himself the rest of the way into the dubious protection of the gable end.

Two Hell-Hounds trotted down the street below, paused momentarily at the corner and gave a whistle which was answered from two streets away. Lalo wondered what had happened to the mercenaries. Then a shadow rose from the opposite rooftop, glimmering like silver as it came into the full light of the moon.

"Limner!" Zanderei called, "The soldiers will kill you if they catch you before I do—give yourself up to me now!"

Lalo thought of the blade which he had wedged uncomfortably into his sash and gritted his teeth. *They call us Wrigglies*, he remembered, *Well, I had better do some quick wriggling now!* Cautiously he squirmed across the tiles. A quiver beneath him told him that Zanderei had also crossed the gap, and he scrambled for the opposite stair.

But there was none. Unable to stop, Lalo leaped to the balcony in a crash of breaking crockery, and swung himself from the railing to the street below. The upper way would not save him, but as he had lain gasping he had remembered an alternative, darker and more dangerous both to the pursuer and the pursued.

Shards of terra cotta smashed and rattled in the street behind him as the owner of the balcony glimpsed Zanderei and pelted him with his broken wares. Lalo sped down the street and past a group wavering along from the direction of the Vulgar Unicorn.

I wanted to be a hero—he thought, forcing his legs to more speed, *but how do you tell the difference between a dead hero and a dead fool?* The singing behind him faltered and someone screamed. Zanderei—for a moment Lalo saw the assassin clearly in the moonlight—he had shed his grey silk and his shirt was torn—he looked as

if he had been bred to the streets of Sanctuary.
And as if he had felt Lalo's gaze, he turned, and
his teeth flashed in a brief smile.

Lalo took a deep breath and stared around
him—he dared not move too quickly now lest he
miss the spot, though every sense was clamoring
to him to flee. There, at the end of the alley—a
wooden cover that capped a circle of crumbling
stones. Lalo pulled it free—the covers were usually left unbolted in hopes that people would
throw refuse directly in—then, gritting his teeth,
he lowered himself down the shaft.

It was not so deep as a well. Lalo landed with a
splash in a sluggish stream slippery with things
he would rather not try to name. Fighting his
stomach, he realized that the Prince's garbage
had been fragrant compared to the sewers which
were his last hope against his enemy.

He slogged grimly forward, counting his steps
and putting out a reluctant hand to the slimy
walls to guide his passage, listening behind him
for the small sounds that would tell him that
Zanderei had followed him even here. Catching
his breath, he felt for the knife, but in all his
scrambling it had been lost.

Just as well—he told himself, *I would not have
known how to use it anyway!*

"You—Limner, you've done well, but what
made you think you could win this game against
me?" The voice echoed dankly from water-
scoured stone walls. "I'll catch up with you
soon—wouldn't you have preferred to have died
cleanly?"

Lalo shook his head, though the other man
could not see. He had reckoned his achieve-
ments and found them wanting, but if he died

now at least he had tried to act like a man. He forced his way onward, fingers questing for the next break in the stone. What if he was wrong? Had he misremembered, or had the tunnels changed in thirty years?

"You will die, you know. This is the last bolthole. Your end is here."

An end for both of us then, Lalo thought numbly. *I will not mind*—Then his trembling fingers found the crack. He moved his hand along the wall, lips whispering the numbers that had become a litany—*sixty-six, sixty-seven steps . . . Please, Lord Ils, let it be here . . . sixty-eight. . . . Shalpa help me, sixty-nine, seventy!*

His fingers closed on a rusting semicircle of iron, and stifling a gasp of relief he hauled himself upward, though his fingers slipped on the rungs. The splashing behind him slowed as if his enemy had paused to listen, then became a tumult as Zanderei began to run.

Lalo gained the top, shoved the wooden cover aside, and heart bursting, rolled over the edge into the clean air. But he could not rest now, not yet, not until the trap was sprung. Summoning strength where he had thought there could be no more, he hauled the cover over the shaft and drove home the wooden bar. And without waiting to see if it would hold, he staggered back to the first shaft and did the same thing there.

Then he sank to the cobbles beside it, pulse hammering, knowing that this last, god-given strength was gone and he could do not more. This was the only place in the network of sewers where two shafts entered the conduits so close together. Zanderei was trapped there now.

How sweet the air was to his lungs. From some

upper room Lalo heard the tinkle of a gittern and a woman's low laughter. A soft wind comforted his burning cheeks—a sea wind. And then Lalo remembered with mingled satisfaction and horror that Zanderei was doubly doomed. With the sea wind would come a rush of dark water from the Swamp of Night Secrets, propelled by the tidal bore.

"You—Assassin—you've done well—but what made you think you could win this game with me?" Lalo whispered through cracked lips. Laughter rasped his throat, and he sat shaking by the locked well-mouth while the slime of the tunnel dried on his skin. A stray pickpocket, passing by, made the sign against madness and scuttled away. He heard a whistle and then the clink of a sword as a Hell-Hound passed the mouth of the alley, but he supposed he looked like nothing human, crouching there.

"Limner, are you there?"

Lalo jumped, hearing the voice so close to him. The wood of the shaft-top shuddered as it was struck from below, and Lalo leaned on the bar. Hanging from the rungs by one hand, there was no way Zanderei could gain enough leverage to break free. That was what Lalo had heard in dark tales whispered by childhood friends, and later, over winecups in the Vulgar Unicorn. If he lived, he too would have a tale to tell. . . .

"Assassin, I am here and you are there and there you will stay," croaked Lalo when the dull hammering finally stilled.

"I will give you gold—I have never broken my word . . . You could establish yourself in the capital."

"I don't want your gold." *I don't even want to*

go to Ranke, his thought continued, *not anymore.*

"I will give you your life . . ." said Zanderei. "Coricidius won't believe you, you know, and the Hell-Hounds will have your skull for a drinking bowl. At the very least they will strike off your hands . . ."

Involuntarily, Lalo's fingers clasped protectively around his wrists, as if a bright blade were already descending. It was true—surely he had lost all he had ever gained. Better to meet Zanderei's knife than to live without being able to take brush in hand. *If I cannot paint I am nothing,* he thought. *I will surely die.*

But he did not move. Shivering with exhaustion and despair, still he would not throw away this victory, even though he hardly understood his reasons anymore.

"Limner, I will give you your soul . . ."

"You can only give death, foreigner! You cannot trick me!"

"I do not need to—" the voice seemed very tired. "I only need to ask you a question. Have you ever painted your own portrait, Limner with the sorcerer's eye?"

The silence stretched into eternity while Lalo tried to understand. He felt a subtle quiver in the earth that told him the tide was beginning to turn. What did Zanderei mean? Of course he had done self-portraits by the dozen, when he could get no one else to pose for him—

—In the old days, before Enas York had taught him to paint the soul . . .

I've been too busy—no . . . the awareness came reluctantly, *I was afraid.*

"What will you see on your canvas when you

have murdered me?" The voice echoed his fear.

"Stop it! Leave me alone!" Lalo cried aloud. He heard a deep voice shout orders in the street beyond the alley, and saw for a moment the flicker of lanterns bobbing by, pallid in the moonlight.

In a few minutes the poisoned waters would be driven from their bed by the inexorable pressure of the tide, and rush through the sewers of Sanctuary like a host of angry serpents seeking their prey. In a few minutes Zanderei would be dead.

If he disappears, maybe they will blame Zanderei for the Fire. When the stir dies down I'll be free to paint again. His hand twitched as if he held a brush, but the motion triggered Zanderei's words in his memory.

"Have you ever painted your own portrait?"

Lalo shuddered suddenly, violently. Could even Enas Yorl lift the curse this man had laid upon his soul? He heard the irregular tramp of men trying to march in close order over an uneven road. The sound was louder now—in a few moments they would pass his alleyway. In a few moments the waters would be here.

"What will you see when you have murdered me?"

Without conscious decision, Lalo found himself running stiffly towards the Serpentine.

"Ho there! Guards—he is hiding in the sewers—down this alley!" He held his ground while they debated, knowing that they could not recognize him under the sodden clothes and mud, and motioned to them to follow him.

Then he pounded down the alley, bent to

wrestle the bar from the shaft-cover and ran on until he found the dark overhang of a staircase to shelter him. Below he felt a trembling and heard the hiss of many waters, and, just as the wooden lid of the shaft was knocked aside, the hollow boom of water forced upward through too narrow a way.

Something dark clung to the rim of the shaft, like a rat flooded from its hole, then clambered the rest of the way out once the fury of the waters had passed. But now the Hell-Hounds surrounded the shaft. There was a flurry of movement and Lalo heard swearing and a cry of pain. Among the voices he distinguished the soft tones of the Emperor's Commissioner.

"Is that who you say you are?" A deep voice, Quag's voice, replied. "Well, if we've lost the dauber, at least we have you. My Lord Prince will be interested to learn what sharp-toothed rats his brother keeps to guard his granaries! Come along, you!"

Lalo sank back against the post of the stair. It was over. The Hell-Hounds were dragging Zanderei away as once they had dragged him into the night.

He would find a way to let Coricidius know what the painting had shown and what Zanderei had confessed to him. Would they call him into court to prove it? Would they dispose of the assassin quietly, or send him back to Ranke to report his failure? With a dim wonder Lalo realized that it did not matter anymore.

Gilla would have harsh words for him when he reached home, but her arms would be soft and comforting . . .

But still he did not move, for below the surface questions in his mind pulsed one more perplexing—*Why did I let Zanderei go?*

Today he had faced death, and fought for his life, and conquered fear. He had realized that the evil of the world was not confined to Sanctuary. But if he could do all this, he was not the person that he had thought he knew.

He held out his magic hands, his painter's hands, so that the moonlight silvered them, staring as if they held his answer. And perhaps that was true, for if he had beaten Zanderei, the other man's final question had also vanquished him. And he could only answer it by facing his mirror with a paintbrush in his hand.

The moon was poised above the tattered rooftops, resting after the labor of drawing in the tide. Like a silver mirror, she blessed the tortured streets of Sanctuary, and the tear-streaked face of the man who gazed at her, with the reflected splendor of the hidden sun.

*   *   *

STEEL

by

Lynn Abbey

Walegrin listened carefully to the small noises carried on the night breeze. His survival depended on his ability to untangle the sounds of the night—and on the steel sword he clutched, unsheathed, at his side. Ambushers crept toward his small camp in the darkness.

Two bright Enlibar wagons sat, unguarded and garish, in the ruddy light of a neglected fire. Their cargo had been scattered in tempting disarray; chunks of aquamarine ore shimmered in the moonlight. Walegrin's cloak lay close by the fire, covering an armload of thorny sticks—a ruse to convince the brigands that he and his men were more weary than careful and valued sleep above their lives.

They'd had little enough rest since leaving the ruined mine with the precious ore; and of the twenty-five men who had left Sanctuary only

seven remained. But Walegrin trusted his six
stalwarts against four times that many hillmen.

Walegrin's thoughts were stopped by the
warning cry of a mountain hawk; Malm, who
had a shepherd's eye for ominous movements,
had spotted the enemy. Walegrin held his
ground until the camp swarmed with dark,
scuttling shapes, until someone stabbed a cloak
and heard wood splintering, not bone. Then,
sword raised, he led his men out of the shadows.

These outlaws were better armed and bolder
than any the soldiers had encountered before,
but Walegrin had no time to consider this discovery. His men were hard-pressed, without
their usual advantage over the hill-bred fighters.
His sword stole the lifeblood of two men, but
then he was cut himself and fought defensively,
unaware of the fate of his men or the tide of
battle. He was forced to retreat another step; the
open back of a wagon pressed against his hips.
The one who bore down on him was as yet un-
wounded. It was time for a soldier's last
prayers.

Snarling, the attacker took his sword in both
hands for a decapitating cut. Walegrin braced to
take the force of the stroke on his sword which he
held in a bent, injured arm. His weapon fell from
his suddenly numb hand, but his neck was intact. The brigand was undaunted, his smile
never wavered; Walegrin was unarmed now.

Steadying himself to face death with courage,
Walegrin's leaden fingers found an object left
forgotten in the wagon: the old Enlibar sword
they had found in the dust of the mine. The
silver-green steel showed no rust, but no-one

had exchanged his serviceable Rankan blade for one forged five hundred years before his birth—until now. Walegrin brought the ancient sword around with a bellow.

Blue-green sparks surged when the swords met. The Enlibar metal *clanged* above the other sounds of battle. The brigand's swordblade shattered and, with a reflex born of experience not thought, Walegrin took his assailant's head in a single, soft stroke.

The fabled steel of Enlibar!

His mind glazed with the knowledge. He did not hear the hillmen take flight, nor see his men gather around him.

The Steel of Enlibar!

Three years of desperate, often dangerous searching had brought him to the mine. They'd filled two wagons with the rich ore and defended it with their lives—but in the depths of his heart Walegrin had not believed he'd found the actual steel: a steel that could shatter other blades; a steel that would bring him honor and glory.

He found his military sword in the dust at his feet and offered it to his lieutenant.

"Take this," he ordered. "Strike at me!"

Thrusher hesitated, then took a half-hearted swipe.

"No! Strike, fool!" Walegrin shouted, raising the Enlibrite blade.

Metal met metal with the same resounding *clang* as before. The shortsword did not shatter, but it took a mortal nick to its edge. Walegrin ran his fingers along the unmarred Enlibrite steel and whooped for joy.

"The destiny of all Ranke is in our hands!"

His men looked at one another, then smiled
with little enthusiasm. They believed in their
commander but not necessarily in his quest.
They were not cheered to see their morose, intense officer so transformed by an off-color
sword—however good the metal and even if it
had saved his life. Walegrin's exaltation, however, did not last long.

They found Malm's body some twenty paces
from the fire, a deep wound in his neck. Walegrin closed his friend's eyes and commended
him to his gods—not Walegrin's gods; Walegrin
honored no gods. Malm was their only casualty,
though they could ill afford the loss.

In grim silence Walegrin left Malm and returned to ransack the headless corpse by the
wagon. Its belt produced a sack of gold coins,
freshly minted in the Rankan capital. Walegrin
thought of the letters he had sent to his rich
patron in the Imperial hierarchy, and of the re-
plies he had not received. In anger and suspicion
he tore at the dead man's clothes until he found
what he knew must be there: a greasy scrap of
parchment with his mentor's familiar seal em-
bossed upon it. While his men slept he read the
treachery into his memory.

Kilite's treasury had financed his quest almost
from the start. The ambitious aristocrat had said
that the Enlibrite steel, if it could be found,
would assure the Empire swift, unending vic-
tories—and swift, unending fortune for whom-
ever made the legend reality. Walegrin had duti-
fully informed the Imperial Advisor of all his
movements and of his success. He cursed and
threw the scrap of parchment into the fire. He'd
told Kilite his exact route from Enlibar to Ranke.

He should have known the moment his first man died—or at least when he lost the second. The hill tribes had been peaceful enough when they'd come up through the mountains and they, themselves, could make no use of the raw ore. He counted the dead man's gold into his own pouch, calculating how far he and his men could travel on it.

Things could have been worse. Kilite might have been able to bribe the tribesmen, but it was still unlikely he could find the abandoned mine. Walegrin had never entrusted *that* secret to paper. And Kilite had never known that Walegrin's final destination had not been the capital, but back in Sanctuary itself. He'd never told Kilite the name of the ugly, little metal-master in the back alleys there who could turn the ore to finest steel.

"We'll make it yet," he said to the darkness, not noticing that Thrusher had come to sit beside him.

"Make it to where?" the little man asked. "We don't dare go to the capital now, do we?"

"We're headed toward Sanctuary from this moment on."

Thrusher could scarcely contain his surprise. Walegrin's intense dislike of the city of his birth was well-known. Not even his own men had suspected they would ever return there. "Well, I suppose a man can hide from anything in Sanctuary's gutters," Thrusher temporized.

"Not only hide, but get our steel too. We'll head south in the morning. Prepare the men."

"Across the desert?"

"No-one will be looking for us there."

His orders given and certain to be obeyed,

Walegrin strode into the darkness. He was used
to sleepless nights. Indeed, he almost preferred
them to his nightmare-ridden slumber. And
now, with thoughts of Sanctuary high in his
mind, sleep would be anything but welcome.

Thrusher was right—a man could hide in
Sanctuary. Walegrin's father had done it, but
hiding hadn't improved him any. He'd ended his
life reviled in a city that tolerated almost anything, hacked to pieces and cursed by the
S'danzo of the bazaar. It was his father's death,
and the memory of the curse that haunted
Walegrin's nights.

By rights it wasn't his curse at all, but his
father's. The old man was never without a doxy;
Rezzel was only the last of a long, anonymous
procession of women through Walegrin's childhood. She was a S'danzo beauty, wild even by
their gypsy standards. Her own people foresaw
her violent death when she abandoned them to
live four years in the Sanctuary garrison, matching Walegrin's temper with her own.

Then one night his father got drunk, and more
violently jealous than usual. They found Rezzel,
what remained of her, with the animal carcasses
outside the charnel house. The S'danzo took
back what they had cast out and, by dead of
night, returned to the garrison. Seven masked,
knife-wielding S'danzo carved the living flesh of
his father, and sealed their curses with his blood.
They'd found two children, Walegrin and Rezzel's daughter, Illyra, hiding in the corner.
They'd marked them with blood and curses as
well.

He'd run away before the sun rose on that

night—and was still running. Now he was running back to Sanctuary.

2

Walegrin patted his horse, ignoring the cloud of dust around them both. Everything, everyone was covered with a fine layer of desert grit; only his hair seemed unaffected, but then it had always been the color of parched straw. He'd led his men safely across the desert to Sanctuary but weariness had settled upon them like dust and though the end of their travels was in sight, they waited in silence for Thrusher's return.

Walegrin had not dared to enter the city himself. Tall, pale despite the desert sun, his braided hair roughly confined by a bronze band, he was too memorable to be an advance scout. He was an outlaw as well, wanted by the prince for abandoning the garrison without warning. He had Kilite's pardon, the scrolls still carefully sealed in his saddlebag, but using it would eventually let Kilite know he was still alive. It was better to remain an outlaw.

Hook-nosed, diminutive Thrusher was a man no-one would remember. Able and single-minded, he'd never run afoul of the town's dangers nor succumb to its limited temptations. Walegrin would have a roof over his men's heads by nightfall and more water than they could drink to set before them. Wine too, but Walegrin had almost forgotten the taste of wine.

As the afternoon shadows lengthened,

Thrusher appeared on the dunes. Walegrin
waved him safe conduct. He put his heels to his
horse and galloped the last stretch of sand. Both
man and beast had been cleansed of yellow grit.
Walegrin suppressed a pang of jealousy.

"Ho, Thrush! Do we sleep in town tonight?"
one of the other men called.

"With full trenchers and a wench on each
knee," Thrusher laughed.

"By the gods, I thought we're bound for
Sanctuary, not paradise."

"Paradise enough—if a man's not choosy,"
Thrusher told them all as he dismounted and
made his way to Walegrin.

"You seem satisfied. Is the town that much
changed since we left it?" Walegrin asked.

"Yes, that much. You'd think the Nisibisi rode
this way. There are more mercenaries in
Sanctuary than in Ranke. We'll never be noticed.
The usual scum fears to leave the shadows—and
if a man knows how to use his sword there's any
number who'll hire him. Kittycat's gold hasn't
been the best for many a month now. He's got to
rely on a citizen's militia to take up the slack
from the Hell-Hounds. Wrigglies—every last one
of them: pompous and—"

"What manner of mercenaries?" Walegrin interrupted.

"Sacred Banders," Thrusher admitted with
noticible reluctance.

"Vashanka's bastards. How many? And who
leads them—if they're led by a man?"

"Couldn't say how many; they camp Downwind. Banders're worse than Hounds; a handful
of 'em's worse than a plague. Some say they
belong to the Prince now that their priest's dead.

Most say it's Tempus at the root of it. They train
for the Nisibisi, but Tempus is building a new
fortress Downwind."

Walegrin looked away. He had no quarrel with
Tempus Thales. True, he was inclined to arrogance, sadism and he was treachery incarnate,
but he moved in the elite circles of power and, as
such, Walegrin could only admire him. Like
everyone else he had heard the Tempus-tales of
self-healing and psuedo-divinity; he professed
to doubt them—but had Tempus gone in search
of Enlibar steel, no-one would have dared stand
in his way.

"They call themselves Stepson—or something
like that," Thrusher continued. "They're all in
Jubal's turf; and neither hide nor hair of Jubal
seen these last months. No hawkmasks on the
streets either, 'cept the ones found nailed to
posts here and there."

"Sacred Banders; Stepsons; Whoresons."
Walegrin shared the prejudices of most in the
Imperial army towards any elite, separate group.
Sanctuary had been the dead-end of the world as
long as anyone could remember. No right-
thinking Rankan citizen passed time there. It
boded ill if Sanctuary had become home to not
only Tempus but a contingent of Sacred Banders
as well. The Empire was in worse shape than
anyone thought.

What was bad for Sanctuary and all of Ranke,
though, was not necessarily bad for the re-
discoverer of Enlibar steel. With luck Walegrin
would find good men in town, or good gold, or
simply enough activity to hide behind. But
whenever Walegrin thought of luck he thought
of the S'danzo. They had marked him for ill-

fortune: if he had good luck it could have been better and when his luck turned sour, the less said about it the better.

"What about that house I asked you about?" Walegrin asked after the conversation had lulled a moment.

The scout was relieved to speak of something else. "No trouble—it wasn't hidden, though no-one knew much about it. Right off the Street of Armorers, like you said it'd be. This metal-master, Balustrus, he must be a pretty strange fellow. Everyone thought he'd died until the Torch—" Thrusher stopped abruptly, slapping himself on the forehead.

"—Gods takes take me for an idiot! *Nothing* is the same in Sanctuary; the gods have discovered it! Vashanka's name was blasted from the pantheon over the palace gate. Vashanka! Sacred Band's Storm God burned clean. The stone steamed for a day and a night. The god himself appeared in the sky—and Azyuna, too."

"Wrigglies? Magicians? Were the Whoresons involved?" Walegrin asked, but without interrupting the flow of Thrusher's theological gossip.

"The Torch himself was nearly killed. Some say a new god's been born to the First Consort and the War of Cataclysm's begun. Officially the priests are blaming everything on the Nisibisi—and not saying why the Nisibisi would wage magical war in Sanctuary. The Wrigglies say it's the awakening of Ils Thousand Eyes. And the mages don't say much of anything because half of them're dead and the rest hiding. The local doomsayers're making fortunes.

"But our Prince Kittycat, bless his empty, little

head, had an idea. He marches out on his balcony
and proclaims that Vashanka is angry because
Sanctuary does not show proper respect to his
consort and her child and that he has blasted his
own name off the pantheon rather than be as-
sociated with the town. Then Kittycat proclaims
a tax on every tavern—a copper a tot—and says
he's going to make an offering to Vashanka.
Sanctuary will apologize by ringing a new bell!"

Walegrin empathized with Sanctuary's naive,
blundering young governor. Actually his idea
wasn't bad; much better than involving the
mageguild or setting the Wrigglies against the
outnumbered Rankans. That was Kittycat's problem; his ideas weren't half bad, but he wasn't
even half the man it would take to have people
listen to them without laughing.

A new idea grew in Walegrin's thoughts. The
Prince had turned to Balustrus, metal-master, to
cast the bell for Vashanka. Now he, Walegrin,
would approach Balustrus to make Enlibar
steel—for the Prince, perhaps, but not Vashanka.
A pattern of fortune might emerge—might be
stronger than the S'danzo curse. He imagined
himself with the Prince; the two of them together
might make one irresistable force.

"Did you see this bell of the metal-master's? Is
it worthy?" he asked Thrusher.

"Worthy of what?" Thrusher replied, not following Walegrin's thoughts at all.

3

Dawn's first light pierced the shadows and
sent the denizens of the night scurrying. The

streets of Sanctuary were almost quiet. Flocks of
seabirds wheeled silently over the town, swooping suddenly as, one after another, the houses
opened their doors to jettison nightslops into the
street. A cowled, burdened monk slipped out the
upper window of a tavern and disappeared
down a still-dark alley. The brief moment of
calm magic faded; the day had begun.

The establishment of Balustrus, metal-master,
was among the first in the armorer's quarter to
come to life. A young woman opened the upper
half of the front door and struggled to raise the
huge, dingy slops-ewer to her shoulder. She
froze, nearly dropping the noisome thing, when
a man stepped out of the shadows. He wore a
monk's garb, but the cowl had fallen back to his
shoulders. A warrior's torc held his straw-blond
hair over his brow.

Walegrin had had three days' rest and washed
the desert from his face, but he was still an ominous figure. The woman gave a small yelp when
he took the ewer from her and carried it some
distance before upending it. When he returned
to the doorway, the metal-master himself stood
there.

"Walegrin, isn't it?"

If the young soldier was ominous, then Balustrus was positively demonic. His skin was the
color of mottled bronze—not brown, nor gold,
nor green—nor human at all. It was wrinkled like
dried fruit, but shone like metal itself. He was
hairless, with features that blended into the convolutions of his skin. When he smiled, as he
smiled at Walegrin, the dark eyes all but vanished.

Walegrin swallowed hard. "I've come with business for you."

"So early?" the bronze man chided. "Well, come right in. A soldier in monk's-cloth is always welcome for breakfast." He hobbled back from the door.

Walegrin retrieved his sack and followed him into the shop. A single oil lamp set over a counting-table cast flickering shadows on the metal-master's face. He rested a pair of iron crutches against the wall behind the table and seemed to hover there, unsupported. Walegrin's eyes adjusted to the dimmer light. He saw the price sheets nailed to the wall and the samples of bronze, iron, tin and steel; he saw the saddle-like perch in which the metal-master sat. But his first impression of the eerie place did not change and he would have left if he could.

"Tell me what you've got in your sack, and why I should care?" the metal-master demanded.

Forcing himself not to stare, Walegrin hoisted the sack to the table-top. "I've found the secret of the steel of Enlibar—"

The bronze man shook with laughter. "What secret? There's no secret to Enlibar steel, my boy. Any fool can make Enlibar steel—if he's got Enlibar ore and Ilsig alchemy."

Walegrin untied the sack, dumping the blue-green ore onto the table. Balustrus stopped laughing. He snatched up a chunk of ore and subjected it to an analysis that included not merely striking it with a mallet, but tasting it as well.

"Yes," the wizened metal-master crooned.

"This is it. Heated and ground and tempered this will be *steel!* Not since the last alchemist of Ilsig sank into his grave has there been steel like the steel I will make."

Whatever else Balustrus was, he was at least mad. Walegrin had first heard the name in the library at Coombs, where he'd gotten the shard of Enlibrite pottery Illyra had read. Kemren, the Purple Mage, had been supposed to read the inscription and Balustrus would make the steel and both men swelt in Sanctuary. Kemren had been dead when Walegrin arrived in the city, but not Balustrus.

It was said the metal-master had been mad when he first came to the city, and Sanctuary had never improved anyone. He claimed he knew everything about any metal but he made his living mending plates and recasting stolen gold.

"I have another ten sacks like this one," Walegrin explained, taking back the ore. "I want swords for my men and myself. I don't have much gold; and fewer friends, but I'll give you a quarter of my ore if you'll make the swords." He continued refilling his sack.

"It will be my priviledge," the cripple agreed, touching the stones one last time before they disappeared. "Perhaps when you have the swords you'll tell me where you found this. At least you'll tell what friends you have that it was the Grey Wolf who forged their weapons."

"You've no need to know where the mine is," Walegrin said firmly, looking directly at Balustrus' legs. "You couldn't go there yourself. You'd have to send others; you'd spread my secret around. Already too many people know." The sack thumped to the floor. "When can I have my swords?"

The metal-master shrugged. "It is not like telling a cloth-cutter to make a tunic, boy. The formula is old; the ore is new. It will take time. I must melt and grind carefully; tempering is an art to itself. It could take years."

Walegrin's blue eyes came alive with anger. "It will not take years! There's war in the north. Already the Emperor has called for men to fill the legions. I will have my swords by summer's end or I'll have your life."

"I have," the metal-master said with bitter irony, "been threatened by experts. You'll have your swords, my boy, as soon as I'm ready to give them to you."

The blond soldier had a ready reply, but withheld it as commotion rose in the street and someone hammered loudly on the bolted doors.

"Open up! Open up in the Prince's name! Open your doors, merchant!"

Walegrin snatched up the sack. He glanced around the room, aware for the first time that it offered no hiding places.

"You look as if you'd seen a ghost, boy. If you don't want to see the Prince's man, just step behind the curtain. Take your ore with you. I'll be but a moment with these fools."

Unable to force coherent words through his tight throat, Walegrin simply nodded and, still clutching the sack, eased behind a curtain and into a dark passageway. He could see narrowly into the room he had left without, he prayed, being seen in return.

Balustrus struggled with the heavy bolts. He got the door open just before the Prince's man

threatened to break it down. Three men immediately surged past: two huge brutes in dirty
rags and a third man in common dress.

"Balustrus? Metal-master?" the third man
demanded.

The man might be dressed commonly, but he
wasn't common. Once Walegrin's suspicions
were aroused, other incongruities became obvious: clean, fresh-curled hair; sturdy boots with
gold buckles; hands that had never been truly
dirty.

Unreasoning fear gripped him. He did not
pause to wonder why a Rankan lord, for such the
visitor must be, would enter the metal-master's
shop in such a disguise; he knew. The S'danzo
curse and his false friends in Ranke had merged.
By sundown he'd be just so much meat on the
torturer's rack. They'd have his secrets, his steel
and, if he got lucky, his life.

". . . It has cooled without a crack," Balustrus
said when Walegrin had regained enough control over his fear to listen again.

"My men will come for it this afternoon," the
lord said, resting his forearms on the table where
Walegrin had spilled his sack of ore.

"As you wish, Hierarch Torchholder. I'll tell
my lads to hoist it up. You'll need a strong cart,
my Lord. She's as heavy as the god."

Both men laughed heartily. Then, looking
mildly annoyed, the High Priest of Vashanka in
Sanctuary stood up and rubbed his arm. A tiny
object dropped to the floor. Walegrin felt bitter
bile surge up his throat as the Rankan retrieved
the bit and examined both it and his arm.

"It broke my skin," he said.

"Scraps," the metal-master replied, taking the

small flake from the priest's hand.

"Sharp scraps. We should put them on the edges of our swords," Torchholder laughed, and took back the offending object. "Not glass either . . . Some new project of yours?"

"No—"

Walegrin could not hear the rest of Balustrus' reply. His fear-clouded mind had finally placed the Lord and his name: the Torch himself, Wargod Priest. As if it were not bad enough to have the regular Imperial hierarchy sniffing along his trail, now here was the Wargod too—and the Sacred Bands? Walegrin was numb from the waist down, unable to move closer or run away. Damn the S'danzo and their curses. Damn his father, if he weren't already damned, for killing Rezzel and incurring supernatural wrath.

But Molin Torchholder was laughing now, giving the metal-master a small coin purse and a brief, casual blessing on his work. Walegrin, whose panicked thoughts always moved too quickly, knew he'd been sold. When the priest and his bodyguards had disappeared out the door, Walegrin confronted the withered, smiling, metal-master.

"Was it worthwhile?" he demanded.

"The palace has the best money in the city. Some of it was truly minted in Ranke and not cut three times since with lead or tin." Balustrus looked up from his counting and studied Walegrin's face. "Now, son, whatever you've done to get Ranke on your tail—don't go thinking I'd be on their side. Your secrets are safe from Ranke with me."

Walegrin tried to laugh, but the attempt failed. "I'm to believe that the Torch himself just hap-

pened to wander down here—and that he just
happened to find a piece of ore stuck to his arm
and then he just happened to give you a double-
handful of gold?"

"Walegrin, Walegrin," Balustrus swung down
from the stool and tried to approach the angry
soldier, but Walegrin easily eluded him. "Molin
Torchholder has only paid me what is due
me—for the work on Vashanka's bell. Now it
might seem strange to you that such a man
would come here himself—but the Hierarch has
taken a personal interest in this project from the
beginning. Anyone in town can tell you that.
Besides, did I know you were going to be here
this morning? Did I suspect that today I'd hold
Enlibrite ore in my hands? No.

"Now, I expect you'll believe exactly what you
want, but it was happenstance, all of it. And
Torchholder's suspicions are not aroused; if
they were he would still be here, believe that.
Mark me well: I know him and the rest better
than you imagine."

It was not the first time Balustrus hinted that
he knew more than he was saying, and the notion
did nothing to reassure Walegrin. Kilite had
often done the same thing—and Kilite had finally betrayed him. "Truly, metal-master, when
can I have my swords?" he asked in a slightly
calmer voice.

"Truly lad, I do not know. The bell is finished,
as you heard. I have no other commissions waiting at my foundry. I'll start testing your ore as
soon as the priest claims his bell. But, Walegrin,
even if I stumble upon the right temperatures
and the right proportions at once—it will still
take time. I've only two lads to help me. I've

agreed to payment in kind—but I cannot hire men with unforged swords. Besides, would you want me to contract day-labor from the taverns?"

Walegrin shook his head. He'd relaxed. His body could not stand the tension he brought to it. He was exhausted and knew his hands would shake if he moved them. What Balustrus said was true enough, except—He paused and a measure of his confidence returned. "I've five men with me: good men; more than equal to day-labor. They sit idle until the swords are ready. They'll work for you."

It was the metal-master's turn to hesitate. "I'll not pay them," he announced. "But they can stay in the outbuildings of the foundry. And Dunsha will make food for them as she does for the rest of us." He seated himself in his stool and smiled. "How about that, son?"

Walegrin winced, not from the offer which was all he had desired, but from Balustrus' attempts at friendship and familiarity. Of course the smith hadn't been in Sanctuary when Walegrin was a youth. He hadn't known Walegrin's father and could not know that Walegrin allowed no-one to call him 'son.' So, Walegrin controlled his rage and grunted affirmatively.

"I'll give you another piece of advice—since you're already in my debt. You've got a hate and fear about you that draws trouble like a magnet. You think the worst, and you think it too soon. You'll be doing neither yourself nor your men any good by going north. But, now listen to me, the Sacred Band of Stepsons and probably the Hounds as well will *have* to go—and then there'll be no-one of any power and ability here. Jubal's gone—you know that—don't you?"

Walegrin nodded. Tales of the night assault on
the Downwind estate of the slaveholder circu-
lated in numerous variations, but everyone
agreed that Jubal hadn't been seen since. "But I
don't want to spend my life in Sanctuary looking
after gutter-scum!" he snarled back at his
would-be benefactor.

"Mark me—and let me finish. You're fresh
back. Things have changed. There're no more
blue hawks to roam the streets. That's not to say
that them as wore the masks are gone—not all of
them, not yet. Only Jubal's gone. Jubal's men and
Jubal's power are there for the taking. Even if he
should return to this town, he'll be in no condition to raise his army of the night again. Let
Tempus, Zalbar—" Balustrus spat for emphasis,
"and all their ilk fight for Ranke. With them gone
and your steel you could be master of this place
for life—and give it on to your children as well.
Kittycat would surrender in a day."

Walegrin didn't answer. He didn't remember
sliding the bolts back before opening the door,
and perhaps he hadn't. He was ambitious to gain
glory, but he had no real thoughts for the future.
Balustrus had tempted him, but he'd frightened
him more.

The morning sun brought no warmth to the
young man. He shivered beneath his borrowed,
monk's cloak. There weren't many people on the
narrow streets and those took pains to stay out of
his path. His cloak billowed out to reveal the
leather harness of a soldier beneath it, but no-one
stopped him to ask questions.

The taverns were boarded up as the barkeeps
and wenches alike caught a few hours rest.
Walegrin pounded past them, head erect, eyes

hard. He reached the Wideway without seeing a welcoming door. He headed for the wharves and the fishermen whose day began well before dawn. They would be ready for refreshment by now.

He wandered into a slant-walled den called the Wine Barrel; Fish Barrel would have been a more appropriate name. The place stank of fish oil. Ignoring the pervasive stench, Walegrin approached the rough-hewn bar. The room had fallen silent and, though a swordsman like himself had nothing to fear from a handful of fishermen, Walegrin was uncomfortable.

Even the ale was rank with fish-oil, but he gagged it down. The thick brew brought the clouds of dullness his mind craved. He ordered another three mugs of the vile, potent stuff and belched prodigiously while the fisherfolk endured him.

Their meek, offended stares drove him back onto the wharf before he was half as drunk as he wanted to be. The tangy air of the harbor undid him; he vomited into the water and found himself almost completely sober. In an abysmal mood, he tugged the priest's cowl over his head and held the cloak shut with a death-grip. His path wound toward the bazaar where Illyra lived and saw the future in the S'danzo cards.

It was a market day at the bazaar, with every extra stall crammed with winter's produce: jellies, sweet breads and preserved fruits. He shoved past them, untempted, until he reached the more permanent part of the bazaar and could hear the ringing of Dubro's hammer above the din. She had found herself an able protector, at least. He stopped before the man who was his own age and height but whose slow strength was unequalled.

"Is Illyra inside?" he asked politely, knowing he would be recognized. "Is she scrying for someone or can I talk to her?"

"You're not welcome here," Dubro replied evenly.

"I would like to see my sister. I've never done anything to hurt her in the past and I don't intend to start now. Stand guard beside me, if you must. I *will* see her."

Dubro sighed and set his tools carefully back in their proper places. He banked the fire and moved buckets of water close by the cloth door of the simple structure he and Illyra called home. Walegrin was about to burst with impatience when the plodding giant lifted the cloth and motioned him inside.

"We have a visitor," Dubro announced.

"Who?"

"See for yourself."

Walegrin recognized the voice but not the woman who moved in the twilight darkness. It was Illyra's custom to disguise her youth with cosmetics and shapeless clothing—still it seemed that the creature who walked toward him was far too gross to be his half-sister. Then he saw her face—his father's face for she took after him that way—and there could be no doubt.

She slouched ungracefully in the depths of Dubro's chair, and Walegrin, though he had little knowledge of these things, guessed she was late in pregnancy.

"You're having a child," he blurted out.

"Not quite yet," she replied with a laugh. "Moonflower assures me I have some weeks to wait yet. I'm sure it will be a boy, like Dubro. No girl-child would be so large."

"And you're well enough?" Walegrin had always assumed she was barren: doubly cursed. It did not seem possible that she should be so robustly breeding.

"Well enough. I've lost my figure but I've got all my teeth, yet," she laughed again. "Did you find what you were looking for?"

"Yes—and more," Walegrin didn't trust the smith who stood close behind him, but Illyra would tell him everything he said anyway. "I've brought back the ore. We were betrayed by treachery—I lost all but five of my men. I have made powerful enemies with my discovery. I need your help, Illyra, if I'm to protect myself and my men."

"You found the steel of Enlibar?" Dubro whispered while Illyra sought a more dignified position in the chair.

"I found the ore," Walegrin corrected, suddenly realizing that the great ox of a monger probably expected to make the swords himself.

"What do you need from me?" Illyra asked. "I'd think you'd need Dubro's help, not mine."

"No," Walegrin spat out quickly. "I've found one to make my steel for me—Balustrus, metal-master. He knows forging, grinding and tempering—"

"And Ilsig alchemy," Dubro added. "Since he cast the Prince's god-bell it would seem good fortune falls to him."

Walegrin did not like to think that Dubro knew of Balustrus and the making of steel. He attempted to ignore the knowledge and the smith. " 'Lyra, it's your help I need: your sight. With the cards you can tell me who I can trust and what I can do in safety."

She frowned and smoothed her skirts over her great belly. "Not now, Walegrin. Not even if I could use the cards for such things. The baby-to-be takes so much from me; I don't have the sight. Moonflower warns me that I must not use the gifts so close to my time. It could be dangerous."

"Moonflower? What is moonflower?" Walegrin complained, and heard a giggle from Dubro.

"She is S'danzo. And she takes care of me, now—"

"S'danzo?" Walegrin said in disbelief. "Since when do the S'danzo help you?"

Illyra shrugged. "Even the S'danzo cannot remember forever, you know. The women have the sight, so the men feel free to wander with the wind. The women stay in one place all their lives; the men—It is forgotten."

"Forgotten?" Walegrin leaned forward to whisper to her. "Illyra, this Moonflower who tells you not to use your sight—does she see those who used to come to you?"

"She—or her daughter," Illyra admitted.

"Illyra, breeding has clouded your mind. They will squeeze you out. They never forget."

"If that were true, so much the worse for them. Since the mercenaries came to town scrying is not pleasant, Walegrin. I do not enjoy looking into the future of soldiers. I do not enjoy their reactions when I tell them the truth." She shifted again in the chair. "But, it is not true. When my son is born the danger will be past and I will see again. Moonflower and Migurneal will not keep what is rightfully mine," she said with the calm confidence of one who has the upper hand. "You need not worry for me. I will not send you to Moonflower, either. I'll answer your questions myself, if I can, after my son is born—if you can wait that long."

It seemed likely that she would be delivered of her child well before Balustrus finished making the swords, so Walegrin agreed to wait.

4

Balustrus' villa-foundry had fallen from fashionability long before the first Rankans reached Sanctuary. Weeds grew boldly in the mosaic face of Shipri in the attrium. There wasn't a room where the roof was intact and several where it was non-existant. Walegrin and Thrusher threw their belongings into a room once connected to the main attrium but now accessible only through a gaping hole in the wall. Still, it was a better billet than most they'd seen.

The work was hard and dirty, with little time for recreation, though Sanctuary was in sight down the gentle slopes. Balustrus treated Walegrin and his men like ordinary apprentices, which meant they got enough food and more than enough abuse. If Walegrin had not borne his share so stoically there might have been problems, but he was willing to sacrifice anything to the cause of his swords.

For three weeks they lived in almost total isolation. A farmer delivered their food and gossip; an occassional mercenary came seeking Balustrus' services and was turned away. Only once did someone come looking for Walegrin him-

self, and that was after Illyra bore twins: a boy
and a girl. The soldier sent them a gold piece to
insure their registry in the rolls of citizenship at
the palace.

"Is it worth it, commander?" Thrusher asked
as he kneaded a soothing balm into Walegrin's
burnt shoulder. "We're here three weeks and
all we have to show for ourselves is fresh
scars."

"What about full bellies and no problems from
Kittycat? Yes, it's worth it. We should know how
steel is made; I had always thought the smiths
just took the ore and made it into swords. I had
no idea there were so many steps in between."

"Aye, so many steps. We've gone through two
sacks already and what have we got? Three
half-decent knives, a mountain of bad steel and a
demon grinding away in the shed there. Maybe
we would be better running. Sometimes I don't
think we'll ever leave Sanctuary again."

"He's mad, but no demon. And I think he's
getting close to the steel we need. He's as eager to
have the steel as we are—it's his life."

The little man shook his head and eased
Walegrin's tunic over the sore. "I don't like
magic," he complained.

"He only added a little bit of Ilsig silver—
hardly enough to make a difference. We've got to
expect a little magic. We found the mine with
magic, didn't we? Balustrus isn't a magician. He
said he couldn't put a spell on the metal like the
Wrigglies put on steel, so he thought he'd try to
add something to the steel that already had a
spell on it."

"Yeah—the Necklace of Harmony!"

"You went to the temple and looked at the statue of Ils. You yourself said there was a silver necklace on the statue. You yourself said there wasn't a rumor in town to the effect that the necklace had been touched, much less stolen. It's not the Necklace of Harmony."

Thrusher bit his lip and looked away in thought. It was just as well that he didn't look at his commander's face. Walegrin had been present at the moment the smith added the bits of silver to the molten metal. He could truthfully say he didn't believe the metal was the Necklace of Harmony, but after seeing the burst of white-hot flame he knew it was no ordinary piece of jewelry.

The whine of Balustrus' grinding wheel dominated the courtyard. The furnaces had been sealed; the piles of crushed ore glittered in the sunlight. Everyone awaited the results of the latest grinding. It seemed to Walegrin, as he turned away from the sound, that it was different this time. The metal shrieked like an agonized, living thing.

Thrusher gave him a sharp nudge. The courtyard had become silent and an apprentice was running toward them. It was time, the youth shouted, for Walegrin to witness the tempering of the blade.

"Luck," Thrusher added as Walegrin rose.

"Aye, luck. If it's good we can start thinking of leaving."

Balustrus was polishing the freshly ground blade when Walegrin entered the hot, dusty shed. The bronze man's tunic was filthy with sweat and dust from the grinding wheel. His mottled skin glistened more brightly than the metal.

"She's a beauty, isn't she?" he said, giving the blade to Walegrin while he sought his crutches.

Fine, wavy lines of black alternated with thicker bands of a more silvery metal. The old Enlibrite sword he kept rolled in his mattress had no such striations but Balustrus said an iron core would ultimately yield a better steel; so much could be learned from the Rankan armorers. Walegrin thumped the flat of the new blade against his palm, wishing he knew if the metalmaster were correct.

"We've done it, son!" Balustrus exaulted, grabbing the blade back. "I knew the secret would be in that silver."

Walegrin followed him out of the shed to one of the smaller furnaces which the apprentices had already fired. The youths ran when the men approached.

"But there was no silver mentioned on the pottery fragment; and there's no silver in ordinary steel, is there?"

The metal-master spat on a weed. "Wrigglies never did anything without a spell, lad. Spells for cooking food, spells for bedding a whore. Big spells, little spells and special spells for steel. And this time we've got the steel spell."

"With respect—you said that last time and it shattered in the brine."

Balustrus scratched his rutted chin. "I did, didn't I? But this *feels* right, boy. There's no other way to explain it. It feels different and it feels right. And it has to be the silver—that's the only different thing this time."

"Did the silver have a 'steel' spell on it?"
Walegrin asked.

The metal-master thrust the blade into the
glowing coals. "You're smart, Walegrin. Too bad
it's too late; you could have learned—you could
make your own steel." He spat again and the
weed fell over. "No, it wasn't a steel spell—nothing like that. I don't know what the Wrigglies put
on that silver. The Torch brought the necklace
here right after the Prince announced the bell. I
could see it was old, but it was plain silver and
not valuable. I thought he'd want it for the inscription; silver pressed on bronze is quite elegant. But no—the Hierarch gives out that this is
the Necklace of Harmony warm off Ils—no saying how he comes to have it. He wants me to melt
the silver into the bell: 'Let Ils tremble when
Vashanka's name is called!' he says in that
priest's voice of his—"

"But you didn't," Walegrin interrupted.

"Not sayin' I didn't try, boy. Put it in with the
copper; put it in with the tin—the damn thing
floated to the top everytime. I had a choice: I
could cast the bell with the silver buried in the
metal and know that the bell would crack as soon
as the Torch struck it. You can imagine the
omens *that* would bring—and what it'd bring to
me as well. Or, I could set the silver aside and tell
the Torch that everything was exactly according
to his instructions."

"And you set the silver aside?" Walegrin covered his face with his hand and turned away
from the both the metal-master and the furnace.

"Of course, lad. Do you think the heavens're
going to open up and Vashanka stick his head

out to tell Molin Torchholder that Ils' silver isn't in the bell?"

"Stranger things have happened of late." Walegrin faced the metal-master's silence. "The silver should have melted in the bronze, shouldn't it?" he asked softly.

"Aye—and I set it aside very carefully when it didn't. I'll be glad to see the last of it. I don't know what it is that the Torch gave me—and I'll wager he doesn't either. But it is Wrigglie-work and it'd have to be spelled or it would have melted—see? So you come asking for Enlibrite steel. You've got the ore and, all things being equal, steel is steel. But it isn't, so I know we need a spell, a spell for hardness and temper. No-one alive would know that spell, but here I've got silver that doesn't melt with a mighty spell on it—

"And, oh, it feels right, Walegrin, it feels right. She'll take an edge like you've never seen."

Walegrin shrugged and looked at the metal-master again. "If you're right, how many swords can you make?"

"With what's left of your ore and my necklace: about fifty. And as it's my silver, lad, I'll be taking more for myself. There'll be about twenty-five for you and the same for me."

The blond officer shrugged again. It was no worse than he had expected. He watched as Balustrus wrestled the dull, red metal from the fire.

There were conflicting theories on the tempering of fighting steel. Some said a snowdrift was best for cooling the metal, others said plain water would suffice. Most agreed the ideal was the living body of a man, though in practice only Imperial swords were made that way. Balustrus believed in water straight from the harbor, left in the sun until it had evaporated by half. He plunged the blade into a barrel of such brine and disappeared in the acrid steam.

The blade survived.

"Get the old sword," Balustrus urged and with a nod Walegrin sent Thrusher after it.

They compared the blades for weight and balance, then, slowly, they tested them against each other. Walegrin held the old sword and Balustrus swung the new. The first strokes were tentative; Walegrin scarcely felt them as he parried them. Then the metal-master grew confident; he swung the new metal with increasing force and uncanny accuracy. Deep green sparks fell in the late afternoon light, but Walegrin found himself more concerned with the old man who suddenly no longer seemed to need crutches. After a few frantic moments Walegrin backed out of range. Balustrus stopped, sighed and let the blade drag in the dust.

"We found it, lad," he whispered.

He sent the apprentices into Sanctuary for a keg of ale. The soldiers and the apprentices partook lavishly of it, but Balustrus did not. He continued to sit in the courtyard with the fresh-ground blade across his hidden, crippled legs. It was dark when Walegrin came out to join him.

"You are truly a master of metal," the younger man said with a smile, setting an extra mug of ale beside Balustrus.

The metal-master shook his head, declining both the ale and the compliment. "I'm a shadow of what I was," he said to himself. "So, now you have your Enlibrite swords, son. And what will you do with them?"

Walegrin squatted in the moonlight. The ale had warmed him against the night breezes and made him both more expansive and optimistic than usual. "With the promise of swords I can recruit men—only a few at first. But we'll travel north, taking commissions—taking what's necessary. I'll hire more as I go. We'll arrive at the Wizardwall fully mounted and armored. We'll prove ourselves with honor and glory against the Nisibisi, then become the vanguard of a legion."

Chuckling loudly, the metal-master finally took a sip of ale. "Glory and honor, Walegrin, lad—what will you do with glory? What do you gain with honor? What becomes of your men when Wizardwall and the Nisibisi are forgotten?"

Honor and glory were their own rewards for a Rankan soldier and as for war—a soldier could always find a conflict or commission. Of course, Walegrin had neither glory nor honor and his commissions thus far had been pedestrian—like duty at the Sanctuary garrison: the antithesis of honor and glory. "I will be known," he resolved after a moment's thought. "While I'm alive I'll be respected. When I'm dead I'll be memorialized—"

"You're already known, lad, or have you forgotten that? You have rediscovered Enlibar steel. You don't dare show your face because of it. How much honor and glory do you think you'll need before you can walk the streets of Ranke? Twenty-five swords? Fifty swords? Do you think they'll believe you when you tell them we made the steel with bits of an old Wrigglie necklace? Eh?"

Walegrin stood up. He paced a circle around the seated cripple. "I will succeed. I'll succeed now or die."

With a quick, invisible movement of his crutch, Balustrus brought Walegrin sprawling into the dust. "It is impolite to speak to the back of my head. Your fortunes have changed, and could change again. The Empire has never given you anything—and will not ever give you anything. But the Empire means nothing to Sanctuary.

"There is power here, lad, not glory or honor but pure power. Power you can use to buy all the honor and glory you want. I tell you, Walegrin— Jubal's not coming back. His world's ripe for taking."

"You've said that before. So Jubal rots under his mansion. How many bloodied hawkmasks have been nailed to the Downwind bridge? Even if I were tempted, there's nothing left."

"Tempus is culling the ranks for you. The wiser ones are safe, I'm sure. They've heard Jubal isn't dead and they're waiting for his return—but they don't know everything."

There was an evil confidence to Balustrus' tone that made Walegrin wary. He never fully trusted the metal-master and trusted him less when he spoke in riddles.

"I was not always Balustrus. Once I was the Grey Wolf. Only twenty-five years ago I led all the Imperial legions into the mountains and broke the last Ilsig resistance. I broke it because I knew it. I was born in those mountains. The

blood of kings and sorcerors runs in my veins, or
it did. But I knew the days of kings were over and
the days of Empire had come. I destroyed my
own people hoping for honor and glory among
the conquerors—''

Walegrin cleared his throat loudly. There
wasn't a citizen alive who hadn't heard of the
Grey Wolf: a young man clothed in animal hides,
given a hero's welcome in Ranke despite his
Wrigglie past—and tragically killed in a fall
from his horse. The whole capital had turned out
for his funeral.

"Perhaps my friends in Ranke were the fathers
of your friends," Balustrus said to Walegrin's
skepticism. "I watched my own funeral from the
gladiators' galleries where drugged, stripped
and branded I'd been left to die or improve my
one-time friends' fortunes." He laughed bitterly.
"I wasn't your ordinary Rankan general—they'd
forgotten that. I could fight and I could forge
weapons such as they'd never seen. I'd learned
metal-mastery from my betrayed people."

"And Jubal—what's he got to do with this?"
Walegrin finally asked.

"He came later. I'd fought and killed so often
I'd been retired by my owners, but then the Emperor himself bought me, Kittycat's father. I
trained the new slaves and Jubal was one of
them. A paragon—he was born for the death-
duel. I taught him every trick I knew; he was a
son to me. I watched fortunes change everytime
he fought. We soon both belonged to the Emperor. We drank together, whored together—the
life of a successful gladiator isn't bad if you don't
mind the brand and collar. I trusted him. I told
him the truth about me.

"Two days later I was on the sand fighting against him. I hadn't fought for five years; but even at my best I was no match for him. We fought with mace and chain—his choice. He took my legs with his second swing. I had expected that, but I expected a quick, merciful death as well. I thought we were both slaves: equals and friends. He said: 'It's been arranged,' pointed to the Imperial balcony and struck my legs again.

"That was summer. It was winter when I opened my eyes again. A Lizerene healer was at my side congratulating himself on my recovery—but I had become this!"

The metal-master jerked his tunic upward, revealing the remains of his legs. The moonlight softened the horror, but Walegrin could see the twisted remnants of muscle, the exposed lengths of bone, the scaly knobs that had once been knees. He looked away before Balustrus lowered the cloth.

"The Lizerene said he'd been paid in gold. I returned slowly to the capital, as you can imagine, and painfully, as you cannot. Jubal had been freed the day after our battle. I searched for years and found him Downwind, already well-protected by his 'masks. I couldn't adequately thank him for my life so I became Balustrus, his friend. I forged his swords and masks.

"Jubal had enemies, most more able than I; I feared my revenge would be vicarious and his death swift. When Tempus came I thought we were both doomed. But Tempus is cruel; crueler than Jubal, crueler than I. Saliman came here one night to say his master lay alive among the corpses at the charnel house, an arrowhead in each knee. Saliman asked if I would shelter the master until he died—as he was certain to do. 'Of course,' I said, 'but he need not die. We'll send him to the Lizerene.' "

The ale no longer warmed Walegrin. He was no stranger to hate or revenge; he had no sympathy for the slaver. But Balustrus' voice was pure sated, insane malice. This man had betrayed his own people for Ranke—and been betrayed by Ranke in turn. He had called Jubal his son, told him the truth about himself and believed that his son had immediately betrayed him. Walegrin knew he was now Balustrus' 'son.' Did the metal-master expect to be betrayed—or would he betray first?

Balustrus submerged himself in his satisfaction; he said nothing when Walegrin took his mug of ale far across the courtyard to the shadows where Thrusher sat.

"Thrush—can you go into the city tonight?"

"I'm not so far gone that I can't thread the maze."

"Then go. Start looking about for men."

Thrusher shook off the effects of the ale. "What's happened? What's gone wrong?"

"Nothing yet. Balustrus is acting strangely. I don't know how much longer we can trust him."

"What's made you agree with me at last?"

"He told me the story of his life. I can see Illyra in ten days—after the new moon and after she's cleansed. We'll leave for the north the next morning, with the silver and the ore if we don't have swords."

Thrusher was not one to say 'I told you so' more than once. He got his cloak and went over

the outer wall without anyone but Walegrin
knowing he was gone.

5

The metal-master organized his courtyard
foundry with military precision. Within six days
of the successful tempering, another ten blades
had been forged. Walegrin marked the progress
in his mind: so many days until he could visit
Illyra, plus one more before the swords were
finished; yet another to meet with the men
Thrusher was culling out of the city and then
they could be gone.

He watched Balustrus carefully; and though
the metal-master gave no overt sign of betrayal,
Walegrin became anxious. Strangers came more
frequently and the cripple made journeys to
places not even Thrusher could find. When
questioned, Balustrus spoke of the Lizerene who
tended Jubal and the bribes he needed to pay.

On the morning of the eighth day, a rainy
morning when the men had been glad to sleep
past dawn, Walegrin finished his planning. He
was at the point of rousing Thrusher when he
heard sound where there should have been silence beyond the wall.

He roused Thrusher anyway and the two men
crept silently toward the sound. Walegrin drew
his sword, the first Enlibar sword to be forged in
five hundred years.

"You've got the money and the message?"
they heard Balustrus say.

"Yessir."

Balustrus' crutches scraped along the broken

stone. Walegrin and Thrusher flattened against the walls and let him pass. They'd never get the truth from the metal-master, but the messenger was another matter. They crept around the wall.

The stranger was dressed in dark clothes of unfamiliar style. He was adjusting the stirrup when Walegrin fell upon him, wrestling him to the ground. Keeping a firm hand over the stranger's mouth and a tight hold on his arm, Walegrin dragged him a short distance from his horse.

"What've we got?" Thrusher asked after a cursory check of the horse.

"Too soon to tell," Walegrin replied. He twisted the arm again until he felt his prisoner gasp, then he rolled him over. "Not local, and not Nisibisi by the looks of him."

The young man's features were soft, almost feminine and his efforts to free himself were laughably futile. Walegrin cuffed him sharply then yanked him into a sitting position.

"Explain yourself."

Terrified eyes darted from one man to the other and came to rest on Walegrin, but the lad said nothing.

"You'll have to give him a search, eh?" Thrusher threatened.

"Aye—here's his purse."

Walegrin ripped the pouch from the youngster's belt, noticing as he did that the youth carried no evident weapon, not even a knife. He did, however, have some large heavy object under his jerkin. Walegrin tossed the purse to Thrusher and sought the hidden object. It proved to be a medallion, covered with a foreign-seeming script. He had made nothing of the inscription before Thrusher yelped with surprise and a dazzle of light flashed between them.

As Walegrin looked up a second flash erupted. Their prisoner needed no more time to effect his escape. They heard the youth mount and gallop off, but by the time either man could see clearly again the trail was already becoming mud.

"Magic," Thrusher muttered as he got to his feet.

Walegrin said nothing as he got his legs under him. "Well, Thrush—what else was in that purse?" he asked after several moments.

Thrusher checked it cautiously again. "A small ransom in gold and this." He handed Walegrin a small silver object.

"One of the Ilsig links, by the look of it," Walegrin whispered. He looked back toward the villa. "He's up to something."

"The magician wasn't Rankene," Thrusher offered in consolation.

"That only means we have new enemies. C'mon. It's time to find my sister. She'll make at least as much sense as the metal-master."

The rain had kept the bazaar crowds to a minimum, but so close to the harbor there was fog, too, and Walegrin got them lost twice before he heard the sound of Dubro's hammer. Two mercenaries, a Whoreson pair by the look of them, waited beneath the awning. Dubro was mending their shield.

"You're putting in more dents than you're taking out, oaf," the younger, taller of the pair complained, but Dubro went on hammering.

Walegrin and Thrusher moved closer without

being noticed. A rope was tied across the doorway, usually a sign that Illyra was scrying. Walegrin tried to find the scent of her incense in the air but found only the smell of Dubro's fire.

There was a scream and a crash from the inside. Dubro dropped his hammer and bumped into Walegrin at the doorway. A third Stepson yanked the rope loose and attempted, unsuccessfully, to bully his way past both Dubro and Walegrin. The smith's hands closed on the Stepson's shoulder. The other pair reached for their weapons, but Thrusher already had his drawn. Everyone froze in place.

Illyra appeared in the doorway. "Just let them go, Dubro," she asked wearily. "The truth hurts him more than you can." She noticed Walegrin, sighed and retreated back into the darkness.

"Lying S'danzo bitch!" the third Stepson shouted after her.

Dubro changed his grip and shook the small man. "Get out of here before I change my mind," he said in a low voice.

"You haven't finished with the shield yet," the young one complained, but his companions hushed him, grabbed the shield and hurried into the rain.

Dubro turned his attention to Walegrin. "One might expect you to be here when something like this happens."

"You shouldn't let her see men like that."

"He wouldn't," Illyra explained from the doorway. "But that's the only kind that comes anymore—for mongering and scrying. The Stepsons scare anything else away."

"What about the women you used to see? The lovers and the merchants?" Walegrin's tone was harsh. "Or did the S'danzo not give them back?"

"No, Migurneal was not untrue. It's the same everywhere. No woman would venture this close Downwind anymore—and not many merchants either. They don't need me to tell them their luck if they run afoul of the Sacred Band."

"And you need the money because of the babes?" Walegrin concluded, then realized he didn't hear the normal infantile sounds.

Illyra looked away. "Well, yes—and no," she said angrily. "We needed a wet-nurse—and we found one. But it's not safe for her or the babies here. They're bullies. Worse than the hawk-masks were—those at least stayed in the gutters where they belonged. Arton and Lillis are at the Aphrodesia House."

It was not uncommon to foster a child at a well-run brothel where young women sold their milk. Myrtis, proprietor of the Aphrodesia, had an unquestionable reputation. Even the palace women kept their children in the Aphrodesia nursery. But fostering wasn't the S'danzo way and Walegrin could see Illyra had agreed to it only because she was scared.

"Have you been threatened?" he asked, sounding like the garrison office he had been.

Illyra didn't answer, but Dubro did. "They make threats everytime she tells them the truth. She tells them they're cowards—and their threats prove it. 'Lyra's too honest; she shouldn't answer the questions men shouldn't ask."

"But I'll answer your questions now, Wale-grin," she offered, not facing her husband.

The incense holders were still scattered across the carpets. Her cards had been thrown against the wall. Walegrin watched while she set her things in order and seated herself behind the table. She had recovered from the birth of the twins, Walegrin judged. There was a pleasant maturity in her face but otherwise she was the same—until she took up the cards again.

"What do you seek," she asked.

"I have been betrayed, but I am still in danger. I wish to know whom I should fear most and where I might be safe."

Illyra's face relaxed into unemotional blankness. Her expressionless eyes stared into him. "The steel brings enemies, doesn't it?"

Though he had seen her in scrying trances before, the change chilled Walegrin. Yet he believed totally in her gifts since she had read the pottery fragment which had led him to the ore. "Yes, the steel brings enemies. Will it be the death of me? Is it the final link in a S'danzo forged chain?"

"Give me your sword," she demanded.

He handed her the Enlibar blade. Illyra stared at it a while then ran her palms along the flat and touched the edge tenderly with her fingertips. She set the metal on her table and sat motionless for so long that Walegrin began to fear for her. He had started for the door when her eyes widened and she called his name.

"The future has been clouded since I gave birth, Walegrin, but your future is as the fog to the sun.

"Steel belongs to no man but to itself alone— this steel even more so. It reeks of gods and magic, places the S'danzo do not see. But unless your betrayers work through the gods they will have no power over you. There is intrigue, treachery—but none of it will harm you or the steel."

"What of the men of Ranke? Have they forgotten me? When I go north—"

"You will not go north," she said, taking hold of the sword again.

" 'Lyra, I'm going north with my men and the swords."

"You will not go north."

"That's nonsense."

Illyra put the sword on the table again. "It is the clearest thing I've seen in a week, Walegrin. You will not go north; you will not leave Sanctuary."

"Then you cannot say no harm will come to me. What of the spy we trapped this morning. The stranger who got away. Do you see him?"

"No—he can mean nothing to you, but I'll try my cards." She picked up the deck, took his hand and pressed it against the cards. "Perhaps your future is distinct from the steel. Make three piles then turn over the top card of each."

He placed the three piles where she pointed and flipped over the cards. The first showed two men dueling. Though blood dripped from their blades neither seemed injured. It was a card Walegrin had seen before. The second was unfamiliar and damaged by water running through the colors. It seemed to show a great mass of ships on the open sea. The third card showed an armored hand clutching a sword-hilt that changed to flame halfway up the blade. Without thinking Walegrin moved to touch the flame. Illyra's fingers closed over his and restrained him.

"Your first: the Two of Ores: steel. It means many things, but for you it is simply this steel itself. But you already know this.

"'Your second: this is the Seven of Ships, or it was the Seven of Ships. It was the fishing fleet, but it has become something else." She squeezed his hand. "Here is all danger and opportunity. Not even the gods see this card as we see it now. The Seven of Ships sails out of the future; it sails for Sanctuary and nothing will be the same. Remember it!" she commanded and overturned the card again. "We were not meant to see what the gods have not yet seen.

"Your third is not a sword, though you thought it was. It is the Lance of Flames—the Oriflamme: leader's card. Coming with steel and the revealed future it places you in the vanguard. It is not a card for a man who believes in S'danzo curses."

"Don't speak in riddles, Illyra."

"It is simple. You are not cursed by the S'danzo—if you ever were. You have been marked by the gods; but remember what we say about the gods: it is all the same whether they curse or favor you. Since the birth of my children this is the first future which is not clouded. I see a huge fleet sailing for Sanctuary—and I see the Oriflamme. I will not interpret what I see."

"The men in Ranke will not reach me and Balustrus will not sell me?"

The S'danzo woman laughed as she gathered her cards. "Raise your eyes, Walegrin. It doesn't matter. Ranke is to the north and you're not

going north. The steel, the fleet and the oriflamme are right here."

"I do not understand."

The incense had burned down. Sunlight came
in through the roped-off door. Illyra emerged
from the aura of mystery to be herself again.
"You are the only one who can understand,
Walegrin," she told him. "I'm too tired, now. It
doesn't really matter; I don't feel your doom—
and I've felt doom often enough since the mercenaries started coming. Who knows. Maybe you
aren't the one who understands. Things happen
to you, around you, and you just muddle
through. Tell Dubro I'll see no-one else today
when you leave."

She stood up and went behind a curtain. He
heard her lie down; he left quietly. Thrusher was
helping Dubro with a wheelrim, but both men
stopped when they saw him.

"She wishes to be left alone the rest of the
day," he said.

"Then you best begone from here."

Walegrin headed out from the awning without
argument. Thrusher joined him.

"Well, what did you learn?"

"She told me that we will not go north and that
a great fleet is headed for Sanctuary."

Thrusher stopped short. "She's mad," he
exclaimed.

"I don't think so, but I don't understand either.
In the meantime we'll follow our original plans.
We'll come back to the city tonight and speak to
the men you've found. There should be twenty-five swords finished by now—if there aren't,
we'll cut our losses and leave with what we've
got. I want to be out of here by sunrise."

6

The light in the tiny, upper room was provided by two foul-smelling candles. A man stood uncomfortably in the center of the room, the only place where he could stand without striking his head on the rough-hewn beams. Walegrin, deep within the corner shadows, fired questions at him.

"You say you can use a sword—do you fight in skirmish or battle?"

"Both. Before I came to Sanctuary, two years back, I lived a time at Valtostin. We fought the citizens by night and the Tostin tribes by day. I've killed twenty men in a single day, and I've got the scars to prove it."

Walegrin didn't doubt him. The man had the look of a seasoned fighter, not a brawler. Thrusher had seen him single-handedly subdue a pair of rowdies without undue injury or commotion. "But you left Valtostin?"

The man shifted his weight nervously. "Women—a woman."

"And you came to Sanctuary to forget?" Walegrin suggested.

"There's always work for such as me; especially in a city like this."

"So you found work here, but not with the garrison. What did you do?"

"I guarded the property of a merchant . . ."

Walegrin did not need to hear the rest of the explanation; he'd heard it often enough. It was as if the surviving hawkmasks had settled on a single excuse for their past involvement with Jubal. In a way there was truth in it; Jubal's trade wasn't fundamentally different from the activities of a legitimate merchant—especially here in Sanctuary.

"You know what I'm offering?" Walegrin asked flatly when the man had fallen silent. "Why come to me when Tempus needs Stepsons?"

"I'd die before I served him."

That too was the expected response. Walegrin emerged from the shadows to embrace his new man. "Well, die you might, Cubert. We quarter in a villa to the north of town. A sign says 'Sighing Trees,' if you read Wriggle. Otherwise you'll know it by the smell. We're with Balustrus, metal-master, for one more night."

Cubert knew the name and did not flinch at the sound of it. Perhaps he did not have the abhorence of magic and near-magic that most mercenaries had. Or he was simply a good soldier and accepted his lot with resignation. Thrusher emerged to open the door.

"Was that the last?" Walegrin asked when they were alone again.

"The best, anyway. There's one more, another hawkmask, and—" Thrusher paused, "—a woman."

Walegrin's sigh made the candles flicker. "Very well—send her in."

It was not the custom of the army, even here in the hinterlands, to consider a woman fit for anything but cooking and fornicating. Jubal's rejection of this time-honored attitude was, to Walegrin, far more outrageous than any of his other activities. Unfortunately, with the Stepsons changing the face of the Downwind side of town, Walegrin was forced to consider these distaff aberations if he was to leave town with a dozen men—soldiers—swords, whatever, in his command.

The last candidate entered the room. Thrusher slid back under the eaves as soon as he had shut the door.

There were two types to these women Jubal had hired. The first was small-built, all teeth and eyes and utterly devoid of the traditional virtues almost every soldier brought into battle. The second type was a man save for accident of birth—big and broad, strong as any man of equal size, but as lacking in military honor as her scrawny sister.

This one was of the first type; her head barely reached Walegrin's chest. In a way she reminded him of Illyra and the resemblence was almost enough for him to order her out on the spot.

She was shaking out her short kilt; repairing a knot at the shoulder of her tunic which tried to conceal a small breast as grimy as the rest of her. Walegrin judged she hadn't eaten for two or three days. A half-healed slash stiffened her face; another wound ran down her hard, bare arm. Someone had tried to kill this woman and failed. She tugged wide-spread fingers through her matted, dark hair, doing nothing to improve it.

"Name," he demanded when she stood still again.

"Cythen." Her voice was remarkably pleasant for one so callused.

"You use a sword?"

"Well enough."

"A lad's sword, not a man's, I suppose."

Cythen's eyes flashed from the insult. "I learned the sword from my father and my brothers, my uncles and cousins. They gave me theirs when the time came."

"And Jubal?"

"And you," she stated defiantly.

Walegrin was impressed by her spirit—and wished he could hire her relatives instead. "How have you survived since Jubal's death—or don't you think he's dead?"

"There's not enough of us left for it to make a difference. We always had more enemies than friends. The hawkmask days are over. Jubal was our leader and no-one could take his place, even for a few weeks. Myself, I went to the Street of Red Lanterns—but it's not to my taste. I was not always like this.

"I saw your man face down a Stepson—so I've come to see you and what you're worth."

A man shouldn't look at his prospective officer that way—not that she was flirting. Walegrin felt she was trying to reverse their roles.

"Jubal was smart and strong—maybe not as smart and strong as he thought he was; Tempus got him in the end. I put a high price on my loyalty and who I give it to. What are your plans? It's rumored you have hard steel. Who do you use it for?"

Walegrin did not reveal his surprise; he just stared back at her. He had far less experience than the slaver, fewer men and far less gold. Ranke, in the form of Tempus, had brought Jubal down—what chance, truly, did he have? "I have the steel of Enlibar forged into swords. The Nisibisi do not fight in neat ranks and files; they

ambush and we will ambush them in turn until
we've made our names. Then with more
swords—"

She sighed loudly. For one raging moment
Walegrin thought she would turn on her heels
and leave. Had she honestly expected him to
scrabble for Jubal's lost domain? Or did she
sense the hollowness of his confidence?

"I doubt it—but at least I'll be out of
Sanctuary," she offered him her hand as she
spoke.

A mercenary captain welcomed his men with
a hand-shake and a comrade's embrace. Walegrin did not embrace women as comrades. When
he needed to he found some ordinary slut, laid
her on her back and, with her skirts up to hide
her face, took what he needed. He had seen
women, ladies, that he would not treat in such a
manner—but they had never seen him.

Cythen was no slut, and she'd hurt him if he
treated her that way. She was no lady, either—
not with her clothes half-gone and covered with
dirt. Still, he wasn't about to set her back on the
streets—at least not until she had a good meal.
After quickly wiping his hand on his hip, Walegrin took hers.

She had a firm grip, not man-strong but strong
enough to wield a sword. Trying to make it seem
natural, Walegrin raised his other arm for the
embrace and was saved from the deed itself by a
thumping, shouting commotion on the stairs
outside.

Thrusher was flat against the wall. Walegrin
had a knife out of its forearm sheath and just
enough time to see Cythen remove a nasty assas-

sin's blade from somewhere in her skirt before
the door burst open.

"They've taken her!"

The light from the torch on the landing
blinded Walegrin to the details of the scene before him. There was a central figure, huge and
yelling; writhing attachments to it, also yelling
and presumably his guards, and finally Thrusher,
leaping out of the darkness to wrap lethal arms
around the neck of the unsubdued invader. The
dark hulk groaned. It fell back, squeezing
Thrusher against the wall. It twisted, freeing its
right arm, then calmly peeled someone off its left
side and threw him into the eaves.

"Walegrin!" it bellowed. "They've taken her!"

Cythen was crouched on the balls of her feet,
beneath the giant's notice but not Walegrin's.
She was ready to strike when he laid a hand on
her shoulder. She relaxed.

"Dubro?" Walegrin asked cautiously.

"They've taken her!" The smith's pain was not
physical, but it was real nonetheless. Walegrin
did not need to ask who had been taken, though
he could not imagine how they had gotten past
the smith in the first place.

"Tell me slowly: Who took her? How long
ago? Why?"

The smith drew a shuddering breath and mas-
tered himself. "It was just past sundown, a
beggar-lad came up. He said there'd been an
accident on the wharf. 'Lyra bid me help if I
could, so I followed the lad. I lost him almost at
once; there was nothing on the wharf—" he
paused, taking Walegrin's wrist in a bone-
crushing grip.

"It was a trap?" Walegrin suggested, grateful for the gauntlet that protected his wrists from the full power of Dubro's despair.

The smith nodded slowly. "She was gone!"

"She hadn't simply followed you and gotten lost—or gone to visit the other S'danzo?"

A deep-pitched groan forced its way out of Dubro's throat. "No—no. T'was all torn about. She fought, but she was gone—without her shawl. Walegrin, she goes nowhere without her shawl."

"She might have escaped to hide somewhere?"

"I've searched—else I'd have been here sooner," the smith explained, shifting his grip from Walegrin's wrist to his less-protected shoulder. "I roused all the S'danzo—and they searched with me. We found her shoe behind the farmer's stall by the river, but nothing else. I went home to look for signs." Dubro shook Walegrin for emphasis. "I found this!"

He withdrew an object from his pouch and held it so close that Walegrin couldn't see it. A measure of calm returned to the smith, he released Walegrin and let him study the object. It was a metal gauntlet boss, engraved and distinctive enough to identify its wearer, should he be found. But Walegrin did not recognize it. He handed it to Thrusher.

"Do you recognize it?" he asked.

"No—"

Cythen took the boss from Thrusher's hands. "*Stepson*—" she said with both fear and anger. "See here, the lightning emerging from the clouds? Only they wear such designs."

"You have a plan?" Dubro demanded.

It wasn't only Dubro waiting for a plan. With the mention of the Stepsons, Cubert had re-entered the room, and Cythen was warm for blood; the hawkmasks all had reasons for vengeance. Even Thrusher, still rubbing his sore head, acted as if this were a challenge that must be answered. Walegrin tucked the boss in his belt-pouch.

"We know it was a Stepson, but we don't know who," Walegrin said, though he suspected the one who had overturned Illyra's table earlier. "We don't have time to run them all to ground, and I don't think Tempus would let us. Still, if we had a Stepson hostage or two ourselves, it would be easier—"

"I'll go with Thrusher. I know where they're at at this hour," Cubert asserted. Cythen nodded agreement.

"Remember, a dead Stepson won't do us any good. So if you must kill one, hide the body well—dammit."

"It'll be a pleasure," Cubert grinned.

"See that they get their swords," Walegrin said as Thrusher led the ex-hawkmasks from the room. He was alone with Dubro. "Now, you and I will search the back streets—and hope we find nothing."

Dubro agreed. For one generally reckoned no smarter than the hammer he used, Dubro moved well through the darkness, leading Walegrin rather than being led. The latter had expected him to be a massive hinderence and had kept him apart from the rest, but Dubro knew blind alleys and exposed basements that no-one else suspected.

At length they emerged from the Maze to the

stinking structures of the charnel houses. Butchers worked there, gravediggers and undertakers as well. Slippery mounds of rotting flesh and bones stretched, undisturbed, down to the river. The gulls and the dogs avoided this place, though the shadows of huge rats could be seen scurrying over the filth. They had found Rezzel here that morning—and left her here. For a moment Walegrin thought he saw Illyra lying out there—but no, it was just another jumble of bones, glowing with decay.

"She'd come here every so often," Dubro said softly. "You'd know why, wouldn't you?"

"Dubro—you don't think I—"

"No, she trusted you and she's not wrong in such things. It's just, if she were frightened, if she thought she had no place else to go—she might come here."

"Let's go back to the bazaar. Maybe her people have found something. If not, well—I'll gather my men and whatever they've found in the morning. We'll deal with Tempus from there." Dubro nodded and led the way, carefully, around the eerily glowing things lying on the mud.

Moonflower, who was as large among women as Dubro was among men, sat awkwardly at Illyra's table when they entered the little rooms behind the awning. "She is alive," the immense woman said, rearranging Illyra's cards.

"Walegrin has a plan to get her back from the Stepsons," Dubro said. Between them they almost filled the room.

Moonflower got off the creaking stool and approached Walegrin, a predatory curiosity in her eyes. "Walegrin—you've grown up!"

She wasn't tall; no taller than Cythen, but she was built like a mountain. She wore layers of colorful clothes, more layers and colors than the eye cared to record. Yet she could move quickly to trap Walegrin before he reached the door.

"You will rescue her?"

"I didn't think you S'danzo cared about her," Walegrin snarled.

"She breaks little rules and pays a little price—but not like this. You think of the mother. She broke the big rules and paid the big price. But wouldn't we all like to break the big rules? She paid with her life—but we remember her here," Moonflower pressed a beefy hand over her heart. "You go and bring her back, now. I'll stay with this one." She stepped aside and pushed Walegrin back into the night. She probably wasn't very strong, but at her weight she didn't need to be.

Alone in the bazaar, Walegrin remembered what Illyra had said about the S'danzo. They were two societies, men and women, and their purposes were not the same. It had been the S'danzo men who had dismembered his father—and S'danzo men who had cursed him. But it was the S'danzo women who had the power, the sight—

Walegrin made his way slowly up the hills behind Sanctuary to Balustrus' villa. His energy went into finding the ground with each foot. He'd need food and sleep before he could face Illyra's problems again. It occured to him that he wouldn't be able to leave until she was found, one way or the other.

A woman's weeping caught his attention. His

half-asleep thoughts converged around Illyra as
a shape rose out of the darkness and threw itself
around him. By the smell it wasn't Illyra. He
pushed Cythen aside and studied her in
dawnlight.

The jagged cut along the girl's face had been
re-opened sometime in the night. Fresh clots of
blood had twisted her expression into something
worthy of Balustrus. Tears and sweat made ver-
tical lines across her dirty skin. Walegrin's first
impulse was to toss her headfirst into the brush.
Instead he took her hand and led her to a rock. He
unfastened his cloak and handed it to her, telling
himself he'd do the same for any of his men, and
not entirely believing it.

"They've got Thrusher and Cubert's dead!"
she sobbed.

He took her hands, trying to distract her from
the hysteria that made her all but incoherent.
"What about Thrush?"

Cythen buried her face in her hands, sniffed
loudly then faced Walegrin without the tears.
"We were Downwind, past Momma Becho's. We
were trailing a Stepson pair we'd been told
passed that way after sundown carrying a body.
Thrush was leading, I was in the rear. I heard a
noise. I gave a warning and turned to face it, but
it was a trap and we were outnumbered from the
start. I never got my knife out—they had me from
behind. It was a carry-off; they weren't trying to
kill us. I went down before they hit me hard—but
Thrush and Cubert kept fighting.

"I got my chance once we were back in the
City, near the palace. I didn't linger, but they
only had Thrusher with us—so Cubert's dead."

"How long ago was this?"

"I came straight here, and I haven't been here long."

"And you're sure it was the Prince's palace—not Jubal's?"

She became indignant. "I'd know Jubal's if I saw it. I'd have stayed and gotten Thrush out if it had been Jubal's. The Stepsons and Tempus haven't had enough time to learn what any hawkmask knows about the mansion. But we were attacked by Stepsons, anyway."

"You knew that?"

"By the smell."

Walegrin was too tired to continue sparring. He'd lost Thrusher who'd been with him longer than anyone, who was more friend and family than lieutenant. Moreover, he didn't have a hostage to strengthen his position. It was impossible to believe this scrawny, starving woman could escape where Thrush hadn't—

"You don't believe me, do you?" she said. "Thrush trusted me at his back. He must've fought until they hit him hard, where's I gave up sooner. That's the difference, Walegrin, you say women have no honor because they'll lose first and win later. You men have to win all the time or die trying. If I was in on it, would I have come back like this?"

"To lead me in," Walegrin challenged, but without conviction.

The sun was up when he slid the bolt of the villa-gate and led Cythen into the courtyard. Balustrus was waiting for them. The metal-master already knew some of the night's events.

"Seems you won't be jumping early after all?" he accused.

"Yes, I'd planned to leave," Walegrin agreed. "The longer I stay; the tighter the noose. I'm getting out. I leave you the ore, the necklace and the formula—you don't need anything else."

"It won't be that easy unless you've replaced Thrusher with that bone-bag behind you. Word's come from the palace." Balustrus handed him a scroll with its seal broken.

The writing confirmed Cythen's story that they'd been taken to the palace by Stepsons. The Prince commanded Walegrin's presence in the Hall of Justice. Walegrin crumpled the paper and threw it into the dirt. He could have abandoned Thrusher; he could have abandoned Illyra—but he could not abandon them both.

"Cythen," he whispered to her as they entered the room he shared with Thrusher. He looked about for a cleaner tunic. "No matter what, don't stop looking for Illyra, hear me? If you find her you take her back to the bazaar. The S'danzo will help, and Dubro. They won't ask about your past. Do you understand?"

She nodded and watched without interest as he cast his filthy tunic aside and pulled another one over his head.

"You should wash first," she told him. "You shouldn't stink before the Prince. You won't win any bargains."

Walegrin glared at her, dropping the second tunic to the floor as he stormed toward the stream where they washed.

"I wasn't always like this," she shouted after him.. "I know better ways."

Dripping, but clean, Walegrin returned to the room to find his tunic lying neatly on the mattress. Somehow the girl had gotten the extra

wrinkles out. His bronze circlet had been given a
quick polish and some of the mud was gone from
his sandals. But Cythen herself was gone from
the shed, the courtyard and the villa. Coming on
top of the loss of Illyra and Thrusher it was almost more than he could endure. Had he found
her right then he would have cheerfully beaten
her.

But the girl had been right, damn her. He felt
better clean. His few men straightened up as he
assembled them in the courtyard. He told them
what he'd told Cythen. They grumbled and he
doubted they'd wait more than a day before
going their separate ways if he did not return. He
looked for Balustrus too, and found only his
share of the swords. The ore, the necklace and
the metal-master had vanished. He was getting
used to that.

Knots of people ducked out of his path once he
was on the streets. He was recognized, but
no-one stopped him. With eyes fixed forward, he
walked past the gallows, not chancing a glance
at the corpses. The gatekeeper took his name
without ceremony and a lad appeared to conduct
him to the Hall of Justice.

He was left alone there in the echoing
chamber. Kadakithus himself was the first to enter, accompanied by two slaves. The young
prince dismissed the slaves and took his place on
the throne.

"So, you're Walegrin," he began simply. "I
thought I might recognize you. You have been no
small amount of trouble."

Walegrin had intended to be quiet and
meek—to do whatever was necessary to free
Thrush. But this was Kittycat and he invited

disrespect. "Finding your clothes each morning must be equal trouble. You've got my man in your dungeons. I want him freed."

The Prince fidgetted with the ornate hem of his sleeve. "Actually I don't have your man. Oh, he's been taken all right, and he's alive—but he's Tempus' prisoner, not mine."

"Then I should be talking to Tempus, not you."

"Walegrin, I may not have your man—but I have you," the Prince said forcefully.

Walegrin swallowed his reply and studied the Prince.

"That's better. You're entitled to your opinion of me—and I'm sure I've earned it. There's a lot to be said for playing one's part in life. Now, you'll talk to Tempus after you've talked to me—and you'll be glad of the delay.

"I've had gods know how many letters from Ranke about you—starting before you disappeared. I got my most recent one with the recent delegation from the capital. Zanderei—as cunning an assassin as they could find. I know how much money you got from Kilite. Don't look so surprised. I was raised in the Imperial Household—I wouldn't be alive at all if I didn't have some reliable friends. The chief viper in my brother's nest is always asking for you. He seems to think you've discovered Enlibar steel; I assure him that you haven't, though I know you have. I know how much he said he'd pay you for the secret; so I know you're not in Sanctuary looking for a better price. But then, I also know what Balustrus said about your progress with the steel. Does any of this surprise you?"

Walegrin said nothing. He was not truly surprised, though he hadn't expected this. Nothing was truly surprising today.

The prince misunderstood his silence. "All right, Walegrin. Kilite's faction found you, paid you, pardoned your absence and then tried to have you killed. I've run afoul of Kilite a few times and I can promise you you'll never outsmart him on your own. You need protection, Walegrin, and you need protection from a special sort of person—the sort of person who needs you as much as you need him. In short, Walegrin, you need me."

Walegrin remembered thinking the same thing once, though he'd envisioned this interview under different circumstances. "You have the Hounds, Tempus and the Sacred Bands," he remarked sullenly.

"Actually, they have me. Face it, Walegrin: you and I are not well-equipped. Alone with only my birth or your steel, we're nothing but pawns. But, put my birth with your steel and the odds improve. Walegrin, the Nisibisi are armed to the teeth. They'll tie up the armies for years before the surrender—if they surrender. Your handful of Enlibar swords won't make any difference. But the Empire is going to forget about us while they're fighting in the north."

"Or, you want my men and my steel here instead of on the Wizardwall?"

"You make me sound just like Kilite. Walegrin, I'll make you my advisor. I'll care for you and your men. I'll tell Kilite we found you floating in the harbor—and make sure he believes it. I'll keep you safe while the Empire exhausts itself in the north. It may take twenty years, Walegrin, but when we return to Ranke, we'll own it."

"I'll think about it," Walegrin said, though actually he was thinking of Illyra's visions of an invading fleet and her warning that he would not go north.

The Prince shook his head. "You don't have time. You've got to be my man before you see Tempus. You might need me to pry your man loose."

They were alone in the room and Walegrin still had his sword. He thought of using it; perhaps the Prince thought the same thing for he sat far back in the throne, playing with his sleeve again.

"You might be lying," Walegrin said after a moment.

"I'm known for many things, but not lying."

That was true enough. Just as much of what he'd said was true. And there was Thrusher's safety, and Illyra's to think of. "I'll want a favor, right away," Walegrin said, offering his hand.

"Anything in my power, but first we talk to Tempus—and don't tell him we've made an agreement."

The Prince led the way along unfamiliar corridors. They were in the private part of the palace and the surroundings, though crude by capital standards, dazzled Walegrin. He bumped into the Prince when the latter stopped by a closed door.

"Now, don't forget—we haven't agreed to anything. No, wait—give me your sword."

Feeling trapped, Walegrin unbuckled his sword and handed it to the Prince.

"He's arrived, Tempus," Kadakithus announced in his most innane voice. "Look, he gave me a present! One of his steel swords."

Tempus looked around from a window. He had some of the god's presence to him. Walegrin felt distinctly outclassed and doubted that Kitty-cat could do anything to help him. He doubted that even the metal boss in his pouch could help him free Thrusher or Illyra.

"The steel is Sanctuary's secret, not Kilite's?" Tempus demanded.

"Of course," the Prince assured him. "Kilite will never know. The entire capital will never know."

"All right, then. Bring him in," Tempus shouted.

Five Stepsons crowded into the room, a hooded prisoner with them. They sent the man sprawling to the marble floor. Thrusher pulled the hood loose and scrambled to his feet. A livid bruise covered one side of his face, his clothes were torn and revealed other cuts and bruises, but he was not seriously hurt.

"Your man—I should have let my men have him. He killed two last night."

"Not men!" Thrusher spat out. "Whoresons; men don't steal women and leave them for the rats!"

One of the Stepsons moved forward. Walegrin recognized him as the one who had overturned Illyra's table. Though he felt the rage himself, he restrained Thrusher. "Not now," he whispered.

The Prince stepped between all of them with the sword. "I think you should have this, Tempus. It's too plain for me—but you won't mind that, will you?"

The Hell-Hound examined the blade and set it aside without comment. "I see you can control your man," he said to Walegrin.

"As you cannot." Walegrin tossed the Hound the boss Dubro had found. "Your men left it behind when they stole my sister last night." They were of a height, Walegrin and Tempus, but it cost Walegrin to look into Tempus' eyes and for once he understood what it meant to be cursed, as Tempus was.

"Yes, the S'danzo. My men disliked the fortune she told for them. They bribed some Downwind to frighten her. They don't understand the Downwind yet. They hadn't intended her to be kidnapped, any more than they'd intended to get robbed themselves. I've dealt with my men—and the Downwinders they hired. Your sister is already back in the bazaar, Walegrin, a bit richer for her adventures and off-limits to all Stepsons. No one guessed you were her brother—certain men are assumed not to have family, you know." Tempus leaned forward then, and spoke only to Walegrin. "Tell me, is your sister worth believing?"

"I believe her."

"Even when she rattles nonsense about invasions from the sea?"

"I believe her enough that I'm remaining in Sanctuary—against all my better judgement."

Tempus turned away to take up Walegrin's sword. He adjusted the belt for his hips and put it on. The Stepsons had already departed. "You won't regret helping the Prince," he said without looking at anyone. "He's favored of the gods, you know. You'll do well together." He followed his men out the door leaving the Prince alone with Walegrin and Thrusher.

"You might have told me you were going to give him my sword!" Walegrin complained.

"I wasn't. I only meant to distract him—I didn't think he'd take it. I'm sorry. What was the favor you wanted?"

With Illyra and Thrusher safe, and his future mapped out, Walegrin didn't need a favor, but he heard his stomach rumbling and knew Thrush was hungry too. "We'll have a meal fit for a king—or Prince."

"Well, at least that's something I can provide you."

WIZARD WEATHER

by

Janet Morris

1

In the archmage's sumptuous purple bed-room, the woman astride him took two pins from her silver-shot hair. It was dark—his choice; and damp with cloying shadows—his romanticism. A conjured moon in a spellbound sky was being swallowed by effigy-clouds where the vaulted roof indubitably yet arced, even as he shuddered under the tutored and inexorable attentions of the girl Lastel had brought to his party. She had refused to tell him her name because he would not give his, but had told him what she would do for him so eloquently with her eyes and her body that he had spent the entire evening figuring out a way the two of them might slip up here unnoticed. Not that he feared her escort's jealousy—though the drug dealer might con-ceivably entertain such a sentiment, Lastel no longer had the courage (or the contractual pro-tective wardings) to dare a reprisal against a Hazard-class mage.

Of all the enchanters in wizard-ridden Sanctuary, only three were archmages, nameless adepts beyond summoning or responsibility, and this Hazard was one. In fact, he was the very strongest of those three. When he had been young, he had had a name, but he will forget it, and everything else, quite promptly: the domed and spired estuary of venality which is Sanctuary, nadir of the empire called Ranke; the unmitigated evil he had fielded for decades from his swamp-encircled Mageguild fortress; the compromises he had made to hold sway over curmudgeon, courtesan and criminal (so audacious that even the bounds of magics and planeworlds had been eroded by his efforts, and his fellow adepts felled on occasion by demons roused from forbidden defiles to do his bidding here at the end of creation where no balance remains between logic and faith, law and nature, or heaven and hell); the disingenuous methods through which his will was worked, plan by tortuous plan, upon a town so hateful and immoral that both the flaunted gods and magicians' devils agreed that its inhabitants deserved no less dastardly a fate—all of this, and more, will fade from him in the time it takes a star to burn out, falling from the sky.

Now, the First Hazard glimpses her movement, though he is close to ejaculation, sputtering with sensations that for years he has assumed he had outgrown, or forgotten how to feel. Senility creeps upon the finest flesh when a body is maintained for millenia, and into the deepest mind, through thousands of years. He does not look his age, or tend to think of it. The years are his, mandated. Only a very special kind of enemy could defeat him, and those were few and far between. Simple death, morbidity or the spells of his brothers were like gnats he kept away by the perfume of his sweat: merely the proper diet, herbs and spells and consummated will, had long ago vanquished them as far as he was concerned.

So strange to lust, to desire a particular woman; he was amused, joyous; he had not felt so good in years. A tiny thrill of caution had horripilated his nape early on, when he noticed the silvering of her nightblack hair, but this girl was not old enough to be—"Ahhhh!" Her premeditated rippling takes him over passion's edge, and he is falling, place and provenance forgotten, not a terrible adept wrenching the world about to suit his whim and comfort, but just a man.

In that instant, eyes defocused, he sees but does not note the diamond sparkle of the rods poised above him; his ears are filled with his own breathing; the song of entrapment she sings softly has him before he thinks to think, or thinks to fear, or thinks to move.

By then, the rods, their sharp fine points touching his arched throat, owned him. He could not move; not his body nor his soul responded; his mind could not control his tongue. Thinking bitterly of the indignity of being frozen like a rearing stallion, he hoped his flesh would slump once life had fled. As he felt the points enter into his skin and begin to suck at the thread binding him to life, his mortification marshaled his talents: he cleared his vision, forced his eyes to obey his mind's command. Though he was a great sorcerer, he was not omnipotent: he could not manage to make his lips frame a curse to cast upon her, just watched the free agent Cime— who had slipped, disguised, into so many mages' beds of late—sip the life from him relishingly. So slow she was about it he had time to be thankful she did not take him through his eyes. The song she sings has cost her much to learn, and the death she staves off will not be so kind as his. Could he have spoken, then, resigned to it, he would have thanked her: it is no shame to be brought down by an opponent so worthy. They paid their prices to the same host. He set about composing his exit, seeking his meadow, star-shaped and ever green, where he did his work when meditation whisked him into finer awarenesses than flesh could ever share. If he could seat himself there, in his established place of power, then his death was nothing, his flesh a fingernail, overlong and ready to be pared.

He did manage that. Cime saw to it that he had the time. It does not do to anger certain kinds of powers, the sort which, having dispensed with names, dispense with discorporation. Some awful day, she would face this one, and others whom she had guided out of life, in an afterlife which she had helped populate. Shades tended to be unforgiving.

When his chest neither rose nor fell, she slid off him and ceased singing. She licked the tips of her wands and wound them back up in her thick black hair. She soothed his body down, arranged it decorously, donned her party clothes, and kissed him once on the tip of his nose before heading, humming, back down the stairs to where Lastel and the party still waited. As she passed the bar, she snatched a piece of citrus and crushed it in her palms, dripping the juice upon her wrists, smearing it behind her ears and in the hollow of her throat. Some of these folk might be clumsy necromancers and thrice-cursed mer-chants with store-bought charms-to-ward-off-

charms bleeding them dry of soul and purse, but
there was nothing wrong with their noses.

Lastel's bald head and wrestler's shoulders,
impeccable in customed silk velvet, were easy to
spot. He did not even glance down at her, but
continued chatting with one of the prince/
governor Kadakithis' functionaries, Molin
Something-or-other, Vashanka's official priest.
It was New Year's holiday, and the week was
bursting with festivities which the Rankan overlords must observe, and seem to sanction: since
(though they had conquered and subjugated
Ilsig lands and Ilsig peoples so that some Rankans dared call Ilsigs "Wrigglies" to their faces)
they had failed to suppress the worship of the
god Ils and his self-begotten pantheon, word had
come down from the emperor himself that Rankans must endure with grace the Wrigglies'
celebration of Ils' creation of the world and re-
newal of the year. Now, especially, with Ranke
pressed into a war of attrition in the north, was
no time to allow dissension to develop on her
flanks from so paltry a matter as the perquisites
of obscure and weakling gods.

This uprising among the buffer states upon
Upper Ranke's northernmost frontier and the in-
flated rumors of slaughter coming back from
Wizardwall's mountainous skirts all out of
proportion to reasonable numbers dominated
Molin's monologue: "And what say you, es-
teemed lady? Could it be that Nisibisi magicians
have made their peace with Mygdon's barbarian
lord, and found him a path through
Wizardwall's fastness? You are well-traveled, it
is obvious. . . . Could it be true that the border
insurrection is Mygdonia's doing, and their

hordes so fearsome as we have been led to believe? Or is it the Rankan treasury that is suffering, and a northern incursion the cure for our economic ills?"

Lastel flickered puffy lids down at her from ravaged cheeks and his turgid arm went around her waist. She smiled up at him reassuringly, then favored the priest: "Your Holiness, sadly I must confess that the Mygdonian threat is very real. I have studied realms and magics, in Ranke and beyond. If you wish a consultation, and Lastel permits—" she batted the thickest lashes in Sanctuary "—I shall gladly attend you, some day when we both are fit for 'solemn' discourse. But now I am too filled with wine and revel, and must interrupt you—your pardon please—that my escort bear me home to bed." She cast her glance upon the ballroom floor, demure and concentrating on her slippered feet poking out under amber skirts. "Lastel, I must have the night air, or faint away. Where is our host? We must thank him for a more complete hospitality than I had thought to find. . . ."

The habitually pompous priest was simpering with undisguised delight, causing Lastel to raise an eyebrow, though Cime tugged coquettishly at his sleeve, and inquire as to its source: "Lord Molin?"

"It is nothing, dear man, nothing. Just so long since I have heard court Rankene—and from the mouth of a *real* lady. . . ." The Rankan priest, knowing well that his wife's reputation bore no mitigation, chose to make sport of her, and of his town, before the foreign noblewoman did. And to make it more clear to Lastel that the joke was on them—the two Sanctuarites—and for the

amusement of the voluptuous gray-eyed woman,
he bowed low, and never did answer her genteel
query as to the whereabouts of the First Hazard.

By the time he had promised to give their
thanks and regards to the absent host when he
saw him, the lady was gone, and Molin Torchholder was left wishing he knew what it was that
she saw in Lastel. Certainly it was not the dogs he
raised, or his fortune, which was modest, or his
business . . . well, yes, it might have been just
that . . . drugs. Some who knew said the best
krrf—black and Caronne-stamped—came from
Lastel's connections. Molin sighed, hearing his
wife's twitter among the crowd's buzz. Where
was that Hazard? The damn Mageguild was getting too arrogant. No one could throw a bash as
star-studded as this one and then walk away
from it as if the luminaries in attendance were
nonentities. He was glad he had not prevailed on
the prince to come along. . . . *What* a woman!
And what *was* her name? He had been told, he
was sure, but just forgot. . . .

Outside, torchlit, their breath steaming white
through cold-sharpened night air, waiting for
their ivory-screened wagon, they giggled over
the distinction between "serious" and "solemn": the First Hazard had been serious, Molin
was solemn; Tempus the Hell-Hound was serious, Prince Kadakithis, solemn; the destabiliza-
tion campaign they were undertaking in
Sanctuary under the auspices of a Mygdonian-
funded Nisibisi witch (who had come to Lastel,
alias One-Thumb, in the guise of a comely caravan mistress hawking Caronne drugs) was
serious; the threat of northern invasion, down-
country at the Empire's anus, was most solemn.

As her laughter tinkled, he nuzzled her: "Did
you manage to . . . ?"

"Oh, yes. I had a perfectly lovely time. What a
wonderful idea of yours this was," she whispered, still speaking court Rankene, a dialect she
had been using exclusively in public ever since
the two of them—the Mazedweller One-Thumb
and the escaped sorcerer-slayer Cime—had decided that the best cover for them was that which
her magic provided: they need not do more. Her
brother Tempus knew that Lastel was actually
One-Thumb, and that she was with him, but he
would hesitate to reveal them: he had given his
silence, if not his blessing, to their union. Within
reasonable limits, they considered themselves
safe to bargain lives and information to both
sides in the coming crisis. Even now, with the
war barely under way, they had already started.
This night's work was her pleasure and his
profit. When they reached his modest east-side
estate, she showed him the portion of what she
had done to the First Hazard which he would
like best—and most probably survive, if his heart
was strong. For her service, she demanded a
Rankan soldat's worth of black krrf, before the
act. When he had paid her, and watched her melt
it with water over a flame, cool it, and bring it to
him on the bed, her fingers stirring the viscous
liquid, he was glad he had not argued about her
price, or about her practice of always charging
one.

*   *   *   2   *   *   *

Wizard weather blew in off the sea later that
night, as quickly as one of the Sanctuary whores

could blow a client a kiss, or a pair of Stepsons
disperse an unruly crowd. Everyone in the suddenly mist-enshrouded streets of the Maze ran
for cover; adepts huddled under beds with their
best warding spells wrapped tighter than blan-
kets around shivering shoulders; east-siders
bade their jesters perform and their musicians
play louder; dogs howled; cats yowled; horses
screamed in the palace stables and tried to batter
their stallboards down.

Some unlucky ones did not make it to safety
before a dry thunder roared and lightning
flashed and in the streets, the mist began to glitter, thicken, chill. It rolled headhigh along
byway and alley, claws of ice scrabbling at shuttered windows, barred doors. Where it found
life, it shredded bodies, lacerating limbs, stealing away warmth and souls and leaving only
flayed carcasses frozen in the streets.

A pair of Stepsons—mercenary special forces
whom the prince's marshal, Tempus, commanded—was caught out in the storm, but it
could not be said that the weather killed one: the
team had been investigating uncorroborated reports that a warehouse conveniently situated at a
juncture of three major sewers was being used by
an alchemist to concoct and store incendiaries.
The surviving partner guessed that his teammate
must have lit a torch, despite the cautions of
research: human wastes, flour, sulphur and more
had gone in through those now-nonexistent
doors. Though the problem the team had been
dispatched to investigate was solved by a con-
cussive fireball that threw the second Stepson,
Nikodemos, through a window into an intersection, singeing his beard and brows and

eyelashes, the young Sacred Band member re-lived the circumstances leading to his partner's death repeatedly, agonizing over the possibility that he was to blame throughout the night, alone in the pair's billet. So consumed was he with grief at the death of his mate, he did not even realize that his friend had saved his life: the fireball and ensuing conflagration had blown back the mist and made an oven of the wharfside; Wideway was freed from the vicious fog for half its length. He had ridden at a devil's pace out of Sanctuary home to the Stepsons' barracks, which once had been a slaver's estate and thus had rooms enough for Tempus to allow his hard-won mercenaries the luxury of privacy: ten pairs plus thirty single agents comprised the team's core group—until this evening past. . . .

Sun was trying to beat back the night, Niko could see it through his window. He had not even been able to return with a body. His beloved spirit-twin would be denied the honor of a hero's fiery bier. He could not cry; he simply sat, hud-dled, amputated, diminished and cold upon his bed, watching a sunray inch its way toward one of his sandaled feet.

Thus he did not see Tempus approaching with the first light of day haloing his just-bathed form as if he were some god's own avatar, which at times—despite his better judgment—his curse, and his battle with it, forced him to become. The tall, autumnal figure stooped and peered in the window, sun gilding his yarrow-honey hair and his vast bronze limbs where they were free of his army-issue woolen chiton. He wore no arms or armor, no cloak or shoes; furrows deepened on his brow, and a sere frown tightened his willful

mouth. Sometimes, the expression in his long,
slitted eyes grew readable: this was such a time.
The pain he was about to face was a pain he had
known too well, too often. It brought to features
not brutal enough by half for their history or
profession the slight, defensive smile which
would empty out his eyes. When he could, he
knocked. Hearing no reply, he called softly,
"Niko?" And again. . . .

Having let himself in, he waited for the Stepson, who looked younger than the quarter-
century he claimed, to raise his head. He met a
gaze as blank as his own, and bared his teeth.

The youth nodded slowly, made to rise, sank
back when Tempus motioned "stay" and joined
him on his wood-framed cot in blessed shadow.
Both sat then, silent, as day filled up the room,
stealing away their hiding place. Elbows on
knees, Niko thanked him for coming. Tempus
suggested that under the circumstances a bier
could still be made, and funerary games would
not be out of order. When he got no response, the
mercenary's commander sighed rattlingly and
allowed that he himself would be honored to
perform the rites. He knew how the Sacred Banders who had adopted the war name "Stepsons"
revered him. He did not condone or encourage it,
but since they had given him their love and were
probably doomed to the man for it—even as their
original leader, Stepson, called Abarsis, had
been doomed—Tempus felt responsible for
them. His instructions and his curse had sent the
gelded warrior-priest Abarsis to his death, and
such fighters as these could not offer loyalty to a
lesser man, to a pompous prince or an abstracted

cause. Sacred Bands were the mercenaries' elite; this one's history under the Slaughter Priest's command was nearly mythical; Abarsis had brought his men to Tempus before committing suicide in a most honorable fashion, leaving them as his parting gift—and as his way of ensuring that Tempus could not just walk away from the god Vashanka's service: Abarsis had been Vashanka's priest.

Of all the mercenaries Rankan money had enabled Tempus to gather for Prince/Governor Kadakithis, this young recruit was the most singular. There was something remarkable about the finely made slate-haired fighter with his quiet hazel eyes and his understated manner, something that made it seem perfectly reasonable that this self-effacing youngster with his clean long limbs and his quick canny smile had been the right-side partner of a Syrese legend twice his age for nine years. Tempus would rather have been doing anything else than trying to give comfort to the bereaved Stepson Nikodemos. Choosing a language appropriate to philosophy and grief (for Niko was fluent in six tongues, ancient and modern), he asked the youth what was in his heart.

"Gloom," Niko responded in the mercenary-argot, which admitted many tongues, but only the bolder emotions: pride, anger, insult, declaratives, imperatives, absolutes.

"Gloom," Tempus agreed in the same linguistic pastiche, yet ventured: "You will survive it. We all do."

"Oh, Riddler . . . I know. . . . You did, Abarsis did—twice," he took a shivering breath; "but it is not easy. I feel so naked. He was . . . always on my left, if you understand me—where you are now.''

"Consider me here for the duration, then, Niko.''

Niko raised too-bright eyes, slowly shaking his head. "In our spirits' place of comfort, where trees and men and life are one, he *is still there*. How can I rest, when my rest-place holds his ghost? There is no *maat* left for me . . . do you know the word?''

Tempus did: balance, equilibrium, the tendency of things to make a pattern, and that pattern to be discernible, and therefore revivifying. He thought for a moment, gravely, not about Niko's problem, but about a youthful mercenary who spoke offhandedly of adept's refreshments and archmagical meditations, who routinely transported his spirit into a mystical realm and was accustomed to meeting another spirit there. He said at last: "I do not read it ill that your friend waits there. Why is it bad, unless you make it so? Maat, if you have had it, you will find again. With him, you are bound in spirit, not just in flesh. He would be hurt to hurt you, and to see that you are afraid of what once you loved. His spirit will depart your place of relaxation when we put it formally to rest. Yet you must make a better peace with him, and surmount your fear. It is well to have a friendly soul waiting at the gate when your time comes around. Surely, you love him still?''

That broke the young Stepson, and Tempus left him curled upon his bed, so that his sobs need not be silent, and he could heal upon his own.

Outside, leaning against the doorjamb, the planked door carefully closed, Tempus put his fingers to the bridge of his nose and rubbed his eyes. He had surprised himself, as well as the boy, offering Niko such far-reaching support. He was not sure he dared to mean it, but he had said it. Niko's team had functioned as the Stepsons' ad hoc liaisons, coordinating (but more usually arbitrating disputes among) the mercenaries and the Hell-Hounds (the Rankan Imperial Elite Guards), the Ilsig regular army and the militia Tempus was trying to covertly make out of some carefully-chosen street urchins, slit purses, and sleeves—the real rulers of this overblown slum and the only people who ever knew what was going on in Sanctuary, a town which might just become a strategic staging area if war did come down from the north. As liaisons, both team-mates had come to him often for advice. Part of Niko's workload had been the making of an adequate swordsman out of a certain Ilsig thief named Hanse, to whom Tempus had owed a debt he did not care to personally discharge. But the young backstreeter, emboldened by his easy early successes, had proved increasingly irascible and contentious when Niko—aware that Tempus was indebted to Hanse and Kadakithis inexplicably favored the thief—endeavored to lead him far beyond slash-and-thrust infantry tactics into the subtleties of Niko's own expertise: cavalry strategies, guerrilla tactics, western fighting forms that dispensed with weaponry by accenting surprise, precision, and meditation-honed instinct. Though the thief recognized the value of what the Stepson offered, his pride made him sneer: he could not admit his need to

know, would not chance being found wanting,
and hid his fear of failure behind anger. After
three months of justifying the value of methods
and mechanics the Stepson felt to be self-
explanatory (black stomach blood, bright lung
blood, or pink foam from the ears indicates a
mortal strike; yarrow root shaved into a wound
quells its pain; ginseng, chewed, renews
stamina; mandrake in an enemy's stewpot in-
capacitates a company, monkshood decimates
one; green or moldy hay downs every horse on
your opponents' line; cheese wire, the right
handhold, or a knife from behind obviates the
need for passwords, protracted dissembling, or
forged papers) Niko had turned to Tempus for a
decision as to whether instruction must continue. Shadowspawn, called Hanse, was a natural
bladesman, as good as any man wishing to wield
a sword for a living needed to be—on the ground,
Niko had said. As far as horsemanship, he had
added almost sadly, niceties could not be taught
to a cocky novice who spent more time arguing
that he would never need to master them than
practicing what he was taught. Similarly, so far
as tradecraft went, Hanse's fear of being labelled
a Stepson-in-training or an apprentice Sacred
Bander prevented him from fraternizing with the
squadron during the long evenings when shop-
talk and exploits flowed freely, and every man
found much to learn. Niko had shrugged,
spreading his hands to indicate an end to his
report. Throughout it (the longest speech Tempus had ever heard the Stepson make), Tempus
could not fail to mark the disgust so carefully
masked, the frustration and the unwillingness to
admit defeat which had hidden in Nikodemos'

lowered eyes and blank face. Tempus' decision
to pronounce the student Shadowspawn
graduated, gift him with a horse, and go on to
new business had elicited a subtle inclination of
head—an agreement, nothing less—from the
youthful and eerily composed junior mercenary.
Since then, he had not seen him. And, upon
seeing him, he had not asked any of the things he
had gone there to find out: not one question as to
the exact circumstances of his partner's death, or
the nature of the mist which had ravaged the
Maze, had passed his lips. Tempus blew out a
noisy breath, grunted, then pushed off from
where he leaned against the whitewashed barracks wall. He would go out to see what headway
the band had made with the bier and the games,
set for sundown behind the walled estate. He did
not need to question the boy further, only to
listen to his own heart.

He was not unaware of the ominous events of
the preceding evening: sleep was never his. He
had made a midnight creep through the sewage
tunnels into Kadakithis' most private apart-
ments, demonstrating that the old palace was
impossible to secure, in hopes that the boy-
prince would stop prattling about "winter
palace/summer palace" and move his retinue
into the new fortress Tempus had built for him
on the eminently defensible spit near the lighthouse with that very end in mind. So it was that
he had heard firsthand from the prince (who all
the while was making a valiant attempt not to
bury his nose in a scented handkerchief he was
holding almost casually but had fumbled desperately to find when first Tempus appeared,
reeking of sewage, between two of his damask

bedroom hangings) about the killer mist and the
dozen lives it claimed. Tempus had let his silence agree that the mages must be right, such a
thing was totally mystifying, though the "thunder without rain" and its results had explained
itself to him quite clearly. Nothing is mysterious
after three centuries and more of exploring life's
riddles, except perhaps why gods allow men
magic, or why sorcerers allow men gods.

Equally reticent was Tempus when Kadakithis, wringing his lacquer-nailed hands,
told him of the First Hazard's unique demise,
and wondered with dismal sarcasm if the adepts
would again try to blame the fall of one of their
number on Tempus' *alleged* sister (here he
glanced sidelong up at Tempus from under his
pale Imperial curls), the escaped mage-killer
who, he was beginning to think, was a figment of
sorcerers' nightmares: When they had had this
"person" in the pits, awaiting trial and sentence,
no two witnesses could agree on the description
of the woman they saw; when she had escaped,
no one saw her go. It might be that the adepts
were purging their Order again, and didn't want
anyone to know, didn't Tempus agree? In the
face of Kadakithis' carefully thought-out policy
statement, meant to protect the prince from involvement and the soldier from implication,
Tempus refrained from comment.

The First Hazard's death was a welcome surprise to Tempus, who indulged in an active, if
surreptitious, bloodfeud with the Mageguild.
Sortilege of any nature he could not abide. He
had explored and discarded it all: philosophy,
systems of personal discipline such as Niko
employed, magic, religion, the sort of eternal

side-taking purveyed by the warrior-mages who wore the Blue Star. The man who in his youth had proclaimed that those things which could be touched and perceived were those which he preferred had not been changed by time, only hardened. Adepts and sorcery disgusted him. He had faced wizards of true power in his youth, and his sorties upon the bloody roads of life had been colored by those encounters: he yet bore the . curse of one of their number, and his hatred of them was immortal. He had thought that even should he die, his despite would live on to harass them—he hoped that it were true. For to fight with enchanters of skill, the same skills were needed, and he eschewed those arts. The price was too high. He would never acknowledge power over freedom, eternal servitude of the spirit was too great a cost for mastery in life. Yet a man could not stand alone against witchfire-hatred. To survive, he had been forced to make a pact with the Storm God, Vashanka. He had been brought to collar like a wild dog. He heeled to Vashanka, these days, at the god's command. But he did not like it.

There were compensations, if such they could be called. He lived interminably, though he could not sleep at all; he was immune to simple, nasty war-magics; he had a sword which cut through spells like cheese and glowed when the god took an interest. In battle he was more than twice as fast as a mortal man—while they moved so slowly he could do as he willed upon a crowded field which was a melee to all but him, and even extend his hyper speed to his mount, if the horse was of a certain strain and tough constitution. And wounds he took healed quickly—

instantly if the god loved him that day, more slowly if they had been quarreling. Only once—when he and his god had had a serious falling-out over whether or not to rape his sister—had Vashanka truly deserted him. But even then, as if his body were simply accustomed to doing it, his regenerative abilities remained—much slowed, very painful, but *there*.

For these reasons, and many more, he had a mystique, but no charisma. Only among mercenaries could he look into eyes free from the glint of fear. He stayed much among his own, these days in Sanctuary. Abarsis' death had struck home harder than he cared to admit. It seemed, sometimes, that one more soul laying down its life for him and one more burden laid upon him would surpass his capacity and he would crack apart into the desiccated dust he doubtless was.

Crossing the whitewashed court, passing the stables, his Trôs horses stuck steel-gray muzzles over their half-doors and whickered. He stopped and stroked them, speaking soft words of comradeship and endearment, before he left to let himself out the back gate to the training ground, a natural amphitheatre between hillocks where the Stepsons drilled the few furtive Ilsigs wishing to qualify for the militia-reserves Kadakithis was funding.

He was thinking, as he closed the gate behind him and squinted out over the arena (counting heads and fitting names to them where men sat perched atop the fence or lounged against it or raked sand or counted off paces for sunset's funerary games), that it was a good thing no one had been able to determine the cause of the ranking Hazard's death. He would have to do something about his sister Cime, and soon—something substantive. He had given her the latitude befitting a probable sibling and childhood passion, and she had exceeded his forbearance. He had been willing to overlook the fact that he had been paying her debts with his soul ever since an archmage had cursed him on her account, but he was not willing to ignore the fact that she refused to abstain from taking down magicians. It might be her right, in general, to slay sorcerers, but it was not her right to do it here, where he was pinned tight between law and morality as it was. The whole conundrum of how he might successfully deal with Cime was something he did not want to contemplate. So he did not, just then, only walked, cold brown grass between his toes, to the near side of the chest-high wooden fence behind which, on happier days, his men schooled Ilsigs and each other. Today they were making a bier there, dragging dry branches from the brake beyond Vashanka's altar, a pile of stones topping a rise, due east, where the charioteers worked their teams.

Sweat never stayed long enough to drip in the chill winter air, but breaths puffed white from noses and mouths in the taut pearly light, and grunts and taunts carried well in the crisp morning air. Tempus ducked his head and rubbed his mouth to hide his mirth as a stream of scatological invective sounded: one of the branch-draggers exhorting the loungers to get to work. Were curses soldats, the Stepsons would all be men of ease. The fence-sitters, counter-cursing the work-boss gamely, slipped to the ground; the

loungers gave up their wall. In front of him, they
pretended to be untouched by the ill omen of
accidental death. But he, too, was uneasy in the
face of tragedy without reason, bereft of the glory
of death in the field. All of them feared accident,
mindless fortune's disfavor: they lived by luck,
as much as by the god's favor. As the dozen men,
more or less in a body, headed toward the altar
and the brake beyond, Tempus felt the god rus-
tling inside him, and took time to upbraid Vashanka for wasting an adherent. They were not
on the best of terms, the man and his god. His
temper was hard-held these days, and the gloom
of winter quartering was making him fey—not to
mention reports of the Mygdonians' foul depre-
dations to the far north, the quelling of which he
was not free to join. . . .

First, he noticed that two people sauntering
casually down the altar's hillock toward him
were not familiar; and then, that none of his
Stepsons were moving: each was stock-still. A
cold overswept him, like a wind-driven wave,
and rolled on toward the barracks. Above, the
pale sky clouded over; a silky dusk swallowed
the day. Black clouds gathered; over Vashanka's
altar two luminous, red moons appeared high up
in the inky air, as if some huge night-cat lurked
on a lofty perch. Watching the pair approaching
(through unmoving men who did not even know
they stood now in darkness), swathed in a pale
nimbus which illuminated their path as the
witchcold had heralded their coming, Tempus
muttered under his breath. His hand went to his
hip, where no weapon lay, but only a knotted
cord. Studying the strangers without looking at

them straight-on, leaning back, his arms outstretched along the fencetop, he waited.

The red lights glowing above Vashanka's altar
winked out. The ground shuddered; the altar
stones tumbled to the ground. *Wonderful,* he
thought. *Just great.* He let his eyes slide over his
men, asleep between blinks, and wondered how
far the spell extended, whether they were ensorceled in their bunks, or in the mess, or on their
horses as they made their rounds in the country
or the town.

Well, Vashanka? he tested. *It's your altar they
took down.* But the god was silent.

Besides the two coming at measured pace
across the ground rutted with chariot tracks,
nothing moved. No bird cried or insect chittered,
no Stepson so much as snored. The companion
of the imposing man in the thick, fur mantle had
him by the elbow. Who was helping whom,
Tempus could not at first determine. He tried to
think where he had seen that austere face—
soul-shriveling eyes so sad, bones so fine and yet
full of vitality beneath the black, silver-starred
hair—and then blew out a sibilant breath when
he realized what power approached over the rutted, Sanctuary ground. The companion whose
lithe musculature and bare, tanned skin were
counterpointed by an enameled tunic of scale-
armor and soft low boots was either a female or
the prettiest eunuch Tempus had ever seen—
whichever, she/he was trouble, coming in from
some nonphysical realm on the arm of the entelechy of a shadow lord, master of the once-in-
a-while archipelago that bore his name: Askelon,
lord of dreams.

When they reached him, Tempus nodded carefully and said, very quietly in a noncommittal way that almost passed for deference, "Salutations, Ash. What brings you into so poor a realm?"

Askelon's proud lips parted; the skin around them was too pale. It *was* a woman who held his arm; her health made him seem the more pallid, but when he spoke, his words were ringing basso profundo: "Life to you, Riddler. What are you called here?"

"Spare me your curses, mage." To such a power, the title alone was an insult. And the shadow lord knew it well.

Around his temples, stars of silver floated, stirred by a breeze. His colorless eyes grew darker, draining the angry clouds from the sky: "You have not answered me."

"Nor you, me."

The woman looked in disbelief upon Tempus. She opened her lips, but Askelon touched them with a gloved hand. From the gauntlet's cuff a single drop of blood ran down his left arm to drip upon the sand. He looked at it somberly, then up at Tempus. "I seek your sister, what else? I will not harm her."

"But will you cause her to harm herself?"

The shadow lord whom Tempus had called Ash, so familiarly, rubbed the bloody trail from his elbow back up to his wrist. "Surely you do not think you can protect her from me? Have I not accomplished even this? Am I not real?" He held his gloved hands out, turned them over, let them flap abruptly down against his thighs. Niko, who had been roused from deep meditation in the barracks by the cold which had spread sleep over the waking, skidded to a halt and peered around the curve of the fence, his teeth gritted hard to stay their chatter.

"No." Tempus had replied to Askelon's first question with that sensitive little smile which meant he was considering commencing some incredible slaughter; "Yes" to his second; "Yes, indeed" to the third.

"And would I be here now," the dream lord continued, "in so ignominious a state if not for the havoc she has wrought?"

"I don't know what havoc she's wrought that could have touched you out there. But I take it that last night's deadly mist was your harbinger. Why come to me, Ash? I'm not involved with her in any way."

"You connived to release her from imprisonment, Tempus—it *is* Tempus, so the dreams of the Sanctuarites tell me. And they tell me other things, too. I am here, sleepless one, to warn you: though I cannot reach you through dreams, have no doubt: I *can* reach you. All of these, you consider yours. . . ." He waved his hand to encompass the still men, frozen unknowing upon the field. "They are mine now. I can claim them any time."

"What do you want, Ash?"

"I want you to refrain from interfering with me while I am here. I will see her, and settle a score with her, and if you are circumspect, when I leave, your vicious little band of cutthroats will be returned to you, unharmed, uncomprehending."

"All that, to make sure of me? I don't respond well to flattery. You will force me to a gesture by trying to prevent one. I don't care what you do about Cime—whatever you do, you will be doing me a favor. Release my people, and go about your quest."

"I cannot trust you not to interfere. By noon I shall be installed as temporary First Hazard of your local Mageguild—"

"Slumming? It's hardly your style."

"Style?" he thundered so that his companion shuddered and Niko started, dislodging a stone which clicked, rolled, then lay still. "Style! She came unto me with her evil and destroyed my peace." His other hand cradled his wrist. "I was lucky to receive a reprieve from damnation. I have only a limited dispensation: either I force her to renege on murdering me, or make her finish the job. And you of all men know what awaits a contractee such as myself when existence is over. What would you do in my place?"

"I did not know how she got here, but now it comes clearer. She went to destroy you in your place, and was spat out into this world from there? But how is it she has not succeeded?"

The Power, looking past Tempus with a squint, shrugged. "She was not certain, her will was not united with her heart. I have a chance, now, to remedy it . . . bring back restful dreaming in its place, and my domain with it. I will not let anything stop me. Be warned, my friend. You know what strengths I can bring to bear."

"Release my people, if you want her, and we will think about how to satisfy you over breakfast. From the look of you, you could use something warm to drink. You do drink, don't you? With the form come the functions, surely even here."

Askelon sighed feelingly; his shoulders

slumped. "Yes, indeed, the entire package is mine to tend and lumber about in, some little while longer . . . until after the Mageguild's fete this evening, at the very least. . . . I am surprised, not to mention pleased, that you display some disposition to compromise. It is for everyone's benefit. This is Jihan." He inclined his head toward his companion. "Greet our host."

"It is my pleasure to wish that things go exceedingly well with you," the woman said, and Niko saw Tempus shiver, a subtle thing that went over him from scalp to sandals—and almost bolted out to help, thinking some additional, debilitating spell was being cast. He was not fooled by those polite exchanges: bodies and timbres had been speaking more plainly of respectful opposition and cautious hostility. Distressed and overbalanced from long crouching without daring to lean or sit, he fell forward, catching himself too late to avoid making noise.

Niko heard Tempus remonstrate, "Let him be, Askelon!" and felt a sudden ennui, his eyelids closing, a drift toward sleep he fought—then heard the dream lord reply: "I will take this one as my hostage, and leave Jihan with you, a fair trade. Then I will release these others, who remember nothing—for the interim. When I am done here, if you have behaved well, you may have them back permanently, free and unencumbered. We will see how good your faith can be said to be."

Niko realized he could still hear, still see, still move.

"Come here, Nikodemos," Tempus summoned him.

He obeyed. His commander's mien implored
Niko to take all this in his stride, as his voice sent
him to see to breakfast for three. He was about to
object that only by the accident of meditation
had he been untouched by the spell—which
sought out waking minds and could not find his
in his restplace, and thus the cook and all the
menials must be spellbound, still—when men
began to stir and finish sentences begun before
Askelon's arrival, and Tempus waved him im-
peratively on his way. He left on the double,
ignoring the stares of those just coming out of
limbo, whistling to cover the wheeze of his fear.

*   *   *   3   *   *   *

So it was that the Sacred Bander Nikodemos
accompanied Askelon into Sanctuary on the
young Stepson's two best horses, his ears ringing
with what he had heard and his eyes aching from
what he had seen and his heart clandestinely
taking cautious beats in a constricted chest.

Over breakfast, Askelon had remarked to
Tempus that it must be hell for one of his tem-
perament to languish under curse and god. "I've
gotten used to it." "I could grant you mortality,
so small a thing is still within my power." "I'll
limp along as I am, thanks, Ash. If my curse
denys me love, it gives me freedom." "It would
be good for you to have an ally." "Not one who
will unleash a killing mist merely to make an
entrance," Tempus had rejoined, his fingers
steepled before him. "Sorcery is yet beneath
your contempt? You are hardly nonaligned in
the conflict brewing." "I have my philosophy."
"Oh? And what is that?" "A single axiom, these

days, is sufficient to my needs." "Which is?" " 'Grab reality by the balls and squeeze.' " "We will see how well it serves you, when you stand without your god." "Are you still afraid of me, Ash? I have never given you cause, never vied with you for your place." "Whom do you think to impress, Riddler? The boy? Your potential, and dangerous proclivities, speak for themselves. I will grant no further concessions. . . ."

Riding with the dream lord into Sanctuary in broad daylight was a relief after the tension of his commander's dining table. Being dismissed by Askelon before the high-walled Mageguild on the Street of Arcana was a reprieve he had not dared to hope for, though the entelechy of the seventh sphere decreed that Nikodemos must return to the outer gates at sundown. He watched his best horse disappear down that vine-hung way without even a twinge of regret. If he never saw that particular horse and its rider again, it would be too soon.

And he had his orders, which, when he had received them, he had despaired of successfully carrying out. When Askelon had been absorbed in making his farewells to the woman whose fighting stature and muscle tone were so extraordinary, Tempus had bade Niko warn certain parties to spread the word that a curfew must be kept, and some others not to attend the Mageguild's fete this evening, and lastly find a way to go alone to the Vulgar Unicorn, tavern of consummate ill repute in this scabrous town, and perform a detailed series of actions there.

Niko had never been to the Vulgar Unicorn, though he had been by it many times during his tours in the Maze. The east-side taverns like the

Alekeep at the juncture of Promise Park and
Governor's Walk, and the Golden Oasis, outside the Maze, were more to his liking, and he
stopped at both to fortify himself for a sortie into
Ilsig filth and Ilsig poverty. At the Alekeep, he
managed to warn the father of a girl he knew to
keep his family home this evening lest the killing mist diminish his house should it come
again; at the Oasis, he found a Hell-Hound and
the Ilsig captain Walegrin gaming intently over a
white-bladed knife (a fine prize if it were the
"hard steel" the blond-braided captain claimed
it was, a metal only fabled to exist), and so had
gotten his message off to both the palace and the
garrison in good order.

Yet, in the Maze, it seemed that his luck deserted him as precipitately as his sense of direction had fled. It should be easy to find the
Serpentine—just head south by southwest . . .
unless the entelechy Askelon had hexed him! He
rode tight in his saddle under a soapy, scum-
covered sky gone noncommittal, its sun
nowhere to be seen, doubling back from Wideway and the gutted wharfside warehouses where
serendipity had taken his partner's life as suddenly as their charred remains loomed before
him out of a pearly fog so thick he could barely
see his horse's ears twitch. Rolling in off the
water, it was rank and fetid and his fingers
slipped on his weeping reins. The chill it
brought was numbing, and lest it penetrate to his
very soul, he fled into a light meditation, clear-
ing his mind and letting his body roll with his
mount's gait while its hoofbeats and his own
breathing grew loud and that mixed cadence
lulled him.

In his expanded awareness, he could sense the folk behind their doors, just wisps of passion and subterfuge leaking out beyond the featureless mudbrick façades from inner courts and wizened hearts. When glances rested on him, he knew it, feeling the tightening of focus and disturbance of auras like roused bees or whispered insults. When his horse stopped with a disapproving snort at an intersection, he had been sensing a steady attention on him, a presence pacing him which knew him better than the occasional street-denizen who turned watchful at the sight of a mercenary riding through the Maze, or the whores half-hidden in doorways with their predatory/cautious/disappointed pinwheels of assessment and dismissal. Still thoroughly disoriented, he chose the leftward fork at random, as much to see whether the familiar pattern stalking him would follow along as in hopes that some landmark would pop out of the fog to guide him—he did not know the Maze as well as he should, and his meditation-sensitized peripheral perception could tell him only how close the nearest walls were and a bit about who lurked behind them: he was no adept, only a western-trained fighter. But, being one, he had shaken his fear and his foreboding, and waited to see if Shadowspawn, called Hanse, would announce himself: should Niko hail the thief prematurely, Hanse would almost certainly melt back into the alleys he commanded rather than own that Niko had perceived himself shadowed—and leave him lost among the hovels and the damned.

He had learned patience waiting for gods to speak to him on wind-whipped precipices while heaving tides licked about his toes in anticipation. After a time, he began to see canopied stalls and hear muted haggling, and dismounted to lead his horse among the splintered crates and rotten fruit at the bazaar's edge.

"Psst! Stealth!" Hanse called him by his warname, and dropped, soundless as a phantom, from a shuttered balcony into his path. Startled, Niko's horse scrabbled backward, hind hooves kicking crates and stanchions over so that a row ensued with the stall's enraged proprietor. When that was done, the dark slumhawk still waited, eyes glittering with unsaid words sharper than any of the secreted blades he wore, a triumphant smile fierce as his scarlet sash fading to his more customary street-hauteur as he turned figs in his fingers, pronounced them unfit for human consumption, and eased Niko's way.

"I was out there this morning," Niko heard, bent down over his horse's left hind hoof, checking for splinters caught in its shoe; "heard your team lost a member, but not who. Pissass weird weather, these days. You know something *I* should know?"

"Possibly." Niko, putting down the hoof, brushed dust from his thighs and stood up. "Once when I was wandering around the backstreets of a coastal city—never mind which one—with an arrow in my gut and afraid to seek a surgeon's help there was weather like this. A man who took me in told me to *stay* off the streets at night until the weather'd been clear a full day—something to do with dead adepts and souls to pay their way out of purgatory. Tell your friends, if you've got any. And do me a favor, fair exchange?" He gathered up his reins and took a handful of mane, about to swing up on his horse, and thus he saw Hanse's fingers flicker: *state it*. So he did, admitting that he was lost, quite baldly, and asking the thief to guide him on his way.

When they had walked far enough that Shadowspawn's laughter no longer echoed, the thief said, "What's wrong? Like I said, I was out at the barracks. I've never seen *him* scared of anything, but he's scared of that girl he's got in his room. And he's meaner than normal—told me I couldn't stable my horse out there, and not to come around—" Shadowspawn broke off, having said what he did not want to say, and kicked a melon in their path, which burst open, showing the teeming maggots within.

"Maybe he'd like to keep you out of troubles that aren't any of your business. Or maybe he estimates his debt to you is paid in full—you can't keep coming around when it suits you and still be badmouthing us like any other Ilsig—"

A spurt of profanity contained some cogent directions to the Vulgar Unicorn, and some other suggestions impossible to follow. Niko did not look up to see Hanse go. If he failed to take the warning to heart, then hurt feelings would keep him away from Niko and his commander for a while. It was enough.

Directions or no, it took him longer than it should have to find his way. Finally, when he was eyeing the sky doubtfully, trying to estimate the lateness of the hour, he spied the Unicorn's autoerotic sign creaking in the moist, stinking breeze blowing in off the harbor. Discounting Hanse, since Niko had entered the close and ramshackle despair of the shantytown he had seen not one friendly face. If he had been jeered once, he had been cursed a score of times, aloud and with spit and glare and handsign, and he had had more than his fill of Sanctuary's infamous slum.

Within the Unicorn, the clientele did not look happy to see a Stepson. A silence as thick as Rankan ale descended as he entered and took more time to disperse than he liked. He crossed to the bar, scanning the room full of local brawlers, grateful he had neglected to shave since the previous morning. Perhaps he seemed more fearsome than he felt as he turned his back to the sullen, hostile crowd just resuming their drinking and scheming and ordered a draught from the bartender. The big, overmuscled man with a balding head slapped it down before him, growling that it would be well if he drank up and left before the crowd began to thicken, or the barkeep would not be responsible for the consequences, and Niko's "master" would get a bill for any damage to the premises. The look in the big man's eyes was decidedly unfriendly. "You're the one they call Stealth, aren't you?" the barkeep accused him. "The one who told Shadowspawn that one of the best kills is a knife from behind down beside the collarbone, and with a sword, cut up between your opponent's legs, and in general the object is never to have to engage your enemy, but dispatch him before he has seen your face?"

Niko stared at him, feeling anger chase the disquiet from his limbs. "I know you Ilsigs don't like us," he said quietly, "but I haven't time now to charm you into a change of mind. Where's

One-Thumb, barkeep? I have a message for him that cannot wait."

"Right here," smirked the aproned mountain, tossing his rag onto the barsink's chipped pottery rim. "What is it, sonny?"

"He wants you to take me to the lady—you know the one." Actually, Tempus had instructed Niko to tell One-Thumb about Askelon's intention to confront Cime, and wait for word as to what the woman wanted Tempus to do. But he was resentful, and he was late. "I have to be at the Mageguild by sundown. Let's move."

"You've got the wrong One-thumb, and the wrong idea. Who's this 'he'?"

"Bartender, I leave it on your conscience—" He pushed his mug away and took a step back from the bar, then realized he could not leave without discharging his duty, and reached out to pick it up again.

The big bartender's thumbless hand curled around his wrist and jerked him against the bar. He prayed for patience. "And he didn't tell you not to come in here, bold as brass tassels on a witch-bitch whore? He is getting sloppy, or he's forgotten who his friends are. Why didn't you come round the back? What do you expect me to do, leave with you in the middle of the day? I—"

"I was lucky I found your pisshole at all, Wriggly. Let me go or you're going to lose the rest of those fingers, sure as Lord Storm's anger rocks even this god-ridden garbage heap of a peninsula—"

Someone stepped up to the bar, and One-Thumb, with a wrench of wrist, went to serve him, meanwhile motioning close a girl whose breasts were mottled gray with dirt and pinkish white where she had sweated it away, saying to her that Niko was to be taken to the office.

In it, he watched the man called One-Thumb through a one-way mirror, and fidgeted. Eventually, though he saw no reason why it happened, a door he had thought to be a closet's opened behind him, and a woman stepped in, clad in Ilsig doeskin leggings. She said, "What word did my brother send to me?"

He told her, thinking, watching her, that her eyes were gray like Askelon's, and her hair was arrestingly black and silver, and that she did not in any way resemble Tempus. When he was finished with his story and his warning that she not, under any circumstances, go out this evening—not, upon her life, attend the Mageguild fete, she laughed, a sweet tinkle so inappropriate his spine chilled and he stiffened.

"Tell my brother not to be afraid. You must not know him well, to take his terror of the adepts so seriously." She moved close to him, and he drowned in her storm-cloud eyes while her hand went to his swordbelt and by it she pulled him close. "Have you money, Stepson? And some time to spend?"

Niko beat a hasty retreat with her mocking, throaty laughter chasing him down the stairs. She called after him that she only wanted to have him give her love to Tempus. As he made the landing near the bar, he heard the door at the stairs' top slam shut. He was out of there like a torqued arrow—so fast he forgot to pay for his drink, and yet, when he remembered it, on the street where his horse waited, no one had come chasing him. Looking up at the sky, he estimated he could just make the Mageguild in time, if he did not get lost again.

* * * 4 * * *

Thinking back over the last ten months, Tempus realized he should have expected something like this. Vashanka was weakening steadily: something had removed the god's name from Kadakithis' palace dome; the state-cult's temple had proved unbuildable, its grounds defiled and its priest a defiler; the ritual of the Tenslaying had been interrupted by Cime and her fire, and he and Vashanka had begotten a male child upon the First Consort which the god did not seem to want to claim; Abarsis had been allowed to throw his life away without regard to the fact that he had been Vashanka's premier warrior-priest. Now the field altar his mercenaries had built had been tumbled to the ground before his eyes by one of Abarsis' teachers, an entelechy chosen specifically to balance the beserker influence of the god. And he, Tempus, was imprisoned in his own quarters by a Froth Daughter in an all-too-human body intent on exacting from him recompense for what his sister had denied her.

Glumly he wondered if his god could be undergoing a midlife crisis, then if he too was, since Vashanka and he were linked by the Law of Consonance. Certainly, Jihan's proclamation of intended rape had taken him aback. He had not been taken aback by anything in years. "Rapist, they call you, and with good reason," she had said, reaching up under the scale-armor corselet to wriggle out of her loinguard. "We will see how you like it, in receipt of what you're used to

giving out." He could not stop her, or refrain
from responding to her. Cime had interrupted
Jihan's scheduled tryst with Askelon, perhaps
aborted it. The body which faced him had been
chosen for a woman's retribution. Later she said
to him, rubbing the imprint of her scale-armor
from his loins with a high-veined hand: "Have
you never heard of letting the lady win?"

"No," he replied, genuinely puzzled. "Jihan,
are you saying I was unfair?"

"Only arcane, weighting the scales to your
side. Love without feeling, mind-caress, spell-
excitation. . . . I am new to flesh. I hope you are
well chastized and repentant," she giggled, just
briefly, before his words found her ears: "I warn
you, straight-out: those who love me die of it,
and those I favor are fated to spurn me."

"You are an arrogant man. You think I care? I
should have struck you more viciously." Her flat
hand slapped, more than playfully, down upon
his belly. *"He*—" she meant Askelon "—cannot
spare me any of his substance. I do this for him,
that he not look upon me hungry for a man and
know shame. You saw his wrist, where she
skewered him. . . ."

"I don't fancy a gift from him, convenient or
no." He was going to pull her up beside him,
where he might casually get his hands around
her fine, muscular throat. But she sat back and
retorted, "You think *he* would suggest this? Or
even know of it? I take what I choose from men,
and we do not discuss it. It is all I can do for him.
And *you* owe me whatever price I care to
name—your own sister took from me my husband before ever his lips touched mine. When
my father chose me from my sisters to be sent to

ease Askelon's loneliness, I had a choice—yea or nay—and a year to make it. I studied him, and felt love enough to come to human flesh to claim it. To become human—you concede that I am, for argument's sake?"

He did that—her spectacular body, sheathed in muscle, taut and sensuous, was too powerful and yet too shapely to be mortal, but even so, he did not critique her.

"Then," she continued, rising up, hands on her impossibly slim waist, pacing as she spoke in a rustle of armor-scales, "consider my plight. To become human for the love of a demiurge, and then not to be able to claim him. . . . It is done, I have this form, I cannot undo it until its time is up. And since I cannot collect satisfaction from her—he has forbidden me that pleasure—all the powers on the twelfth plane agree: I may have what I wish from you. And what I wish, I have made quite plain." Her voice was deepening. She took a step toward him.

He objected, and she laughed, "You should see your face."

"I can imagine. You are a very attractive . . . lady, and you come with impeccable credentials from an unimpeachable source. So if you are inexperienced in the ways of the world, brash and awkward and ineffective because of that, I suppose I must excuse you. Thus, I shall make allowances." His one hand raised, gestured, scooped up her loinguard and tossed it at her. "Get dressed, get out of here. Go back to your master, familiar, and tell him I do not any longer pay my sister's debts."

Then, finally, she came at him: "You mistake me. I am not asking you, I am telling you." She

reached him, crouched down, thighs together,
hands on her knees, knees on what had once
been Jubal the Slaver's bed. "This is a real debt,
in lieu of payment for which, my patron and the
elementals will exact—"

He clipped her exactly behind her right ear,
and she fell across him, senseless.

Other things she had said, earlier in passion,
rang in his head: that should he in any way
displease her, her duty would then be plain: he
and Vashanka could both be disciplined by way
of the child they had together begotten on one of
Molin Torchholder's temple dancers.

He was not sure how he felt about that, as he
was not sure how he felt about Askelon's offer of
mortality or Vashanka's cowardice, or the posi-
tives and negatives of his sister's self-engen-
dered fate.

He gave the unconscious woman over to his
Stepsons with instructions that made the three
he had hailed grin widely. He could not estimate
how long they would be able to hold her—
however long they managed it, it had better be
long enough. The Stepson who had come from
seeking Niko in Sanctuary found him, garbed for
business, saddling a Trôs horse in the stables.

"Stealth said," the gruff, sloe-eyed commando
reported: " 'She said stay out of it, no need to
fear.' He's staying with the archmage, or whatever it is. He's going to the Mageguild party and
suggests you try and drop by." A feral grin stole
over the mercenary's face. He knew something
was up. "Need anybody on your right for this,
commander?"

Tempus almost said no, but changed his mind

and told the Stepson to get a fresh horse and his best panoply and meet him at the Mageguild's outer gate.

*   *   *   5   *   *   *

There was a little mist in the streets by the time Tempus headed his Trôs horse across the east side toward the Mageguild—nothing daunting yet, just a fetlock-high steaminess as if the streets were cobbled with dry ice. He had had no luck intercepting his sister at Lastel's estate: a servant shouted through a grate, over the barking of dogs, that the master had already left for the fete. He had stopped briefly at the mercenaries' hostel before going there, to burn a rag he had had for centuries in the common room's hearth: he no longer needed to be reminded not to argue with warlocks, or that love, for him, was always a losing game. With his sister's scarf, perhaps the problem of her would waft away, changed like the ancient linen to smoke upon the air.

Before the Mageguild's outer wall, an imprudent crowd had gathered to watch the luminaries arriving in the ersatz-daylight of its ensorceled grounds. Pink clouds formed a glowing canopy to the wall's edge—a godly pavilion; elsewhere, it was night. Where dark met light, the Stepson Janni waited, one leg crooked over his saddlehorn, rolling a smoke, his best helmet dangling by his knee and his full-length dressmantle draped over his horse's croup, while around his hips the ragged crowd thronged and his horse, ears flattened, snapped at Ilsigs who came too near.

Tempus' gray rumbled a greeting to the bay;
the curly-headed mercenary straightened up in
his saddle and saluted, grinning through his
beard.

He wasn't smiling when the Mageguild's pon-
derous doors enfolded them, and three junior
functionaries escorted them to the "changing
rooms" within the outer wall where they were
expected to strip and hand over their armaments
to the solicitously smirking mages-in-training
before donning proferred "fete-clothes" (gray
silk chitons and summer sandals) the wizards
had thoughtfully provided. Askelon wasn't taking any chances, Tempus thought but did not
say, though Janni wondered aloud what use
there was in checking their paltry swords and
daggers when enchanters could not be made to
check their spells.

Inside the Mageguild's outer walls, it was
summer. In its gardens—transformed from their
usual dank fetidness by artful conjure into a
wonderland of orchids and eucalyptus and wil-
lows weeping where before moss-hung swamp-
giants had held sway over quickmires—Tempus
saw Kadakithis, resolutely imperious in a black
robe oversewn with gems into a map of Ranke-
caught-in-the-web-of-the-world. The prince/
governor's pregnant wife, a red gift-gown splen-
did over her child-belly, leaned heavily on his
arm. Kittycat's approving glance was laced with
commiseration: yes, he, too, found it hard to
smile here, but both of them knew it prudent to
observe the forms, especially with wizards. . . .

Tempus nodded and walked away.

Then he saw her, holding Lastel's hand, to

which the prosthetic thumb of his disguise was firmly attached. A signal bade Janni await him; he did not have to look back to know that the Stepson obeyed.

Cime was blond, tonight, and golden-eyed, tall in her adept-chosen robe of iridescent green, but he saw through the illusion to her familiar self. And she knew it. "You come here without your beloved armaments or even the god's amulet? The man I used to know would have pulled rank and held on to his weapons."

"Nothing's going to happen here," he murmured, staring off over her head into the crowd looking for Niko; "unless the message I received was in error and we do have a problem?"

"*We* have no problem—" glowered Lastel/One-Thumb.

"One-Thumb, disappear, or I'll have Janni, over there, teach you how to imitate your bar's sign." With a reproachful look that Tempus would utter his alias here, the man who did not like to be called One-Thumb outside the Maze lumbered off.

Then he had to look at her. Under the golden-eyed illusion, her char-and-smoke gaze accused him, as it had chased him across the centuries and made him content to be accursed and constrained from other loves. *God*, he thought, *I will never get through this without error.* It was the closest he had come to *asking* Vashanka to help him for ages. In the back of his skull, a distant whisper exhorted him to take his sister while he could . . . that bush on his right would be bower enough. But more than advice the god could not give: "*I have my own troubles, mortal, for which you are partly responsible."* With the echo of Vashanka's last word, Tempus knew the god was gone.

"Is Lastel telling the truth, Cime? Are you content to face Askelon's wrath, and your peril, alone? Tell me how you came to *half*-kill a personage of that magnitude, and assure me that you can rectify your mistake without my help."

She reached up and touched his throat, running her finger along his jaw until it found his mouth. "Ssh, ssh. You are a bad liar, who proclaims he does not still love me. Have you not enough at risk, presently? Yes, I erred with Askelon. He tricked me. I shall solve it, one way or the other. My heart saw him, and I could not then be the one who stood there watching him die. His world beguiled me, his form enthralled me. You know what punishment love could bring me. . . . He begged me leave him to die alone. And I *believed* him . . . because I feared for my life, should while he died I come to love him. We each bear our proper curse, that is sure."

"You think this disguise will fool him?"

She shook her head. "I need not; he will want a meeting. This," she ran her hands down over her illusory youth and beauty, "was for the magelings, those children at the gates. As for you, stay clear of this matter, my brother. There is no time for quailing or philosophical debates, now. You never were competent to simply *act*, unencumbered by judgment or conscience. Don't try to change, on my account. I will deal with the entelechy, and then I will drink even his name dry of meaning. Like that!" She snapped her fingers, twirled on her heel, and flounced off in a good imitation of a young woman offended by a forward soldier.

While he watched, Askelon appeared from the crowd to bar her path, a golden coin held out before him like a wand or a warding charm.

That fast did he have her, too fast for Tempus to get between them, simply by the mechanism of invoking her curse: for pay, she must give herself to any comer. He watched them flicker out of being with his stomach rolling and an ache in his throat. It was some little while before he saw anything external, and then he saw Nikodemos showing off his gift-cuirass to Janni.

The two came up to him wondering why it was, when everyone else's armaments had been taken from them, Niko, who had arrived in shabby duty-gear, had been given better than ever he could afford. Tempus drew slowly into his present, noting Molin Torchholder's over-gaudy figure nearby, and a kohl-eyed lady who might easily be an infiltrator from the Mygdonian Alliance talking to Lastel.

He asked his Stepsons to make her acquaintance: "She might just be smuggling drugs into Sanctuary with Lastel's help, but do not arrest her for trifles. If she is a spy, perhaps she will try to recruit a Stepson disaffected enough with his lot. Either of you—a single agent or half a broken pair—could fit that description."

"At the least, we must plumb her body's secrets, Stealth," Janni rumbled to Niko as the two strutted her way, looking virile and predatory.

With a scowl of concern for the Stepson to whom he was bound by ill-considered words, he sought out Torchholder, recalling, as he slid with murmured greetings and apologies through socialites and Hazard-class adepts, Niko's blank and steady eyes: the boy knew his danger, and trusted Tempus, as a Sacred Bander must, to see him through it. No remonstrance or doubt had shown in the fighter called Stealth's open countenance, that Tempus would come here against Askelon's wishes, and risk a Stepson's life. It was war, the boy's calm said, what they both did and what they both knew. Later, perhaps there would be explanations—or not. Tempus knew that Niko, should he survive, would never broach the subject.

"Torchholder, I think you ought to go see to the First Consort's baby," he said as his hand came down heavily on the palace-priest's be-baubled shoulder. Torchholder was already pulling on his beard, his mouth curled with anger, when he turned. Assessing Tempus' demeanor, his face did a dance which ended in a mien of knowing caution. "Ah, yes, I did mean to look in on Seylalha and her babe. Thank you for reminding me, Hell-Hound."

"*Stay with her,*" Tempus whispered sotto voce as Molin sought to brush by him, "*or get them both to a safer place—*"

"We *got* your message, this afternoon, Hound," the privy priest hissed, and he was gone.

Tempus was just thinking that it was well Fete Week only came once yearly, when above him, in the pink, tented clouds, winter gloom began to spread; and beside him, a hand closed upon his left arm with a numbingly painful grip: Jihan had arrived.

* * * 6 * * *

Askelon of Meridian, entelechy of the seventh sphere, lord of dream and shadow, faced his would-be assassin little strengthened. The Hazards of Sanctuary had given what they could of power to him, but mortal strength and mortals' magic could not replace what he had lost. His compassionate eyes had sunken deep under lined and arching brows; his skin was pallid; his cheeks hosted deep hollows like his colossus's where it guarded an unknown sea, so fierce that folk there who had never heard of Sanctuary swore that in those stony caverns demons raised their broods.

It had cost him much to take flesh and make chase. It cost him more to remove Cime to the Mageguild's innermost sanctum before the disturbance broke out above the celebrants on the lawn. But he had done it.

He said to her, "Your intention, free agent, was not clear. Your resolve was not firm. I am neither dead nor alive, because of you. Release me from this torture. I saw in your eyes you did not truly wish my demise, nor the madness that must come upon the world entire from the destruction of the place of salving dreams. You have lived awhile, now, in a world where dreams cannot solve problems, or be used to chart the future, or to heal or renew. What say you? You can change it, bring sanity back among the planes, and love to your aching heart. I will make you lady of Meridian. Our quays will once again rise crystal, streets will glitter gold, and my people will finish the welcoming paean they were singing when you shattered my heart." As he spoke, he pulled from his vestments a kerchief and held it out, unfolded, in his right hand. There on snowy linen glittered the shards of the Heart of Askelon, the obsidian talisman which her rods had destroyed when he wore it on his wrist.

She had them out by then, taken down from her hair, and she twirled them, blue-white and ominous, in her fingers.

He did not shrink from her, nor eye her weapons. He met her glance with his, and held, willing to take either outcome—anything but go on the way he was.

Then he heard the hardness of her laugh, and prepared himself to face the tithe-collectors who held the mortgage on his soul.

Her aspect of blond youthfulness fell away with her laughter, and she stepped near him, saying, "Love, you offer me? You know my curse, do you not?"

"I can lift it, if you but spend one year with me."

"*You can lift it?* Why should I believe you, father of magic? Not even gods must tell the truth, and you, I own, are beyond even the constraints of right and wrong which gods obey."

"Will you not help me, and help yourself? Your beauty will not fade; I can give youth unending, and heal your heart, if you but heal mine." His hand, outstretched to her, quivered. His eyes sparkled with unshed tears. "Shall you spend eternity as a murderer and a whore, *for no*

reason? Take salvation, now it is offered. Take it
for us both. Neither of us could claim such a boon
from eternity again."

Cime shrugged, and the woman's eyes so
much older than the three decades her body
showed impaled him. "Some kill politicians,
some generals, foot soldiers in the field. As for
me, I think the mages are the problem, twisting
times and worlds about like children play with
string. And as for help, what makes you think
either you or I deserve it? How many have you
aided, without commensurate gain? When old
Four-Eyes-Spitting-Fire-And-Four-Mouths-Spit-
ting-Curses came after me, no one did *anything,* not my parents, or our priests or seers.
They all just looked at their feet, as if the key to
my salvation was written in Azehur's sand. *But it
was not!* And oh, did I learn from my wizard!
More than he thought to teach me, since he
crumbled into dust on my account, and that is
sure."

Yet, she stopped the rods twirling, and she did
not start to sing.

They stared a time longer at each other, and
while they saw themselves in one another, Cime
began to cry, who had not wept in thrice a
hundred years. And in time she turned her rods
about, and butts first, she touched them to the
shards of the obsidian he held in a trembling
palm.

When the rods made contact, a blinding flare
of blue commenced to shine in his hand, and she
heard him say, "I will make things right with
us," as the room in which they stood began to

fade away, and she heard a lapping sea and singing children and finger cymbals tinkling while
lutes were strummed and pipes began to play.

*   *   *   7   *   *   *

All hell breaking loose could not have caused
more pandemonium than Jihan's father's blood-
red orbs peering down through shredded clouds
upon the Mageguild's grounds. The fury of the
father of a jilted bride was met by Vashanka in
his full manifestation, so that folk thrown to the
ground lay silent, staring up at the battle in the
sky with their fingers dug deep into chilling,
spongy earth.

Vashanka's two feet were widespread, one
upon his temple, due west, one upon the Mageguild's wall. His lightning bolts rocked the
heavens, his golden locks whipped by his adver-
sary's black winds. Howls from the foreign
Stormbringer's cloudy throat pummeled ear-
drums; people rolled to their stomachs and
buried their heads in their arms as the incon-
ceivable cloud creature enveloped their god, and
blackness reigned. Thunder bellowed; the black
cloud pulsed spasmodically, lit from within.

In the tempest, Tempus shouted to Jihan,
grabbed her arms in his hands: "Stop this; you
can do it. Your pride, and his, are not worth so
many lives." A lightning bolt struck earth beside
his foot, so close a blue sparkling áftercharge
nuzzled his leg.

She jerked away, palmed her hair back, stood
glaring at him with red flecks in her eyes. She
shouted something back, her lips curled in a

flash of light, but the gods' roaring blotted out her words. Then she merely turned her back to him, raised her arms to heaven, and perhaps began to pray.

He had no more time for her; the god's war was his; he felt the claw-cold blows Stormbringer landed, felt Vashanka's substance leeching away. Yet he set off running, dodging cowerers upon the ground, adepts and nobles with their cloaks wrapped about their heads, seeking his Stepsons: he knew what he must do.

He did not stop for arms or horses, when he found Niko and Janni, but set off through the raging din toward the Avenue of Temples, where the child the man and god had begotten upon the First Consort was kept.

Handsigns got them through until speech was useful, when they had run west through the lawns and alleys, coming to Vashanka's temple grounds from the back. Inside the shrine's chancery, it was quieter, shielded from the sky that heaved with light and dark.

Niko shared his weapons, those Askelon had given him: a dirk to Tempus, the sword to Janni. "But you have nothing left," Janni protested in the urgent undertone they were all employing in the shadowed corridors of their embattled god's earthly home. "I have this," Niko replied, and tapped his armored chest.

Whether he meant the cuirass Askelon had given him, the heart underneath, or his mental skills, Tempus did not ask, just tossed the dirk contemptuously back, and dashed out into the murky temple hall.

They smelled sorcery before they saw the sick

green light or felt the curdling cold. Outside the door under which wizardsign leaked like sulphur from a yellow spring, Janni muttered blackly. Niko's lips were drawn back in a grin: "After you, commander?"

Tempus wrenched the doors apart, once Janni had cut the leather strap where it had been drawn within to secure the latch, and beheld Molin Torchholder in the midst of witchfire, wrestling with more than Tempus would have thought he could handle, and holding his own.

On the floor in the corner a honey-haired northern dancer hugged a man-child to her breast, her mouth an "ooh" of relief, as if now that Tempus was here, she was surely saved.

He took time to grimace politely at the girl, who insisted in mistaking him for his god—his senses were speeding much faster than even the green, stinking whirlwind in the middle of the room. He was not so sure that anything was salvageable, here, or even if he cared if girl or priest or child or town . . . or god . . . were to be saved. But then he looked behind him, and saw his Stepsons, Niko on the left and Janni with sword drawn, both ready to advance on hell itself, would he but bid them, and he raised a hand and led them into the lightfight, eyes squinted nearly shut and all his body tingling as his preternatural abilities came into play.

Molin's ouster was uppermost in his mind; he picked the glareblind priest up bodily and threw him, wrenching the god's golden icon from his frozen fist. He heard a grunt, a snapping-in of breath, behind, but did not look around to see reality fade away. He was fighting by himself, now, in a higher, colder place full of day held at bay and Vashanka's potent breath in his right ear. *"It is well you have come, manchild; I can use your help this day."* The left is the place of attack in team battle; a shield-holding line drifts right, each trying to protect his open side. He had Vashanka on his right, to support him, and a shield, full-length and awful, came to be upon his own left arm. The thing he fought here, the Stormbringer's shape, was part cat, part manlike, and its sword cut as hard as an avalanche. Its claws chilled his breath away. Behind, black and gray was split with sunrise colors, Vashanka's blazon snapping on a flag of sky. He thrust at the clouds and was parried with cold that ran up his sword and seared the skin of his palm so that his sweat froze to ice and layers of his flesh bonded to a sharkskin hilt. . . . That gave him pause, for it was his own sword, come from where-ever the mages secreted it, which moved in his hand. Pink glowed that blade, as always when his god sanctified His servant's labor. His right was untenanted, suddenly, but Vashanka's strength was in him, and it must be enough.

He fought it unto exhaustion, he fought it to a draw. The adversaries stood in clouds, typhoon-breaths rasping, both seeking strength to fight on. And then he had to say it: "Let this slight go, Stormbringer. Vengeance is disappointing, always. You soil yourself, having to care. Let her stay where she is, Weather-Gods' Father; a mortal sojourn will do her good. The parent is not responsible for the errors of the child. Nor the child for the parent." And deliberately, he put down the shield the god had given him and peeled the sticky swordhilt from a skinless palm, laying his weapon atop the shield. "Or surmount me, and have done with it. I will not die of exhaustion for a god too craven to fight by my side. And I will not stand aside and let you have the babe. You see, it is me you must punish, not my god. I led Askelon to Cime, and disposed her toward him. It is my transgression, not Vashanka's. And I am not going to make it easy for you: you will have to slaughter me, which I would much prefer to being the puppet of yet another omnipotent force."

And with a growl that was long and seared his inner ear and set his teeth on edge, the clouds began to dissolve around him, and the darkness to fade away.

He blinked, and rubbed his eyes, which were smarting with underworld cold, and when he took his hands away he found himself standing in a seared circle of stinking fumes with two coughing Stepsons, both of whom were breathing heavily, but neither of whom looked to have suffered any enduring harm. Janni was supporting Niko, who had discarded the gift-cuirass, and it glowed as if cooling from a forger's heat between his feet. The dirk and sword, too, lay on the smudged flagstones, and Tempus' sword atop the heap.

There passed an interval of soft exchanges, which did not explain either where Tempus had disappeared to, or why Niko's gear had turned white-hot against the Stormbringer's whirlpool cold, and of assessing damages (none, beyond frostbite, blisters, scrapes and Tempus' flayed swordhand) and suggestions as to where they might recoup their strength.

The tearful First Consort was calmed, and

Torchholder's people (no one could locate the priest) told to watch her well.

Outside the temple, they saw that the mist had let go of the streets; an easy night lay chill and brisk upon the town. The three walked back to the Mageguild at a leisurely pace, to reclaim their panoplies and their horses. When they got there they found that the Second and Third Hazards had claimed the evening's confrontation to be of their making, a cosmological morality play, their most humbly offered entertainment which the guests had taken too much to heart. Did not Vashanka triumph? Was not the cloud of evil vanquished? Had not the wondrous tent of pink-and-lemon summer sky returned to illuminate the Mageguild's fete?

Janni snarled and flushed with rage at the adepts' dissembling, threatening to go turn Torchholder (who had preceded them back among the celebrants, disheveled, loud-mouthed, but none the worse for wear) upside down to see if any truth might fall out, but Niko cautioned him to let fools believe what fools believe, and to make his farewells brief and polite—whatever they felt about the mages, they had to live with them.

When at last they rode out of the Street of Arcana toward the Alekeep, to quench their well-earned thirsts where Niko could check on the faring of a girl who mattered to him, he was ponying the extra horse he had lent Askelon, since neither the dream lord nor his companion Jihan had been anywhere to be found among guests trying grimly to recapture at least a semblance of revelry.

For Niko, the slow ride through mercifully dark streets was a godsend, the deep midnight sky a mask he desperately needed to keep between him and the world awhile. In its cover, he could afford to let his composure, slipping away inexorably of its own weight, fall from him altogether. As it happened, because of the riderless horse, he was bringing up the rear. That, too, suited him, as did their tortuous progress through the ways and intersections thronging intermittently with upper-class (if there was such a distinction to be made here) Ilsigs ushering in the new year. Personally, he did not like the start of it: the events of the last twenty-four hours he considered somewhat less than auspicious. He fingered the enameled cuirass with its twining snakes and glyphs which the entelechy Askelon had given him, touched the dirk at his waist, the matching sword slung at his hip. The hilts of both were worked as befitted weapons bound for a son of the armies, with the lightning and the lions and the bulls which were, the world over, the signatures of its Storm Gods, the gods of war and death. But the workmanship was foreign, and the raised demons on both scabbards belonged to the primal deities of an earlier age, whose sway was misty, everywhere but among the western islands where Niko had gone to strive for initiation into his chosen mystery and mastery over body and soul. The most appropriate legends graced these opulent arms that a shadow lord had given him; in the old ways and the elder gods and in the disciplines of transcendent perception, Niko sought perfection, a mystic calm. And the weapons were perfect, save for two blemishes:

they were fashioned from precious metals, and made nearly priceless by the antiquity of their style; they were charmed, warm to the touch, capable of meeting infernal forces and doing damage upon icy whirlwinds sent from unnamed gods. Nikodemos favored unarmed kills, minimal effort, precision. He judged himself sloppy should it become necessary to parry an opponent's stroke more than once. The templedancing exhibitions of proud swordsmen who "tested each other's mettle" and had time to indulge in style and disputatious dialogue repelled him: one got in, made the kill, and got out, hopefully leaving the enemy unknowing; if not, confused.

He no more coveted blades that would bring acquisitive men down upon him hoping to acquire them in combat than he looked forward to needing ensorceled swords for battles that could not be joined in the way he liked. The cuirass he wore kept off supernal evil—should it prove impregnable to mortal arms, that knowledge would eat away at his self-discipline, perhaps erode his control, make him careless. In the lightfight, when Tempus had flickered out of being as completely as a doused torch, he had felt an inexplicable elation, leading point into Chaos with Janni steady on his right hand. He had imagined he was indomitable, fated, chosen by the gods and thus inviolate. The steadying fear that should have been there, in his mind, assessive and balancing, was missing . . . his maat, as he had told Tempus in that moment of discomfitting candor, was gone from him. No trick panoply could replace it, no arrogance or battle-lust could substitute for it. Without equilibrium, the

quiet heart he strove for could never be his. He
was not like Tempus, preternatural, twice a man,
living forever in extended anguish to which he
had become accustomed. He did not aspire to
more than what his studies whispered a man had
right to claim. Seeing Tempus in action, he now
believed what before, though he had heard the
tales, he had discounted. He thought hard about
the Riddler, and the offer he had made him, and
wondered if he was bound by it, and the
weapons Askelon had given him no more than
omens fit for days to come. And he shivered,
upon his horse, wishing his partner were there
up ahead instead of Janni, and that his *maat* was
within him, and that they rode Syrese byways or
the Azehuran plain, where magic did not vie
with gods for mortal allegience, or take souls in
tithe.

When they dismounted at the Alekeep, he had
come to a negotiated settlement within himself:
he would wait to see if what Tempus said was
true, if his *maat* would return to him once his
teammate's spirit ascended to heaven on a pillar
of flame. He was not unaware of the rhythmic
nature of enlightenment through the precession
of events. He had come to Ranke with his partner
at Abarsis' urging; he remembered the Slaughter
Priest from his early days of ritual and war, and
had made his own decision, not followed blindly
because his left-side leader wished to teach Rankans the glory of his name. When the elder
fighter had put it to him, his friend had said that
it might be time for Nikodemos to lead his own
team—after Ranke, without doubt, the older man
would lay down his sword. He had been dreaming, he had said, of mother's milk and waving

crops and snot-nosed brats with wooden shields, a sure sign a man is done with damp camps and bloody dead stripped in the field.

So it would have happened, this year, or the next, that he would be alone. He must come to terms with it; not whine silently like an abandoned child, or seek a new and stronger arm to lean on. Meditation should have helped him, though he recalled a parchment grin and a toothless mouth instructing him that what is needed is never to be had without price.

The price of the thick brown ale in which the Alekeep specialized was doubled for the holiday's night-long vigil, but they paid not one coin, drinking, instead, in a private room in back where the grateful owner led them: he had heard about the manifestation at the Mageguild, and had been glad he had taken Niko's advice and kept his girls inside. "Can I let them out, then?" he said with a twinkling eye. "Now that you are here? Would the Lord Marshal and his distinguished Stepsons care for some gentle companionship, this jolly eve?"

Tempus, flexing his open hand on which the clear serum glistened as it thickened into scabby skin, told him to keep his children locked up until dawn, and sent him away so brusquely Janni eyed Niko askance.

Their commander sat with his back against the wall opposite the door through which the tavern's owner had disappeared. "We were followed here. I'd like to think you both realized it on your own."

The placement of their seats, backs generously offered to any who might enter, spoke so clearly of their failure that neither said a word, only moved their chairs to the single table's narrow sides. When next the door swung open, One-Thumb, not their host, stood there, and Tempus chuckled hoarsely in the hulking wrestler's face. "Only you, Lastel? I own you had me worried."

"Where is she, Tempus? What have you done with her?" Lastel stomped forward, put both ham-hands flat upon the table, his thick neck thrust forward, bulging with veins.

"Are you tired of living, One-Thumb? Go back to your hidey-hole. Maybe she's there, maybe not. If not . . . easy come, easy go."

Lastel's face purpled; his words rode on a froth of spray so that Janni reached for his dagger and Niko had to kick him.

"Your sister's disappeared and you don't care?"

"I let Cime snuggle up with you in your thieves' shanty. If I had 'cared,' would I have done that? And did I care, I would have to say to you that you aspire beyond your station, with her. Stick to whoremistresses and street urchins, in future. Or go talk to the Mageguild, or your gods if you have the ears of any. Perhaps you can reclaim her for some well-bartered treachery or a block of Caronne krrf. Meanwhile, you who are about to become 'No-Thumbs,' mark these two—" He gestured to either side, to Niko and Janni. "They'll be around to see you in the next few days, and I caution you to treat them with the utmost deference. They can be very temperamental. As for myself, I have had easier days, and so am willing to estimate for you your chances of walking out of here with all appendages yet attached and in working order, though your odds are lessening with every breath I have to watch

you take. . . ." Tempus was rising as he spoke.
Lastel gave back, his flushed face paling visibly
as Tempus proposed a new repository for his
prosthetic thumb, then retreated with surprising
alacrity toward the half-open door in which the
tavern's owner now stood uncertainly, now disappeared.

But Lastel was not fast enough; Tempus had
him by the throat. Holding him off the ground,
he made One-Thumb mouth civil farewells to
both the Stepsons before he dropped him and let
him dash away.

*   *   *   8   *   *   *

At sundown the next day (a perfectly natural
sundown without a hint of wizard weather about
it), Niko's partner's long-delayed funeral was
held before the repiled stones of Vashanka's field
altar, out behind the arena where once had been
a slaver's girl-run. A hawk heading home flew
over, right to left, most auspicious of bird omina,
and when it had gone, the men swore, Abarsis'
ghost materialized to guide the fallen mercenary's spirit up to heaven. These two favorable
omens were attributed by most to the fact that
Niko had sacrificed the enchanted cuirass Askelon had given him to the fire of his left-man's
bier.

Then Niko released Tempus from his vow of
pairbond, demurring that Nikodemos himself
had never accepted, explaining that it was time
for him to be a left-side fighter, which, with
Tempus, he could never be. And Janni stood
closeby, looking uncomfortable and sheepish,
not realizing that in this way Tempus was freed

from worrying that harm might come to Niko on
account of Tempus' curse.

Seeing Abarsis' shade, wizard-haired and
wise, tawny skin quite translucent yet unswept
eyes the same, smiling out love upon the Stepsons and their commander, Tempus almost
wept. Instead he raised his hand in greeting, and
the elegant ghost blew him a kiss.

When the ceremony was done, he had sent
Niko and Janni into Sanctuary to make it clear to
One-Thumb that the only way to protect his dual
identity was to make himself very helpful in the
increasingly difficult task of keeping track of
Mygdonia's Nisibisi spies. As an immediate
show of good faith, he was to begin helping Niko
and Janni infiltrate them.

When the last of the men had wandered off to
game or drink or duty, he had stayed at the shrine
awhile, considering Vashanka and the god's
habit of leaving him to fight both their battles as
best he could.

So it was that he heard a soft sound, half hic-
cough and half sniffle, from the altar's far side, as
the dusk cloaked him close.

When he went to see what it was, he saw Jihan,
sitting slumped against a rough-hewn plinth,
tearing brown grasses to shreds between her fingers. He squatted down there, to determine
whether a Froth Daughter could shed human
tears.

Dusk was his favorite time, when the sun had
fled and the night was luminous with memory.
Sometimes, his thoughts would follow the light,
fading, and the man who never slept would find
himself dozing, at rest.

This evening, it was not sleep he sought to chase in his private witching hour: he touched her scaled, enameled armor, its gray/green/copper pattern just dappled shadow in the deepening dark. "This does come off?" he asked her.

"Oh, yes. Like so."

"Come to think of it," he remarked after a strenuous but rewarding interval, "it is not so bad that you are stranded here. Your father's pique will ease eventually. Meanwhile, I have an extra Trôs horse. Having two of them to tend has been hard on me. You could take over the care of one. And, too, if you are going to wait the year out as a mortal, perhaps you would consider staying on in Sanctuary. We are sore in need of fighting women this season."

She clutched his arm; he winced. "Do not offer me a sinecure," she said. "And, consider: I will have you, too, should I stay."

Promise or threat, he was not certain, but he was reasonably sure that he could deal with her, either way.

GODSON

by

Andrew J. Offutt

Hanse did not want to be a soldier or a member of the Sacred Band of Tempus, the Stepsons, and most especially not a Stepson-in-training or any other dam' thing in-training. He wanted most definitely and most desperately to be Shadowspawn; to be Hanse. That remained elusive. It was a problem, just *being*. He did not know that many spent their lives looking for whoever or whatever it was that they were or might be, and if he had known it would not have helped a midge-worth. He was Hanse, by Ils! Not Hons or Honz or Hanz; *I am Hanse!*

The problem was that he was not sure what that meant.

Who was Hanse? What was Hanse?

O Cudget, if only they had not slain you! You'd have shown me and told me, wouldn't you?

It had used to be so simple. Life was simple. There was the city called Sanctuary, and in it were empty bellies, and some that were full. That was simple: it described lions (or jackals, but never mind that) and prey. And there was Cudget Swearoath, and Hanse his apprentice in whom he was well pleased, and there were the marks—the human sheep. And the shadows, to facilitate their fleecing.

It was all the world there was or needed be; a microcosm, a thieves' world.

And now! Now there were the Rankans who swaggered and Prince Kadakithis who really did not but who ruled, governed; and Tempus—O ye gods, there was Tempus!—and his mercenary friends, who swaggered—and nothing was simple.

Now a god had spoken to Hanse—Hanse!—and then another, and Hanse had rather they just kept to themselves. The business of soldiers was killing and the business of Prince-Governors was ruling and killing and the business of gods was godding and the business of one smallish dark thief of thieves' world was thieving.

But now Shadowspawn was agent for gods.

Sword clanged on sword and well-guided blade slid along brilliantly interposed blade with a screech as loud as the grinding of a personal ax. That shrill ugliness was punctuated by a grunt chorused from two throats.

"Stopped me again, Stealth," one combatant grunted, stepping back and twitching his head sharply to the side. Sweat crept like persistent oil from his black mop under the blood-red sweatband and into his eyebrows. He jerked his head to send it flying; the gesture carried all the constant impatience of youth.

"Barely," the other man said. He was bigger though not much older and in a way his face was more boyish than that of his opponent, who had for years cultivated a mean, menacing look he knew made him look older, and dangerous. The bigger man was fair in contrast to the other. His hair was as if splashed or streaked with silver so that it was cinerous.

"I own it, Shadowspawn: you are good and you are a natural. *Now.* Want to work a bit from the saddle?" His enthusiasm showed in his face and added bright color to his voice.

"No."

The one called Stealth waited a moment; the one called Shadowspawn did not embellish on that word which, when spoken flat and unadorned, was one of the four or five harshest and most unwelcome words in any language.

The man called Stealth masked his disappointment. "All right. How about . . . *your stones, then!*"

His last words emerged in a shout as the paler man moved, at speed. His sword was a silver-gray blur, up-whipping. It rushed on up, too, for the wiry fellow in the dust-colored tunic pounced up and aside, not quite blurring. He simply was not present to receive the upward cut at the source of progeny he might produce, like more bad virus upon the world. The other man arrested his movement to prepare alertly for a counter-stroke.

No counter-stroke was attempted. It did not come. Shadowspawn had quit the game. They looked at each other, the expert teacher called Stealth and the superb student he called Shadowspawn.

The latter spoke. "Enough, Niko. I'm weary of the sham."

"Sham? *Sham,* you weed-sprout? Had you not moved you'd be a candidate for the temple choir of soprano boys, Hanse!"

Hanse called Shadowspawn smiled little and when he did he smiled small, and often the smile was a sneer that fitted and mirrored his inner needs. It was a sneer now. Still, it was not of disdain or contempt for this member of the so-called Sacred Band, the Stepsons, who had taught him so much. He had been a natural fighter and unusually swift. Now he was a trained one, with knowledge and ways of combative science that made him even swifter.

"But I did move, Niko; I did move. Tell Tempus how I move, you he set to teach me to be a bladesman. And tell him that still I have no desire to be a soldier. No desire to do murder, 'nobly' or no."

Niko stared at him.

Damned . . . boy, he mused. Oh, but I'm weary of him and his sneers and his snot. I have known only war. He, who has never known it, dares sneer at it and its practitioners. Neither of us had a father—I because mine was slain—in war—when I was a child; this posturing backstreet blade-bristling night-thief because his mother and his father were nodding acquaintances at best. Nor would I change places with this . . . this little gutter-rat, so happy in his provincial ignorance and his total inconsequence. I had rather be a man.

And I have made him a fighter, a real fighter, so that now he swaggers even more!

"And look you to keep your valuables 'neath your pillow, Niko. Stealth, for I am shadow-spawned stealth, and have seen even the bed of the Prince-Governor . . . and of Tempus."

Niko of the Stepsons showed nothing and did not respond. Inside, he seethed only a little. Petty insults were cheap, cheap. As cheap as

barely nubile yet experienced professional girls
in the shadowy Maze that spawned this naive
youth and served him as nest and den. Niko
stepped back a pace, formally. Holding his blade
up before squinting eyes, he turned it for his
examination before putting it away in one swift
smooth motion.

The Sanctuarite was not so insolent as to keep
his weapon naked in his hand. He too held it out
and turned it for inspection at the squint, and
took hold of his scabbard with his right hand,
and turned his blade toward himself without
ever moving the dark, dark eyes that now gazed
at his teacher. And he housed the blade 'neath
but not through the hand on its sheath. With
pride.

"Nicely done," Niko could not quite help saying.

Not because he felt the need to compliment, or
enjoyed it; but because there was both edge and
gratification in reminding both of them who had
taught this wearer of so many blades the man-
euver he had just demonstrated.

(A man might draw at an untoward sound or to
dispatch an enemy, Niko had told Hanse. And
having done, see to the housing of his blade at
his side. At that moment, while he held scabbard
and looked down to see to its filling, he was
vulnerable. It was then the clever maker of the
"innocent" noise or the hidden confederate of
the new-slain man might pounce, and there was
an end to sheathing and unsheathing, all at once.
Thus a sensible man of weapons learned to bring
his blade up and over and back, its point toward
himself, and guide it into its sheath with a wait-

ing off-hand. Meanwhile his eyes remained alert for the sudden charge.

(Yes, Nikodemos called Stealth had taught even that to Hanse. For Tempus owed him debt, and yet he and Tempus were no longer quite frinds. And so Niko paid as Tempus's agent: he trained this wiry, cocky hawk-nose called Hanse.)

"Your shield!" Hanse called.

Niko glanced at it, leaning against a mud-brick wall with Hanse's buckler beside it. They had slipped them off and set them there a pint of sweat ago, to practice with blades alone. Now Hanse turned and drew and threw all in one motion fluid as a cat's pounce, arm going out long and down in follow-through, and *thunk* one of his damned knives appeared in Niko's shield. It stood there, quivering like a breeze-blown cat-tail.

Hanse pounced after it, all wiry and cat-lithe and dark.

He retrieved the knife, giving his wrist the little twist that plucked forth an inch of flat blade from bossed wood capable of withstanding a good ax-blow. Almost distractedly he slipped it back into its sheath up his right arm.

Hanse half-turned to flash teeth at his teacher-at-arms but not at knife-throwing, and he saluted. Then he turned and faded around the building and was gone, although the sun was still orangey-yellow and the late-day shadows only thinking about gathering to provide him his natural habitat.

"*Shadowspawn*," Niko muttered, and went to retrieve his shield and seek out Tempus. *Deliver*

*me from this insolent Ilsigi in his painful youth,
Tempus! Take away this bitter cup you have had
me lift, and lift to my lips, and lift!*

Hanse moved away, wearing a tight little smile
that really did not enhance his looks.

He was proud. Pleased with himself. Too, he
liked Niko. There was no way he could not, and
not respect him too, just as there was (almost, at
least) no way he could admit or show it.

He had let Tempus know he liked him while
claiming to care about no one, and had gone and
got him out of the dripping hands of that swine,
Kurd. Kurd the vivisectionist. One who sec-
tioned, who sliced, the vibrantly living. Tempus,
for instance. Among others.

After the horror of the house of Kurd, Hanse
was an uncharacteristically pensive fellow; a different Hanse. The eeriness of a regenerated
Tempus was almost more than he could bear.
Immortal! O gods of us all—immortal, a human
newt who survived all and healed all and regrew
even vivisectioned parts—scarless!

Nor had that enigmatic and ever-scornful immortal said aught concerning Hanse's expenses
in freeing him, or his promise to retrieve a certain set of laden moneybags from a certain well
up on Ea—a certain place.

Oh, it had cost.

For weeks Hanse had been idle. He did nothing. No; he did do something; he drank. His
income stopped. He even sold some of his belongings to buy the unwatered wine he had always avoided.

Even so he did not sell the gift of a dead Stepson; an entirely mortal one. It hung now on the

wall of Hanse's lodgings: a fine, fine sword in a silvered sheath. He would not wear it. He would not touch it. Only he was sure that it was not the gift of that dead man but of a god. Tempus's god, Who had spoken to Hanse and rewarded him for his rescue of His servant Tempus—as that god, Vashanka, had promised.*

That sword hung, minus its silver sheath, on Hanse's wall. The scabbard trailed down his right leg. It was wrapped all in dull black leather, knotted and pegged and knotted again. Nor was he one with the mercenaries cluttering the city, bullying the city, and he had no wish to be.

Hanse had another need for becoming proficient with arms, and better than proficient. It was Hanse's secret, and it was bigger than Sanctuary itself.

He collected from Tempus, though not in coin. That immortal had offered to make him a bladesman. (As for the horse . . . well, it was something of value and prestige, at least. Horses and Hanse were not friends and he hoped never never to fight from the back of one. But for a horse, he'd be rich!)*

Tempus did not know why Hanse had changed his mind and sent word that he was minded to learn swordsmanship. He was pleased, Hanse was sure of that. Just as he and his ego were sure that he must be the best student Niko had ever had. Already, he was sure, he was incredibly good. Hanse never needed the same instruction twice. He never repeated an error. He

*"The Vivisectionist," in Shadows Of Sanctuary; Ace Books, 1981.

*"Shadowspawn," in Thieves' World; Ace Books, 1979.

was good. Niko said so, and Niko spoke for Tempus.

Leaving Niko now, the thief called Shadowspawn wore a tight little smile. It was the pleased smile of one on whom a god has smiled; a pleased but enigmatic smile. *He says that I am good.*

I hope so, Vashanka's minion, he mused. *Oh, I hope so. And I hope Vashanka finds me better than good!*

Hanse wended home, compact and lithe and darkly menacing, weighted with blades at leg and hips and arms. There were those who were in the act of departing this place or that but waited within doorways until he had passed; there were those who stepped aside for him though he made no hostile move. They did not like it, or like themselves for doing it, but they would do it again, for this menacing street-tough.

Hanse went home. *I'm ready,* he thought, and tight-smiled.

After that business with Kurd and with Tempus and the absolute ghastliness of Tempus's mutilations—and the ghastlier reality of his complete recovery even unto regrowing several parts—Hanse had taken to drink.

He was not a drinker. Never had been. That was no deterrent to millions of others and it was not to Shadowspawn. So he drank. He drank to find an alternate state, an alternate reality, and he succeeded admirably in achieving the unadmirable.

The problem was that he did not like that. Getting away from everything was getting away from Hanse, and Hanse was the poor wight he was trying to find.

O Cudget, if only they had not slain you—you'd have shown me and told me as always, wouldn't you?

(Put another way, he had been shaken badly and dived for solace into a lake of alcohol. He stayed there, and he was drunk quite a lot of the time. He didn't like that either; he didn't even like the *taste* of the stuff. Most especially he didn't like the way he felt when sleep stopped his body and let it awake with a mouth like vinegar and the desert all at once, a mouth with the feel of a public restroom for horses and a tongue in need of a curry-comb and a stomach he'd willingly have traded for a plate of pigs' trotters and a head he'd have traded for nearly anything at all. Something had come loose in there and was rolling around, and it banged against the inside of his head when he moved it. Alcohol helped. More scales off the snake that had bit him. That merely started the whole process again. Besides, he preferred *control*, control or some feeling of it. Strong drink washed that away on a river of vomit and sank it with explosive belches and retching.

(He had the *need* for control, back there in the barely lighted shadows of his mind. All dark, back in there, in the mind of the bastard son from the wrong side of everything. He had never been in control, and so sought it, or its semblance. He had no need for any drug, and now he knew he had no desire for it either. Not to mention head or stomach.

(That was that. Hanse was off the sauce.)

He returned to being what most others were,

certainly most who were his age: a creature of his
own subconscious, a stranger dwelling within
him, and he lived as its captive.

One day someone mentioned his "obvious
sense of honor"—and it was obvious—as he put
it. Learned, that fellow said, from Hanse's respected mentor Cudget Swearoath, master thief.
And Shadowspawn sneered and looked menacing. That the innocent spewer of insults offered
to buy him a drink did not advance his cause or
Hanse's mental state in the least measure. The
poor fellow soon remembered an important ap-
pointment elsewhere, well apart from Hanse,
and he repaired there at speed. Hanse predicta-
bly spent the rest of that day behaving as if he
had no notion what honor might be.

And still he sought, and remembered.

"Thou shalt have a sword," that voice had
said inside his head, a lion agrowl in the
shadowed corridors of his mind, *"if thou free'st
my valued and loyal ally. Aye, and a fine sheath
for it, as well. In silver!"*

Hanse knew fear and some anger; he wanted
nothing of that incestuous god of Ranke, for it
had to be Vashanka whom Tempus served close.
*No! I serve—I mean . . . I do not . . . No! Tem-
pus is my . . . my . . . I go to aid a fr—a man
who might help me,* he tried to tell that god in his
mind, for he admitted to no friends and had
sworn to Tempus that he had none and wanted
none. He who had friends was vulnerable, and
Hanse much preferred his image of himself as a
separate room, a person apart, an island.

*Leave me and go to him, jealous god of Ranke!
Leave Sanctuary to my patron Shalpa the Swift,*

*and Our Lord Ils. Ils, O Lord of a Thousand Eyes,
why is it not You who speaks to me?*

Yet a miracle surely transpired that night, and it served to save the life of Hanse and thus of Tempus, whom Hanse freed. Hanse knew no pride in having served and been saved by the god of the Rankan overlords, and he found his lake of alcohol. When he emerged and dried out, he was still troubled.

He was not the first in such straits to have turned god-ward.

Not Vashanaka-ward! On four separate occasions he had visited the sanctuaries of Ils and Shipri All-mother, His spouse. Ils, god of the Ilsigi who long ago fled one land and found this one, and founded Sanctuary. (There was no temple to their fourthborn, Shalpa, who shared birthdate with his sister Eshi. Shalpa was He to Whom There is no Temple, and The Shadowed One, in his night-dark cloak. He was Shalpa the Swift, too. Shalpa of the night, and untempled: patron of athletes and of thieves.)

Hanse went avisiting the house of gods, and came the time there he felt his hair quiver and start up while his stomach went chill and as if empty, for he felt sure that one of Them spoke to him. A god, aye.

Ils Himself? Shalpa His son? (Considering his recent drinking, Hanse later wondered if it might more likely have been Anen. He was firstborn of Ils and Shipri, and he was patron of bibbers and taverners.)

Whoever it was spoke to him in his head, it was not Vashanka, not there in the house of the gods of Ilsig.

Hanse of the Shadow, Chosen of Ilsig, Son of the Shadow.

We exist. We are here. Believe. And look for this ring.

He *saw* it. The gaud appeared from nowhere and hung there before his eyes. Now it was as if solid, and now he seemed to see through it, into the temple appointments beyond. A ring that seemed a single piece of gold, unfused, and set all about with twinkling little blue-white stones like stars. In its center a big tiger's-eye, caged in gold bands. And that orange-yellow gemstone, that tiger-eye—seemed to stare at him, as if it was more than merely a chatoyant stone of quartz fibers.

And then it was gone, and so was the voice that had been inside his head, addressing him— hadn't it? Had it?—and he was left slumped and slick all over with sweat. He had to apply his mind and then make conscious effort even to close his mouth. The temple's coolth had become chill.

After a while he felt strong enough to move. Move he did, for he was not minded to remain there in that joint temple of Ilshipri. He departed, all prickly still and wet with sweat even down his legs. He squinted on leaving the dimness of the temple, for the time was mid-afternoon, not night at all.

Had it begun then, even in daylight?—the hallucinations, the false feeling of importance that was a lie swarming up like a nest of spiders from the lees of swilled wine?

Or did I hear—could I have heard . . . a god? The god?

He had walked from the temple, seeing nothing and no one. A person apart and an island indeed! Until, as if a hood had been lifted off his head to bare his eyes, he saw Mignureal.

She came directly toward him, looking at him, that S'danzo daughter of his friend Moonflower of the Seeing eyes. Moonflower who so well knew him—and did not want him having aught to do with her daughter. Mignureal. Heading purposefully toward him, gazing at him. A girl who looked thirteen and was older, long since pubertous and interested in Hanse—fascinated with Hanse as a woman is ever fascinated by and with the rascal. It pleased her to act as if she was thirteen, not a woman of sixteen, most of whose age-peers were wedded or at least bedded.

"My daughter is very young and thinks you are just *so* romantic a figure," that great big woman said, who was such a pretty little woman inside the masses of flesh her husband so loved. "Will you just pretend she is your sister?"

"Oh you would not want *that*," Hanse had assured her, in one of those rare revelations as to the sort of childhood he must have had. "She is my friend's daughter and I shall call her cousin."

Hanse meant that promise. Besides, Mignureal had seen him quaking and blubbering with fear, a victim of that fear-staff of the perverse gods, and he did not care to look her in the eyes. It was she who had rescued him and led him, a tremulous mouse helpless against the power turned on him, back to her mother.

And now here she came, bearing some colorful bundle. Small and dark and yet not at all a creature of night and shadows as he was. Mignureal

was a creature of day and this day in her bright
yellow skirt she wore a strange look, as if she was
drugged.

If she is, Hanse thought fiercely, *I will beat her
and take her home and curse Moonflower for
allowing it to happen to this . . . this dear
maiden.*

But then he stopped thinking. She was before
him, stopping and forcing him to stop. And
when she spoke her voice was odd and flat as her
eyes, emotionless as her face. She spoke as if she
said words she had only learned—the words, not
their meaning—like a girl who had learnt her
part for some temple rite on a god-day.

Dark brown eyes like garnets and just as lacking in softness, she said, *"You are invited to
dinner tomorrow night. You will be in no danger.
Wear this clothing. The place is known to you. It
is long unpeopled, but its water is a silver pool.
The silver is your own, Son of the Shadow, Chosen of Ilsig. Come, tomorrow even as the sun sets,
to the aerie of the great ruler of the air."*

Without blinking, she pressed into his hands
that which she carried, and turned and ran in a
butterfly flurry of yellow skirts and streaming
blue-black hair. Hanse stood, stupidly staring
after her until she rounded a corner and was
gone down another street. Then he looked down
at his gift. All in shades of blue and some green,
with a flash of yellow-gold embroidery. A fine
tunic, and a cloak considerably better than good.
Good clothing!

Clothing so fine existed in Sanctuary, of
course. No S'danzo girl had any of it though, nor
did a youth who gained his living by stealth.

Whence, then, came this soft fabric?

From the same place those words came from, he thought, *for they were not Mignureal's words. And again the phrases Son of the Shadow and Chosen of Ilsig!* A shiver claimed Hanse then, and possessed him for a long moment.

" 'Day to you, Hanse—ah! I see you had a good night, 's more like it, hum?" And that acquaintance went on smiling, for what else could he think? Where else could Hanse have gained such a bundle of finery, save through a bit of climbing and breaking-and-entering on yesternight?

Hanse stood directing thoughts to his feet, and at last they began to respond. He walked on, trying to make his bundle as small as he could, lest some member of the City Watch espy him, or a Hell-Hound from the palace, or someone nosy enough to consider turning him in or blabbing it about that Hanse had stolen good soft, decorated clothing sufficient to pay his room's rent for the next twelvemonth.

Hanse had received coded messages beforetimes, and had devised the meaning. He did so this time. He knew where he was invited. (Invited? Bidden! Summoned!) Away up on the craggy hill now called Eaglebeak was a long untenanted manse. It lay partially in ruins, that magnificent home its long-ago builder and tenant had called Eaglenest. Nearby, beyond scattered fallen columns and tumbled stones, rotted planking marked a well. Down in that well languished two leathern bags. Saddlebags. Hanse knew they were there, for he had put them there, in a way, though it had not been his intent.

He hoped they were there, for they contained a great deal of silver coins, and a few that were gold.

They were the ransom of the Rankan symbol of power, the staff called Savankh, which a thief called Shadowspawn had stolen from the palace of the Prince-Governor. The P-G knew they were there, but had agreed that they would remain Hanse's property. Hanse had, after all, uncovered a spy and a plot and saved Prince Kadakithis's face, if not his life.

But for a horse and a dead man named Bourne, Hanse would have had all that gleaming fortune in his possession, rather than "banked" down in the earth, atop a hill, in a narrow well that was like to have been the death of him!

He was to go to Eaglebeak, then. To dine in dark and deserted aerie: Eaglenest! So he quietly told Moonflower. For aye, once again he betook himself to her in quest of information and advice. (Mignureal was not about when he approached, and neither he nor Moonflower was sorry.)

He sat before her now in his nondescript tunic the color of a field mouse, his feet in dusty buskins, knees up. And only three blades showing on him. He sat on the ground and she on her stool. The fact that she overflowed all around was disguised by her voluminous skirts; Moonflower wore red and green and ochre and blue and another shade of green. Across her lap lay his new clothing.

She fondled and sniffed and tasted it, closed her eyes and drew it through her dimple-backed hands. And all the while she was moving her

lavender-tinted lips. The vastness of her bosom
was almost still as her breathing slowed, her
heartbeat slowed, her muttering slowed and she
slid away from herself, a great gross kitten at her
divining.

No charlatan, this mother of eleven who had
raised nine, but one with the Gift, the power.
Moonflower Saw.

Now she Saw for Hanse as she had before, and
he was not all that happy with it. Nor was she,
even in trance.

"I See you, darling boy, all nobly turned out in
this finery, and I See a great light hosting y—oh!
Oh, oh *Hanse* . . . it is, it is He! Here is Hanse,
aye, and here is He, Himself—Ils, god of gods!
And I See . . . ah! *Hmp.* I like not what else I See,
for it is Mignue, my Mignue, with you and the
Lord of Lords."

He nodded, frowning. That was her pet name
for her daughter. He accepted that somehow
Mignureal was a part of this . . . whatever this
was.

"Ah! Here is Hanse with a sword, and wield-
ing it well, well . . . for a god, Hanse, soldierly
Hanse I See . . . for a god, *against* a god!"

Against a god. *Father Ils, what means this all?
What would you make of me?* And he had an
idea: "Who . . . who gave me the sword?"

"A bas—no, no, a foster son. Ah—a stepson.
Yes. A s—"

"And who gave me the clothing? Is that Mignureal?"

"Mignue? No, oh no, she is a good g—ah. I see
her. Eshi! It is Eshi Herself who has given you
this clothing, Han—" And she shuddered of a

sudden, and sagged, and her eyes came alive to stare into his. "Hanse? Did I See? Was it of value?"

He nodded. He was unable to look other than grim. "You Saw, O Passionflower. This time I must owe you, beyond the binding coin." (Which she had already dropped into that warm crevasse she called her Treasure Chest.)

Eshi, Hanse thought. Eshi!

A jealous and passionate god, Ils created all the world, and from his bodily wastes He peopled it. The gods He created from his two extra toes, and the eons passed and the first-created challenged Ils. This was Gunder, and he lost. He was hurled to the earth. His daughter Shipri, though, was thrice-fair, and her the great Lord Ils spared—and couched. By him Shipri became All-mother; of him she bore Shils, and Anen, and Thufir, and the twins Shalpa and Eshi, their first daughter, and another; the god no one spoke of. Now Anen was called firstborn, for jealous, passionate Ils sinned; in rage he slew his firstborn son, Shils.

Eshi. Much spoken of She was, and prayed to as well, but it was little reverence she gained. Everyone knew that she was a sensuous beauty who sought out and had her way with each of her brothers, and indeed sought to bring to couch even her father. In that She failed; even Ils was not that passionate, and one sin for a god was enough.

Eshi was fond of jewellery, and so gemworkers took a manifestation of her as patron. She was known to love love, and thus lovers, of course. Cows were special to her, and so were cats. Her sign was the liver, which any child learned early was the seat of love and its younger sibling, infatuation. Eshi!

Aye, Hanse thought. She loves jewellery and thus the ring; cats are sacred to her and thus the stone: the eye of a cat. Somehow it was pleasant thus to find some small comfort of logic in all this that clearly had naught to do with logic. Gods! He was involved with the very gods!

Mignureal came along just as he was departing. She asked about the handsome clothing he carried! Obviously she had never seen it before, and Hanse blinked. His eyes swerved in her mother's direction. She was staring at her daughter.

"Into the house, Mignue," she said, with uncommon sharpness. "See to the preparation of the leeks and yeni-sprouts your father fetched home for dinner."

Hanse went away thoughtful and shaken while Moonflower sat staring at nothing. She was a mother, and she too was shaken, and passing nervous.

For Hanse the next twenty-six hours rode by on the backs of snails. He slept not well and his dreams were not for the repeating.

Attired in such a way as to arouse the envy of a successful merchant, Hanse completed his ascent to Eaglebeak just after the sun began sliding off the edge of the world. Continuing cautious and too apprehensive to hurry, he picked his way through a jumble of tumbled columns and jagged stones habited only by spiders and serpents, lizards and scorpions, a few snails, and the most insistent of scrubby plants. These owned Eaglebeak now, and Eaglenest. All here

had been murdered long and long ago. They
were said still to haunt the place, that merchant
and his family. And so the hilltop and once-fine
estate-house were avoided.

Even so a great portion of the manse stood, and
some of it was even under roof. Green-bordered
blue cloak fluttering, his emerald-hued tunic
with its purfling of yellow gold an unwontedly
soft caress on his thighs, Hanse approached a
doorless entry. It yawned dark, and still the ancient dark stains splashed the jamb; the blood of
murder. He cast many anxious looks this way
and that, and he did not hurry. For once he was
not pleased to go into shadows.

He was met and greeted. Not by Ils or a
beauteous woman, either!

Oh she was female, all right, and indeed
shapely in a warm deep pink, a long gown
sashed with red and hemmed with silver. The
dress was lovely and rich and her figure was
lovelier than that but even so the most striking
aspect of her was her face. She had none.

Hanse stopped very abruptly and stared. At
nothing. It was as if his gaze somehow swerved
away from the face of this woman who greeted
him, putting forth one lovely smooth hand.

The hand was adorned with a single ring.
Hanse recognized it. He had seen it yesterday, in
the sky-aspiring temple of Ilshipri.

"Don't be fearful, Hanse of the Shadows, Chosen of Ilsig, Son of Shadows." It was a very nice
voice, and unconditionally female.

"Of one who has no face on her? Oh, of course
not!"

Her laughter was a stream of bright quicksilver

in sunshine. "Choose a face then," she bade him, and proceeded to give him a choice.

The air shimmered above her shoulders and a head formed, and a face. It was not comforting. Hanse was looking at Lirain. Lirain, who had conspired with another against Kadakithis, and sought to use Hanse (and succeeded), and who was dead for her crime, and her pretty face gone with her. It disappeared now, to become the piquant features of the royal concubine who had been unlucky enough to be present the night he stole the Savankh from the Prince-Governor's own bedchamber. When last Hanse had seen this one she was bound as he'd left her. He could not even remember her na—oh. Taya. No matter. She was becoming someone else.

"Uh!"

That gasp was elicited by Taya's vanishing to be replaced by . . . Moonflower! Aye, Moonflower, earrings, chins and all!

"No thank you," Hanse was able to say, and felt better for it.

Far more shocking was the next visage, one he recognized after a few moments of gaping. The woman he had seen murdered for her terror rod out by Farmer's Market, less than two months ago! Before he could protest, she had flickered away after the others, and Hanse swallowed. Now he gazed close upon a face he knew and had always wished could be closer. She was the smiling and truly beautiful daughter of Venerable Shafralain. Esaria her name, a girl of seventeen or eighteen—the *Lady* Esaria! A beauty he had watched and about whom he had entertained phantasies rather more than once or thrice.

"You *know*," Hanse blurted, with more breath than voice. "You bring out these faces from my own memory!"

Already Esaria was becoming Mignureal, sweet-faced Mignureal, who gazed serenely at him—and spoke.

"You are invited to dinner tomorrow night. You will be in no danger. Wear this clothing. The place is known to you. It is long unpeopled, and its water is a silver pool. The silver is your own, Son of the Shadow, Chosen of Ilsig."

And of course now he knew who his greeter was. It was not possible, but then none of it was.

"Whom shall I be to your eyes tonight, Son of Shadow?"

Hanse replied with surely a great stroke of genius, and made the most brilliantly diplomatic utterance of his life.

"The thrice-beauteous face of the Lady Eshi from the statue in the temple of Eshi Radiant," he said—

And She was, smiling delightedly, ever so pleased. She embraced him with warmth and Hanse nearly collapsed.

Her hand clasping his with warmth, she led him into that ruined and murkily-shadowed once-luxury manse . . . and it was again! Everywhere candles sprang into lambence, with constant flashes and continuing unnatural brightness. Bright, bright light, revealing perfect inlaid floors that were works of art and walls all alive and acolor with mosaic-work. Along a high-soaring hall he was led, and into a palatial dining hall, and here too all came alight with the brightness of day.

At the far—far!—end of a genuinely long table of fine inlaid wood sat . . . a shadow. And a man . . .

Hanse tore loose his hand from the warm grasp of a god and backed a pace with a hissing whisper of soft-soled buskins.

"Cudget!" he all but shouted. "Oh no, no, Cudget—they killed you, Cudget!" And his voice broke.

The voice that replied was not Cudget's, but was male, and warmth itself. Somehow it made Hanse feel good; all warm.

"It is in the nature of gods to be self-directed, what you call selfish. Sometimes we forget your mortal attachments, unbroken by death. I thought you would like the face of your mentor and late best friend and foster father, my beloved friend and servant Hanse. My own visage is only Light; Lambence; Candence. For I have not a thousand eyes you know, not really."

"You . . . cannot be . . ."

"Hanse—take the crossed brown pot with you," Cudget said in Mignureal's voice, and only she and Hanse knew that she had said those words to him one night of evil. (Or did she?) And then Cudget was speaking on, in another voice that Hanse did not at first recognize. Then he did—it was his own! He remembered the words, from the night he had gone to Kurd's and nearly died—no! He had not uttered those words! He had but thought them, and only he could know them:

"O Ils, god of my people and father of Shalpa my patron! It is true that Tempus-Thales serves Vashanka Tenslayer. But help us, help us both,

lord Ils, and I swear to do all I can to destroy
Vashanka Sister-wifer or drive him hence, if
only You will show me the way!"

On hearing those words issue in his voice from
the Being at the far end of the long table, Hanse
could only stare.

"Only two could know that prayer of yours,
Hanse. Only two not just in all the world, but in
all the universe. You are one; the other is He who
hears all words directed to him, whether they are
uttered by tongue or mind only."

Pale, Hanse could only gasp forth shaky
words: "Lord . . . God."

"Yes," the warm voice spoke from that lambence.

Hanse had elected not to genuflect on meeting
a prince of Ranke. Now, upon meeting that god
Who was god of gods, he was far too shaken to
think of falling to his knees.

Lord Ils proved that he was no mere king or
emperor or religious leader, to insist upon such
displays. Neither egoism nor egotism marked
gods. They had no need of either. They were
gods. Cudget's face vanished and again Hanse
was forced to squint. Someone still sat at table's
end in that big dining hall, but there was no face
at all now. There was only light.

Eyes almost closed, Hanse was forced to look
away from it—and discovered that now he
looked upon a goddess, all in deep warm pink
bordered with silver and sashed with scarlet.
With jewels flashing in the deep indigo silk of
her hair; or perhaps they were stars.

The voice of warmth spoke.

"Yes," it said again. "Cheated of strength in

my own lands, but not drained, Hanse Son of Shadow. The intensity of belief of one who had sneered at gods, and his loyalty that is not automatic but learned, volunteered—it is you I speak of, Hanse—these aided Me. For gods and mortals are mutually dependent, Hanse.

"My cousin Savankala's son Vashanka has waxed here by the power of belief of one variously called the Riddler, and Thales, and Tempus, as well as the Engineer, and Sea-born. We need not concern you with who he really is. Vashanka wished his freedom one night; wished it enough to bargain with Me. It required only the efforts of Shalpa my son to cloud the skies that night. Because the climate of your land is what it is, both Vashanka's power and Mine were required to send rain that night, when you needed water to survive the plant-that-kills. Naturally I made bargain with Vashanka ere I helped him—because I knew Vashanka would bargain to help you save Tempus!

"Having agreed, Vashanka himself made a concession: Vashanka himself struck his name from the palace of My people. Nor will Vashanka use such power displays here again. It were not wise of Me to raise my murdered temple, which Vashanka struck down; that is the business of you humans. Such edifices please you humans; gods have no need of such aggrandizement for there is no aggrandizement beyond godhead."

Hanse's brain was awhirl and he wished he were sitting down. He said, "And . . . and Mignureal?"

It was Eshi who replied to that. "We have acted through her twice now, and she remains more powerful than she knows. For none can be touched by a god without receiving some of that which is the essence of gods—a form of strength, a form of dominion over time and space. Those are after all creations of gods, and bounded about my mortals. The girl Mignureal remembers nothing of having twice acted for us. But she dreams—O how she dreams, now!"

Now that shadow-presence spoke, at table's end, and its voice was as a shadow might sound; was as a piece of good leather drawn slowly across a whetstone. "The power of Vashanka remains at bay, and now you may make use of Vashanka's servant, who is . . . lost."

"How—why?" Hanse asked, and indeed he was not sure if either question was the right one. Seismic disruptions disturbed his brain and his stomach felt both hollow and drawn together.

Because they needed him, they told him without equivocation, for what was pride to gods?

The Ilsigi his people, and Sanctuary called Thieves' World needed him, and the world needed him. It was not just that Ils and his family would wane and shrink and perish. Ranke would rule supreme over all the world, and Ranke was ruled by men other than good ("for my cousin Savankala is old and weary of the strife of his offspring") and Savankala's warlike, war-loving son ruled Ranke, through its emperor.

"I may not do battle with Vashanka, though," Ils said, light speaking in the voice of warmth, "for son must battle son."

And with that stated He vanished, and much light left with him. Now the big chamber was draped with shadows, and the Shadow at table's end spoke, in the rustly voice of shadows, hooded and cloaked.

"You think you know me, Hanse, and you are right. I am He to Whom There is no Temple. I am the Shadowed One, Hanse who are Son of the Shadow. It is I who must combat Vashanka, for I am son of Ils as he is son of Savankala my uncle. But the presence here of Ranke, and of Vashanka and his so-powerful servant—these have robbed me of abilities. I can act only through you, Hanse, as my sister may act only through Mignureal. With the sword from him called Stepson, Hanse, who is Godson, is to combat a god."

"Vash—Vashanka?"

Hanse saw the shadowy nod that was his only reply, and again he blurted words: "But I am not skilled with a sword!—Lord of Shadows," he added.

That fortunate fact was not to be his succor as he hoped. Fight a god! Shadowspawn? *Hanse?* No no, he wanted only to fly from here and lose himself in that cess-warren called the Maze, forever!

But: "There is one in Sanctuary who is more than expert with the sword and the business of killing, and he allows that he owes you. With him now are those who are skilled at teaching use of the sword, and they are his liege-men, Hanse. Hanse: *use him.* He will see to your instruction, and with pleasure. You shall learn prodigiously and surprise them, for I shall be there with you, Hanse who are the Chosen of Ilsig."

Now Hanse was propping himself with both hands on a high-backed chair, and at last Eshi took notice.

"We are cruel, brother! Shadowspawn—seat yourself."

Shadowspan obeyed with gratitude and alacrity. He almost collapsed into the chair. He took a very deep breath, let part of it out, and was able to form words by letting them ride the breath: "But . . . uh . . . then what?"

"You will know, Hanse."

Then Shadowspawn twitched away at a sound beside him. He looked at the floor beside his chair, at what had only just appeared there, and could not possibly be there. Clinking, dripping, running water, were the bags off the saddle of a dead man named Bourne. Hanse's saddlebags, from the deeps of the well just outside! The ransom of the Savankh, which he had stolen for little purpose other than his own ego and pride—which had soared, then. The ransom Prince Kitty-cat had told him was his—if he could get it out of the well.

It was irresistible. He bent to the bags, opened one, took forth a few wet silver coins. And he sighed. He dribbled them back in, listening to their sweet lovely clink, and he did it again—keeping a few in his fist. Then, staring thoughtfully down at those bags sending wet runnels along the floor, he sighed.

"You are god and my god, Shadowed One. This . . . this is safe in the well. Uh, can you put it back?"

Hanse jerked when the bags vanished, and he wondered if he were not the greatest fool in Sanctuary. *How silly I am going to feel when I wake up from this dream!*

"It is back in the well, Son of the Shadow, and aye, it *is* safe indeed! And we must go, my sister and I. Our time on this plane is necessarily limited."

Hanse raised an expostulating hand, said "But—" and was alone in Eaglenest. The candles remained, burning. So now did food and wine, on the table before him. He glanced down. The puddles and dark run-stains of water remained. And so did the coins in his hand, a few pieces of silver.

Did that mean it had all indeed happened?

No, of course not. When I wake, the coins will be gone.

The food he took with him, eating as he left, tasted very good in his dream, and the wine was the very best he had ever sipped. Only sipped; the sack remained heavy as he climbed the steps to his room deep in that area of Sanctuary called the Maze. (It was even more dangerous now than ever before, what with all these damned swaggering soldiers, all foreigners; that was one reason he had chosen to leave his money in the well. Even the Maze could no longer be considered safe, Hanse thought.)

He entered his room and closed the door with care, and bolted it with as much care. A window leaked in a little moonlight, and by the time he had the cloak unclasped and off and the tunic over his head, he was able to see pretty well. That was how he discovered that a woman waited in his bed.

A girl, rather. The truly beautiful Lady Esaria. In his bed. She sat up, showing that all she wore was the bedspread, and held out her arms.

Hanse was somehow able to avoid yelling or collapsing. He made it to the bed. She was real. She was waiting for him. It was wonderful, all of it with her. Even his wondering, *Is she Eshi?*, did not inhibit him or her or his enjoyment or hers. What matter whether she was the Esaria she appeared to be or the goddess; she was higher than he could have aspired, and the experience was supernal.

He deduced that it really was Esaria, not Eshi (in his dream, of course, he reminded himself) because surely Eshi wouldn't have been eating so much garlic.

She was gone in the morning, and he lay smiling, thinking about his dream. Lying on his back, he rolled his head.

He could see cloak, tunic, and wine-sack from here. That brought him wide awake, and sent his hand swinging down beside the pallet to check his buskins. The silver coins were still there. Hanse demonstrated the cliché of sitting bolt upright. Hurling back the spread, he inspected his bed. That required no effort. The evidence of Esaria's visit and her late virginity were vehemently present.

I was not dreaming, he thought, and then he spoke aloud: "*I see and I believe. I will do it, O Swift-footed One, O All-father Ils! I will do it, holiest-but-one Lady Eshi, and Venerable Lady of Ladies Shipri!*"

The voice was there, inside his head: *All depend on you, son.*

Not "all depends," Hanse realized later. "All depend." Meaning "all the gods of Ilsig and the Ilsigi!"

He took up the last of the strong drink he had used all too much since That Night, the night at Kurd's, and he poured it out onto the sheet on the floor, which already showed the scarlet of another form of sacrificial outpouring.

"A libation to the gods of Ilsig!" Hanse said firmly, and he meant it.

From the secret hiding place it had occupied for a month and more, somehow resisting alcoholic urges to sell it, he took out a packet. It was the one he had brought away the morning after That Night. It contained the shining and obviously valuable surgical instruments of Kurd the vivisectionist, whom Tempus had lately sent off to another plane of existence or inexistence. Thieving was out of the question now, and such excellent tools would bring him plenty of coin, the naked Hanse thought, and he opened the package on the rickety little table.

And he stared.

The surgical instruments were gone. The packet contained some forty feet of supple, slim, inch-wide black leather strap; a shirt of superb mail, black; a plain black helmet with nose-, temple-, and neck-guards. And a ring. It was not black. It was of gold, and it was set with a large tiger's-eye, caged in bands of gold and surrounded by small blue-white sones.

He spent a lot of time that day wrapping and tightening the leather strapping around the silver sword-sheath given him by him called Stepson. Thus its ornate value was concealed. He tried on the mailcoat and marveled at its suppleness and spent many many minutes learning to get it off. Over the head, yes, but one could not hoist it up and over as one did a tunic—not just under forty pounds of boiled leather covered with rings of black metal! The helmet fitted perfectly, of course.

The ring he would not try on. It was hers, Hers
and his sign; he could not consider it his ring. It
and four of his five silver coins he carefully
stashed before he went down, rather late in the
afternoon, for something to eat. He wore the old
camel-hued tunic with the raveling hem.

He ate well, drinking only barley water.

"Saw you going out last night, Shadowspawn," the taverner said quietly, admiring the
silver coin and trying to be cool about it. "Musta
been a good night, hmm?"

"Aye. A good night. Aye! Don't forget my
change."

It was too late to do much of anything. He
wandered a bit, hoping to catch sight of Tempus.
He did not, and had to go back. pretending not to
hurry, to check his new possessions.

He did. It was all there. The change from the
silver coin was still in the draw-top bag he was
not stupid enough to wear on his belt. And there
were five silver coins in his stash.

Hanse sat on the edge of his bed, thinking
about that.

*Looks as if my, uh, immortal allies want me to
have no financial worries! They'd maybe not
wish to be served by what I had to remind
Kadakithis I am (or was?)*—"Just a damned
thief!"

Over the next several days he spread the
money around, happily giving a silver coin to
dear old Moonflower ("because you're beautiful,
why else?") and two to a one-armed beggar with
two fingers missing, because Hanse recognized a
victim of Kurd; and he gave to others. The krrf
dealer was suspicious on receiving a silver Rankan Imperial ("for the future, just in case; don't

forget my face, now!") but he took the coin.

And always when the spawn of shadows returned to his room above a tavern, always his secret hiding place offered one ring and five silver coins.

Tempus, meanwhile, had been astonished, but certainly agreed to the training. He assigned Nikodemos called Stealth to the daily duty. And now it had gone on, and on, day after day of practice and sweating and cursing, and now Niko had told him that he was good, and a natural. Elated, Hanse had sunk a knife into the fellow's shield while of course pretending that it was a sneer become action. Then he had saluted and betaken himself around that building while Niko stood looking long-suffering and boyish, and on the way home Hanse had given away a silver coin. He had already spent another this day. And there were five remaining in his room, too.

3

He opened his eyes. He knew absolutely that a moment ago he had been sleeping soundly, and had come instantly awake. There was no time to wonder why; all he had to do was turn his head to see that it was still dark, the middle of the night, and that he had a visitor.

She was Mignureal, looking a bit older and truly beautiful, all in white and palest spring-yellow. And surrounded by a pale glow, a sort of all-body nimbus of twilight.

"Gird thyself, Hanse. It is time."

Weeks and weeks ago, when first he returned from that night up at Eaglenest, he would have shuddered at such words. Not now. Now Hanse

was a trained fighter and he had given it plenty
of thought and he was more than ready. He had
not known it would come this way, but as he rose
to obey he was glad that it had. This way he had
no time to think about it, to worry about what
might happen to him. It was time. He girded
himself.

He donned tights and leathern pants; woolen
footsers and a thief's soft, padded-sole buskins.
Next the new cotton tunic, long, and over that
the padded one. The glow remained in his room;
Mignureal remained, this Mignureal, from attractive moth into beauteous butterfly. The mailcoat jingled into place and he buckled on the
sword. Not the practice sword; the sword of the
Stepson, with which he had privately practiced.

The figure in his room stretched forth a hand.
"Come, Hanse. We have to go now. It is time, Son
of Shadow."

He picked up his helm. "Mignureal? Have you
. . . a brother? A twin?"

"You know that I have."

"And what do you call him?" He took her
hand. It was cool, soft. Too soft, for Mignureal.

"You know what I call him, Hanse. I call him
Shadow, for shadows he rules and births,
Shadowspawn. Come Hanse, Godson."

He went, under the helmet. Surely there were
some awake even at this hour, and surely some
saw the strange couple. As surely, none recognized Hanse the thief in his warlike attire and
under the helm, for anyone who knew him or
knew of him would never expect to see him so
accoutred and so accompanied.

Under a frowning parlous sky, in an eerie
almost-silence kept alive and made bearable

only by insects, they went away out of the Maze, and out of Sanctuary, and up to Eaglenest. And into Eaglenest they went, all dark and ancient now that place of ghosts and gods. Their way was lit by the nimbus of a goddess, whose hand remained soft in Hanse's.

A place of gods indeed, for they went through the manse and out the back and the world changed.

Here was an eerie sky shot through with ribbons of gold and pale yellow and citrine and marred by clouds whose underbellies were mauve. Here was a weird vista from the nightmares of poison. Stone formations rose in impossible shapes, bent and snaked along the ground to rise again; ugly rockshapes in red and burnt ochre and siena, imitating vines fighting their way through an invisible stone wall or plants tortured into convoluted shapes by alkali or lime.

The strange stone-shapes stretched out and out to become only shadows on a plain, a vista that stretched out gray to meet that nacreous sky. And there was no sound. Not the faintest hum of a single lonely insect; not the merest peep of a nightbird or the scuttle of tiny feet or of fronds whispering in a night-breeze. Here was no sun and yet no night, and no flora or fauna either.

Here were only Hanse, armored and armed, and Mignureal, and here came Vashanka, at the charge.

Purple was his armor, hawk-beaked his helm and tall-spiked atop; black his shield and the blade of his sword so that there was no gleam to announce its onrush. Hanse drew, hurriedly shifted his buckler into place, thought of Mig-

nureal and knew he had no time to glance aside.
Here came a god, armed and armored, charging
to end this now, right now.

The god did not, nor did Hanse. Sparks were
struck by a blow parried, and feet shifted and
Vashanka was past and Hanse turning, unharmed.

The god came in with the arrogant precipi-
tousness of a god set to slay a snotty little mortal.
In rushed his dark sword, to be caught and
turned by a round shield so that he was jarred by
the impact and the snotty human's return stroke
nearly bit his leg. Still Vashanka did not learn,
could not respect this wiry little foeman in its
untested mail, and again he struck, his shield
still down from protecting his leg, and this time
Hanse jerked his shield on impact so that the
god's blade was directed aside, drawing Vashanka's arm and thus his body that way, and
only the projections of his unorthodox, twisted
body-armor saved his neck from Hanse's edge.
The god grunted as he was struck but un-
wounded, and Hanse showed him teeth, side-
stepping, back-stepping, feinting with sword
and then with buckler and showing a prepared-
ness that turned another godly attack into a feint.

Vashanka had been taught respect.

They circled, each with his shield-side to the
other, each staring above the arcing rim of the
shield. Pacing, watching. Each a moving target
and moving menace. Arms slightly amove so
that neither blade was still in that dead air.

Somewhere the moon moved in the sky and
hourglasses were turned, while those two circled and stared, paced and glared, paced and
feinted as fighting men with respect each for the

other. Now and again steel hissed and sang and steel rang or wood boomed under the impact of swordblade on reinforced shield. Now and again a man grunted, or a god. One swift awful flurry of strokes traded left each bruised under armor still intact.

How could Hanse knew that they fought so for an hour? Staying alive meant staying alert; being alert meant having no time to think of time or of tiring. It was guard and parry, strike and cover, and pace to seek another opportunity. Silver twinkled as the sword-bitten winding on Hanse's sheath came loose and dangled.

How long was it, ere Vashanka was there no more but become a rock-leopard that snarled and sprang with awful talons extended—

—to be met by Hanse become bear; a big bear that caught the huge cat and squeezed it in mid-leap, staggering back, feeling its claws as he shook it and hurled it from him to hit the ground, hard, and roll, snarling with a whining note, twisting, becoming a cobra.

Both were blooded now, and blood marked the hissing serpent that reared, striking—

It struck neither man nor bear, for neither was there, but a small ferocious collection of teeth and fur and boneless speed that avoided the strike and pounced to clamp its teeth on a hated enemy—

But as soon as the mongoose had the cobra, the serpent swelled huge and then huger so that its tiny antagonist fell away. That still-growing cobra was blooded again, however, and when it became horse with Vashanka atop or part of it, it turned to canter away. And away, prancing easily over ugly shapes of stone . . . only to wheel

and come back at the gallop. Charging, hooves
pounding, striking sparks off stone, bounding
over twisted rock-formations at the small shape
who seemed gone all fearful, scurrying back and
forth in its path, then whirling and racing away,
fleeing on a straight line easily overtaken . . .

The legs of that racing horse rushed into the
long strip of leather Hanse had just bound in
place for it, and it stumbled with a scream and
flew through the air so that Hanse, swerving,
heard its mighty impact behind him. Then he
whirled and rushed back, shield ready and
sword up and back, gathering velocity for the
stroke to carry all.

He was forced to slow. A man-shape stood
there waiting, a god in armor and helm beaked in
imitation of a bird of prey, shield up and ready,
sword a dark silver of death ready in his fist.
Shield took blow and shield took blow, but its
bottom edge was banged in to impact Hanse's
body at the waist so that he groaned and half-
doubled and staggered back, trying not to fall,
but falling, sprawling backward, a grounded
target ready for the death-stroke of a god he never
should have fought. His elbow banged into a
snake-shape of ochreous rock and the sword
leaped from it as if eager to flee.

Hanse had the ridiculous thought *I knew I
should never have done this* as he tried to writhe
and wriggle and watched death rushing at him
with upraised sword. Mignureal saved him,
leaping in from the side with a screech. Hanse,
flailing and groaning, trying to will himself onto
his feet and yet despairing utterly, saw the vicious black-bladed stroke that cut her nearly in
two almost precisely at the waist.

Now it was a god's turn to show his teeth in feral smile worthy of the lowest beast, and after spinning completely around from the exertion of destroying that poor pale-clad body, he came bounding again, sword rising for the second death-blow in seconds, and the absolutely desperate Hanse reverted: he thrust his left hand up his tunic sleeve, half-rolling as he did to free his arm all the way, and hurled the long flat knife.

He watched its rush as he had never tracked a cast before, none of his thousands and thousands of practice casts. The leaf of shining metal seemed to take minutes, floating through eternity to reach the rushing oncoming god who, though racing toward Hanse, took as long to near. Lightning sundered the sky and thunder followed, but it was the voice of enraged, triumphant Vashanka, at the charge.

"I CANNOT BE SLAIN BY WEAPONS OF YOUR PLANE, IDIOT, LITTLE THIEF, POOR DEMI-MORTAL, INCONSEQUENTIAL INSEC—"

And then his charge met the knife's.

The knife struck, beautifully and perfectly point-first, just under the adam's apple. Vashanka shrieked and the shriek burbled. That impossible plane of infinity came alive with blinding and coruscating light.

. . . *down in Sanctuary those up at dawn saw the late-rising moon vanish as the sky was hurled alight by heat lightning bright as day* . . .

that surrounded Vashanka utterly, that was Vashanka, as his bellow of rage and pain was thunder and lightning. Pierced, he went flying backward as if by smashing impact, and the wind of his passage was as the gale of a storm booming in off the sea. And on he went, until he was so distant to the staring, squinting Hanse that he was tiny, and then that tiny Vashanka vanished.

Ils appeared before Hanse then, radiant. His face was that of the statue in the destroyed temple.

At that, Hanse wondered; he saw the radiance and yet dimly. Why was it darker; why was his god not all triumphant in pure lambence?

Why can't I move my damned head, damn it?

"In the end," Ils said, "he was right and yet not wise enough. He said true in that he cannot be slain by weapons of this plane. But the knife flew true, the mortal knife off its proper plane here on the Plane of Infinity, and it struck him a killing blow, so that he began to die. But that was not possible. Thus a paradox existed. That is against the nature of things, Hanse, for the God of Gods who created all existence—aye, and who created Me—that god is Reality. Since my cousin's son Vashanka could not be slain by weapons of your plane, this dimension, he could not die in this chamber of the House of Infinity that is the domain of Lord Reality."

Of course Hanse said, "I don't understand."

"Hmp! I am sure you don't! It's heady stuff for a god! Explanations for all this won't be discovered by your kind for thousands of years, Son of Shadow. Suffice it to say that Vashanka is gone from here, and that meaning of 'here' is a broad one, indeed and in deed! Vashanka is gone from here because he cannot exist here, in this universe. He has been blown backward through a wormhole in space, which is no easier for you to understand, eh? Accept this truth, Hanse: Vashanka is ElseWhere. And though there is an infinity of possibilities, of dimensions or chambers, one is closed to him forever; used up. That one—yours—is impossible to him and does not exist for him.

"That which can never exist is the combination of Vashanka on this plane of Reality. Since he is dead but gods may not die from the weapons of mortals, he cannot be here. He can never return to this chamber of the House of Infinity."

Hanse felt that Ils had said the same thing three several ways, and all were nicely logical and avoided paradox, but . . . A wormhole? In space? Yet he was not concerned with that and could not be. Vashanka was gone; Hanse must have won. He felt fine, too, except that he could not seem to lift his head or feel anything. Yet somehow being a hero made him behave as one; he did not mention that but asked a hero's question:

"And Mignureal?"

"She is asleep in her bed. Was—she is risen now, and seeing to her siblings, for in Sanctuary it is dawn. As I and mine are all-powerful here now. . . . !"

And Eshi rose, whole and unscarred, and rushed to the prostrate Hanse.

She knelt beside him and he knew her hands were on him because he could see them. She looked up at the Lord of Lords.

"I want him, father! I want him!"

"But—me!" Hanse said. "What of me?"

Ils gazed down on him. "You, beloved Son of Shadow, have defeated a god and restored Me to

my own people in Sanctuary. Further, as Vashanka had become the most powerful of the
gods of Ranke, that people's power will wane.
Empires die slowly, but it has begun, as of this
moment."

"Yes," Hanse said almost plaintively, not even
realizing the enormity of his service to gods and
Ilsigi and world, "but . . . now? What of *me*—
now?"

"Fa-*ther*," Eshi said with the sound of accusa-
tion in her voice, "his neck is broken!"

Ils said quietly, "Now, Hanse, hero, you are
dying."

"But—"

"His head struck this nasty damned stone and
he's paralyzed from the neck down! He feels
nothing, nothing!"

"But that cannot be," Ils went on, as if he had
heard neither of them. "You cannot be dying, for
you cannot be dead, for he who did death on you
does not exist on this plane. Therefore a paradox
exists, if you are dying. Therefore you cannot be
dying."

Pain rose up in Hanse then, as again his body
came alive, and he moved his head to look down
at Eshi, whose weight was partially on him, and
then that was all he felt, for all pain fled and so
did each scratch and bruise.

"Uh—pardon me, uh, Lady Goddess," he
grunted, and Hanse rose to face his god. To him
clung the daughter of that god, herself a god.
"And now? After all this, my god—what am *I?*"

"Now, Hanse, you return. For ten circuits of
your world around the s—that is, for ten circuits
of the sun—you shall have what you wish. All
that you desire. We shall not be available to you.

Then we shall, and you will face me again, beloved Hanse, and tell me what is your desire."

"But—"

Eshi clung to him, but her grip was broken, her fingers torn free of the mailed hero of the Ilsigi by the wind of Ils that rushed him back to Sanctuary; back to his own beloved, squalid little Thieves' World.

A glance upward showed him more of the impossible that had lately become all too commonplace for the Son of Shadow. The sky was precisely as it had been when he departed on his mission. He even recognized the oddly formed little cloud 'way out there above Julavain's Hill. It looked just like a—

But even as he paced along the narrow Maze "street," the cloud was coming apart, changing, never to be the same again.

Information was yielded Hanse by that. But it was for realization later, the fact that while hours or days had been consumed in that mighty combat in a chamber of the House of Infinity, in Sanctuary exactly no time had passed at all.

Just now, in the darkness of Slick Walk, an accoster separated itself from the shadows along one wall and glided into his path. The fellow bulked large, too.

"You're not in a hurry are you, little fellow?" the voice said, mocking him. "Carrying a purse?"

"Not tonight," Hanse said, stepping into the light that fell between them.

He drew a long sword from a silver-flashing sheath buckled over fine dark armor that rang softly with the movement of mailed sleeve on chest. At the same time he showed teeth and the

blade moved up to catch the light and the foot-
pad whirled and ran for absolutely all he was
worth.

Chuckling softly, Hanse moved on along
Slick toward the Serpentine.

Now those gods with whom he was so intimate
had a strange way of expressing themselves
sometimes, but he was sure Ils had said that he
could have anything he wished for . . . what did
He mean? Ten circuits of the sun was subject to
interpretation.

Did the god mean only ten days? Surely He
had not meant ten *years*?

Oh well. Ten days or ten months or ten years,
Hanse would take them as they came—each as it
came. *One at a time*, he mused, and he yawned.

To begin with he wished that he were not at all
tired, and then he made another wish as well,
grinning, and when he entered his room there
she was, waiting all low-lashed and smoky-eyed,
in his bed.

(Sleeping entwined, they were awakened later
by a horrific vivid lighting of the sky that quite
occluded the late-rising moon, but that was the
sort of paradox that both Reality and minor gods
such as Vashanka and Ils allowed, and counte-
nanced. It was enough to bring anyone wide
awake and it was frightfully early, but Hanse
found something to do.)

EPILOG

The fishing fleets of Sanctuary made the first sighting.

Haron saw a strange sail and called Omat to show it to him. By the time he had shaded his eyes from the sun's glare and located the strange ship, there were five sails—then twenty, all with the strange lateen rigging he had seen the day of the Old Man's disappearance . . . only these ships were larger, much larger.

He began working quickly, his one arm aching and cramped with the effort of quick-hauling his nets. The alarm spread from boat to boat and soon the entire fleet was on the move to shore. Some abandoned their nets and traps, preferring to lose their equipment to remaining there on the fishing grounds.

By the time they reached the piers, over a hundred sails were in view, all on an unwavering course for the town called Sanctuary.

*   *   *

Word spread through the city like wildfire.

A fleet, a big one—bound for Sanctuary. Some said it was an invasion from the north. Others argued hotly that the design of the ships was not northern; their specific point of origin was unknown, save that they could not be from the Northern Kingdoms.

All that was known for sure was that before nightfall new feet would tread the streets of

Sanctuary. Some panicked, fleeing to the palace or the temples for reassurance. Others, more practical, began boarding up their shops and hiding their valuables.

*   *   *

Hanse Shadowspawn heard the news with mixed feelings, wishing anew he could be certain how long his guarantee of divine protection would last. Finally he decided that discretion really was the better part of valor and headed for the ruined estate that had been the scene of his recent adventures. An estate that was well outside the boundaries of Sanctuary proper. Things had been so much simpler *before* he had anything to lose.

*   *   *

Myrtis, ruling the Street of Red Lanterns from her Aphrodesia House, was perhaps the best prepared of any in town. A few curt orders were all that would be necessary to begin relocating her "staff" to the tunnels beneath the city. Though worried about the chronic shortage of supplies in the chambers below, she was more worried about Lythande. The mage had been absent from town for some time now—and the oncoming fleet boded ill for any traveller's return.

*   *   *

The magical community of Sanctuary viewed the fleet with a mixture of anticipation and dread. There was magic in those ships, strong magic of a type they had never encountered before. Some, like Enas Yorl and Ischade, with nothing to lose, waited with curiosity, eager to add to their already great wealth of knowledge. The rest wove hurried spells of defense around themselves and prayed secretly to varied gods that strength alone would suffice.

*   *   *

Molin Torchholder, head priest of the Temple of Vashanka, had his hands full reassuring his cadre so that they might, in turn, calm the crowds of believers who pressed through the temple doors. Amidst his attempts to organize things, he was haunted by his own fears. He had worked to ground the Storm God's power, leaving the priesthood free to explain and interpret as was their god-given right and duty. He had thought himself successful, for lately Vashanka's presence was noticeably lacking in town.

Now this.

Perhaps his schemings had backfired. Where was the Storm God's protection now that a force threatened them? Just one good windstorm . . .

With a sigh Molin reminded himself that the trouble with the gods was that they were never there when you needed them, but always there when you didn't.

*   *   *

Jubal cursed aloud when Saliman arrived at their new hideout with word of the fleet. Their plans to rebuild a power structure had been

going well, old employees being infiltrated
through the existing structures of the town and
new hirelings being bought or frightened into
co-operation. With only weeks to go before their
first act of power, this new force could mean
complications and disruption of the existing order. He would need to completely re-evaluate
and probably revise all their plans.

After months of painful healing and careful
planning, Jubal was *not* one to accept inconvenience with a smile.

*   *   *

Prince Kadakithis shooed his advisors out of
the meeting chambers so that he might speak
privately with Tempus. It had already been decided that a messenger would be dispatched for
the capital immediately with news of the fleet.
There was no reason to believe they'd be able to
get word out after the fleet landed.

Sanctuary's military situation was bleak.
Counting the Stepsons, the garrison and Walegrin's newly formed company, the city would
muster less than two hundred swords. If this
incoming fleet were indeed hostile, their opposition would likely number in the thousands.

The Prince angrily rejected Tempus' suggestion that he accompany the messenger north to
the safety of Ranke. He was royalty, pledged to
the service and protection of the town. When one
enjoyed the fruits of position, Kitty-cat said, then
one occasionally had to bear the burdens too—
even if that burden included the possibilities of
capture, ransom and worse.

Tempus argued that this was illogical, citing

numerous historic examples, but Kadakithis
remained unswayed. The citizens of Sanctuary
could not flee and, therefore, neither would he.
Good or bad, he would remain with the town and
share its fate.

*   *   *

Confronted with another prophecy come true,
Walegrin sought his half-sister in the bazaar,
only to find his path blocked by silent S'danzo
men. Dubro's appearance averted potential
bloodshed; the smith drew Walegrin aside and
explained what he knew of the situation.

Illyra was in a meeting with the other S'danzo
women—a meeting closed to outsiders. As near
as Dubro could determine, they were pooling the
information each had received through visions
of the approaching ships and arguing over the
best course for the S'danzo to follow. Until the
meeting broke up, there was nothing to do but
wait.

Walegrin fumed but settled back to sweat out
the time until the meeting was over, knowing
full well the value of the information that might
be forthcoming—if he could convince Illyra to
share the tribe's secrets with him.

*   *   *

The Downwinders were jubilant when they
heard the news. As those currently at the bottom
of the social structures, any change would have
to be for the better, though the more imaginative
cautioned that this need not be true. Still, the
scavengers anticipated the fleet's arrival with far

more enthusiasm than could be found anywhere else in town.

*   *   *

The Vulgar Unicorn was crowded with those seeking to stave off the future with a tankard of ale. One-Thumb stoically refused to give either discounts or credit, wishing secretly that he had the courage to raise the prices instead. It took men to man ships, and men drank, especially when they landed in a new town. He could be rich by tomorrow, rich enough to leave this town for good, if . . .

If these low lifes didn't drain his cellars completely before the fleet arrived. With an angry bellow he answered the next request for credit by smashing the asker in the face with a tankard.

*   *   *

The docks were deserted now. The fisherfolk had fled inland, leaving the area free for the garrison troops. The city's soldiers had not yet arrived and there was some doubt that they ever would. Most felt the Prince would keep them at the palace rather than run the risk of having them desert before they reached the enemy.

Only one person kept the seabirds company as they watched the fleet move closer. Hakiem, the storyteller, sat crosslegged on a crate in the shade of a ragged canvas awning that flapped noisily in the stillness of the empty wharf. He had purloined two bottles of good wine from an abandoned tavern and he sipped at them alternately as he squinted at the distant sails.

He had not been idle since his conversation with Omat and he knew now the approaching ships matched the descriptions of those used by the Fish-Eyed-Folk of old legends . . . and that a similar ship had captured the Old Man and his son months before.

Whether friendly or hostile, the fleets' arrival promised to be the most noteworthy event in this generation's history—and Hakiem intended to witness it firsthand. He was not unaware of the potential danger, but he feared even more the possibility of missing the moment of landfall.

It might prove to be the end of the Old Man's story, and it would definitely be the beginning of a new story for Sanctuary. The fact that it might be the end of Hakiem's story was inconsequential.

Shooing away a random fly, the storyteller drank again, and waited.

MURDER, MAYHEM, SKULDUGGERY...
AND A CAST OF CHARACTERS
YOU'LL NEVER FORGET!

THIEVES' WORLD™

EDITED BY
ROBERT LYNN ASPRIN and LYNN ABBEY

··

FANTASTICAL ADVENTURES

One Thumb, the crooked bartender at the Vulgar Unicorn...
Enas Yorl, magician and shape changer...*Jubal,* ex-gladiator and
crime lord...*Lythande the Star-browed,* master swordsman
and would-be wizard...these are just a few of the players you will
meet in a mystical place called Sanctuary™. This is *Thieves' World.*
Enter with care.